THE VERITAS CODEX

Stay curious, always!

THE VERITAS CODEX

BETSEY KULAKOWSKI

BABYLON
BOOKS

For my Mom who always made sure I had books to read, and encouraged me to write my own

CHAPTER 1

LAUREN SCRATCHED HER HEAD AS SHE PEERED DOWN AT THE corpse. It looked more like a chicken than any known animal, but the feet were cloven, like a goat. The stench that wafted from it made Lauren gag. The sickly-sweet aroma of death and decay lingered — evidence that putrefaction remained incomplete.

"What is that?" The escort from the Peruvian government pushed past the camera, jockeying for a better look. Jean-René peered out over the viewfinder at him. He cast a sidelong look at Lauren.

"That's what we're here to find out." Lauren put on her gloves and edged the escort out of her way before reaching into the small indention. She lifted the tiny body from deep within the cavern. She carried it to a nearby rock to examine it. "I need light."

The night-vision cameras were off, so the lighting techs moved in with two high-powered spotlights. After five years of working on the show, Lauren was accustomed to being in front of the cameras, but she became impatient when the production teams got in the way of her work. She wasn't much happier about the inspector, who maintained a stern and sour disposition, barking at her in a language she didn't understand.

She was a scientist first and foremost, a television personality second. It wasn't where she'd thought she'd be at this point in her career, but the television crews paid for her research, and it was better than she'd made working for PBS, or the college where she'd had tenure.

"It doesn't have a head," Rowan observed. Lauren glanced at him but said nothing. Any idiot could see it didn't have a head.

"The body is very light for its size. I need my scale." Lauren pulled her tape measure out of her pocket. She stretched it out, glancing up at Bahati, who was ready to take notes. "Thirty point five centimeters." She measured the length, then turned the tape. "Seventeen point eight centimeters." Rowan handed her the digital scale. She laid the body on the metal plate, tapping a few buttons with her gloved pinkie, waiting for the beep. "Six-hundred-eight point three nine grams." She handed back the scales as she lay the body back on the high, flat stone.

Bahati nodded, documenting the evidence. She handed Lauren the digital camera and everyone waited while Lauren photographed it from every angle, laying out her tape measure for scale. After all these years as a research scientist, she was doing what she knew best.

"Looks like an alien to me," Jean-René recoiled at the stench as he moved over Lauren's shoulder to get a better shot.

She turned and cast a stern look at him. "We don't make conclusions until we've analyzed the evidence." He knew that. They all did. It was hard not to make assumptions, though. The legs had two sets of joints, one that bent opposite the other. Upon closer inspection there were two toes, maybe hooves or toenails.

"Okay. Let's bag it up," she said. "Get me an evidence kit."

"No," the escort said flatly.

Lauren could feel the cameras on her as she recoiled at his refusal. His jaw was set, with his lips pursed and his hands went to his hips. "What?"

"It is the property of the Peruvian government. You cannot take it." His accent made the short, clipped words hard to understand. Lauren knew what he was saying. She just didn't like it.

"We found it," she snapped.

"It is not yours," he countered. "Property of Peruvian government. This is not finders-keepers."

Lauren's brow narrowed. "We came to study what we found. I can't do that here. I need my lab." The heat rose in her cheeks and flickered in her dark eyes.

"What if we agree to bring it back after we're done studying it?" Rowan stepped in, blocking Lauren. She was a logical woman, but he knew how passionately she hated anything that came between her and her work.

"No." The escort stabbed a finger in Rowan's chest, tilting his head back to look him in the eye. Rowan peered down at him, arching a critical eyebrow. The official took a step back. "You Americans are all the same. Take what is not yours, even when you are shown every courtesy. This is our history, and I will not allow you to defile it!"

Lauren took a step closer to the official, who barely came to her shoulders. She stood with her hands on her hips. "Look, Mister." She held the words between clenched teeth. "While this might be part of your history, if you think you can bully me and tell me I can't study something that I traveled 4,000 miles to find, then you better think again. If you keep it up, this won't be the only headless corpse they find in a cavern in Peru."

The man backed up and swallowed hard.

Rowan caught her arm and drew Lauren back. "Hey," he used a soft tone to turn away her wrath. "Let's just back up and take a minute here."

"Excuse me?" Her brow furrowed. "It's bad enough that you drag me into the middle of nowhere and send me down into a dark hole...and then I have to put up with that guy?" Her eyes flashed as she turned her anger on her co-host, who also functioned as the team medic.

"Look," he snapped. "I'm not any happier about this than you are but threatening a government official isn't going to help."

"It wasn't a threat." She lowered her voice. "Only one of us is going to come out of this cavern alive."

Rowan put his hands on his hips and stared at the toe of his hiking boots. He took a deep breath to still his racing thoughts. "Getting angry isn't going to get us very far with this guy, I can tell."

"So, what did you want me to do? Kill him with kindness?"

"Just don't kill him," Rowan pleaded.

She took a deep breath, finding wisdom in his words. She nodded and let go of her anger. Calmly, she turned to the official. "Can I at least take samples?"

He was silent for a moment. "Small." He held up two fingers, spread minutely apart.

She held her hand up with her fingers much farther apart. "Just a small one?"

"Small." He reached up and pinched her fingers down several centimeters.

Lauren stared down at him, her upper lip twitching as she considered her next move. "Small, huh?" She capitulated but rolled her eyes.

"Better than none." Rowan shrugged.

"Okay. I'm going to need a scalpel and tweezers."

Unable to take a rotting, unidentified corpse out of the country, they could only take pictures and a few tissue samples for DNA analysis. It wasn't much, Lauren thought, but it would have to do.

———

After all the trouble they'd gone through to get there, more would have been nice, but it was beyond their control. Lauren carefully collected her samples, then labeled and sealed them in a controlled bag, documenting her evidence with the precision of a forensics expert. She had collected samples of all kinds over the years. As a certified phase-contrast microscopist, she'd even done her own analysis in the lab. She preferred being in the field to hovering over a microscope.

She inspected the corpse and planned her cut carefully. The body was like leather, dry and crumbly on the outside. It had no hair, no scales, nothing remotely resembling external reproductive organs. The ribs were visible through torn flesh. As she poked around, she realized the inside felt more like a meaty sponge. She went deep with the scalpel, hoping to collect a bit of the internal viscera. A bit of liver would be beneficial for analysis. Bone would be better, but when dealing with a cryptid, knowing where to aim was the problem. Not every creature kept its liver in the same place.

She lifted the sample with her tweezers and held it up to the light, inspecting it, before dropping it in the bag Bahati held out for her. She glanced up at the official. "Is it too much to ask for a bit of bone?" Lauren flashed him a saccharine-sweet smile.

"Yes," he said, flatly. He crossed his arms over his chest. "You have enough. *No mas.*"

———

They spent another hour getting footage for the television show before Lauren returned the headless corpse to the depression where they'd found it.

"I wish I could get a sample of that odor." She sniffed into the sleeve of her jacket before peeling off her gloves. "Man, that's vile."

"How long do you think it's been here?" Bahati asked, holding a trash bag for Lauren to dispose her gloves into. Bahati's thick accent was melodic and rich but could be hard to understand sometimes. She rolled the bag up and put it in the pack, along with the carefully labeled samples, making sure they were safely tucked in before zipping them closed.

"It's hard to say," she said. "The lab will have to determine that."

"Let's wrap it up and head home, then," Rowan said.

———

It took another six hours to make their way out of the cavern. Lauren fell asleep in the back of the truck, nested atop their bags and gear, dreaming of tiny alien chicken-men dancing across the star-dappled velvet sky.

"Lauren." A nudge from Rowan woke her abruptly. "Lauren. Look!"

She was immediately awake. Three objects arranged in a V formation circled directly above them. They maneuvered like a flock of geese. Lauren was momentarily blinded by a glowing blue light as the three objects came together into a unified disc. It hovered above, seeming to lower. It kicked up dirt and rock, sandblasting them with grit.

Lauren was mesmerized by the object that glowed brightly as it moved lower across the ravine. Rowan pounded a hand on the top of the truck, and it screeched to a stop, kicking up a cloud of dust that hovered around them. Rowen regained his balance and turned his attention back to the sky.

Unmoving, the unidentified disc cast a white pallor across the sands, looking like a throbbing moon on the earth. It illuminated the dust cloud that settled around them and their breath that hung in the blue-white air.

"What the hell is that?" Lauren's heart pounded in her throat. She didn't wait for an answer. "Get the camera. Get the camera!"

The team, disoriented, roused from sleep by the bizarre glow, raced to get their equipment. In a matter of moments, they had multiple cameras aimed at the sky, and the object that seemingly defied explanation.

"Is it moving?" Jean-René asked, his French accent more pronounced in his heightened state of awe. "I can't tell." He went on to mutter a string of French curses as he took out his camera and pointed it into the night sky, trying to hold the camera steady.

Lauren turned and looked at the camera Chance operated. It wasn't easy, but she did her best to rein in her excitement. Exhaustion tempered her racing heart. "It's four in the morning and we were on our way back from the cavern. We're at least two hours outside of Cusco. Our caravan is still in the middle of nowhere and we have come to find that something unreal … is very real in Peru."

Lauren set out across the expanse between the truck and the disc, hoping Chance would keep the camera on her as she moved silently. He didn't. He was as engrossed with the throbbing object as the rest of the team.

She was a good ten meters across the flat expanse before anyone realized she wasn't beside them. She had her digital camera in her hand. Her finger rested on the button, snapping a string of photographs in rapid succession. She continued to move closer, zooming in on the radiant glow, transfixed on the image as if in a trance. It hovered closer until she stood directly beneath it. Gazing up, she could see subtle details where smaller lights flickered like disco lights at a rave. Her hair lifted off her neck as the vibrations emitting from the object pulsed through her body.

Lauren took a step forward, her head tilted back, transfixed on the disc. She raised her hand to shield her eyes as she moved to try and get a better look. Suddenly, the lights went from blue to red and the pulse rate increased into a rapid tempo. A deafening whine rose around her. She covered her ears and stumbled backwards.

"Lauren!" Bahati leapt from the truck to run after her before she stepped off into the ravine. "Lauren," she gasped, pulling her back. The red light abated, and the whining ceased. Lauren leaned over and peered down into the deep crevice before Bahati hurried her back into the darkness.

"Mind that first step!" Jean-René shouted, grinning wickedly from the back of the truck, watching her through the viewfinder of his video camera "It's a doozie!"

She paused a moment. Her heart pounded in her chest and she was breathless. She cocked a hip to one side and raised a hand with a one-finger salute. She didn't need his smart-ass remarks at the moment.

He returned the camera to the sky, chortling as he filmed. As she moved back to the safety of the group, she returned her attention to her own camera, panning in on the object, switching to infrared. She was amazed to find very little heat signature. It flickered cool shades in a swirling kaleidoscope of energy.

For nearly twenty minutes, they watched and filmed until the disc gradually faded, but never moved away. It finally dissipated into a disintegrating mass of twinkling dust and was suddenly...gone.

"Just tell me you got that." Lauren turned back to Jean-René as he lowered the camera, his jaw slack in disbelief.

"I think so," he said, reviewing the video in the tiny monitor. It cast the same blue-white glow on his face from the screen. "Yeah. I got it."

"Let me see," Lauren said, climbing back into the truck,

taking the camera from him, as the team gathered around, all trying to get a look. "Oh my God," she breathed heavily, her hands trembling as she replayed it over and over.

————

The sky was a pale shade of gray when the convoy came to a stop on the outskirts of the town of Cusco. The dawn brought little relief from the cold. The suburban streets were quiet, but the perfume of baking bread and the rumble of garbage trucks nearby suggested the city's inhabitants were rising from their beds, preparing to face the day.

The crew roused from their nests in the back of the truck, piling out and unloading their equipment. Lauren lifted out her pack. As she dropped it to the ground, she almost plowed into the government escort who stood with his hands on his hips, his lips pursed, and his eyes narrowed. Two *policia* twice his size stood behind him, materializing from one of the dusty red archways.

"Excuse me, Señor Prieta." Lauren had been nothing but courteous since the incident back in the cavern.

The taller of the two police officers said something curtly in Spanish.

Jean-René spoke better Spanish than anyone on the team. "He says you're under arrest for assault and making threats against a government official."

"Arrest?"

"Assault?" Rowan turned. "No one was assaulted."

"You wanna see assault?" Lauren's upper lip curled, and her fists balled.

The police officer said something else and reached over to catch Lauren by the arm. She recoiled, trying to escape his grasp, but found herself pinned against the truck with her arms wrenched behind her. The officer cuffed her. To her right, she found Rowan in the same predicament. "Wait!" she protested. "Why are you arresting him? He didn't do anything."

"You didn't either," Rowan said. "Just take a deep breath. We'll figure this out."

———

Jean-René was led into the room where Lauren sat. Her feet were chained to the chair, and her hands cuffed behind her back. Her head hung heavily. He walked over and put a hand on her shoulder. She looked up at him, one eye swollen shut, her lip split. Her cheek was bruised.

"*Tabernaque!*" he winced. "What happened?

"I sure as hell didn't fall down."

"Boss..." he sat across from her. "I called the Embassy. They're sending an assistant to negotiate your release."

"The Embassy? An assistant? Really?"

"I'm also going to see if I can get you some medical attention," he said. "At least they could let you see the medic from our team."

"I'm fine. I don't need to see the medic." She didn't want Rowan seeing her like this. Apparently, his arrest had been just for a show of power; he'd been released shortly afterward.

Jean-René considered her a moment. "Just hang tight. Let me see what I can do."

———

The next time the door opened, it was one of the two *policia* involved in her arrest. She sat up, but the room spun, and it was everything she could do to hold herself upright. The officer carried one of her equipment bags and rummaged through it without saying a word. He inspected each piece of equipment and set the cameras on the table, tossing everything else carelessly back into the bag, including the specimens collected from the cavern. He pushed the bag off the table, and it landed with a thud. Taking the camera, he turned it on as he sat down then scrolled through the pictures; the camera beeping each time he hit the button to advance. Lauren glowered at the man. She wasn't sure what he was up to, but if he intended to look at every picture on that camera then the joke was on him. She'd taken several thousand pictures since replacing the video card at the beginning of their expedition. At the moment, she was grateful she'd uploaded pictures from the cavern to the Cloud before they loaded into the truck.

"*¿Qué es esto?*" He turned the camera towards her. The image of the corpse appeared.

Lauren sat stone-faced, remaining silent.

"*¿Qué es esto?*" he repeated, more forcefully.

Jean-René had taught her a few useful phrases in Spanish. "*Vete al inffierno.*" She was pretty sure she'd just told him to go to hell.

The man looked up at her soberly. He repeated, "*Una última vez. ¿Qué es esto?*"

"*Tu madre,*" she said. *Your momma.*

He kicked back the chair and rose. He walked around behind her and she tensed, preparing for a blow that never came. Instead, the crashing sound of breaking glass and crushing plastic exploded behind her. She could hear his boot come down on the remains of her camera and he twisted his foot to obliterate what was left. Panic washed through her as the evidence of her work was destroyed. All of her pictures...lost forever.

"In my country, that's called destruction of personal property. Maybe even destruction of evidence." The video of her exchange with the official – the video that might convict or acquit her – was most likely on Jean-René's or Chance's camera. It offered her a small glimmer of hope. She needed the ambassador's assistant to see that video. She never laid a hand on Señor Prieta. On the other hand, he had jabbed Rowan in the middle of the chest with his short, stumpy finger. That's what her counsel needed to see.

———

Rowan walked out of the police station into the blinding sun and biting wind. Jean-René stood waiting with a tall woman with long dark hair. "Mr. Pierce?"

"Yes?"

"I'm Consuela Gonzales." She stuck her hand out. "I'm with the American Embassy."

Rowan grimaced at Jean-René. "You called the Embassy?"

"We needed help." He shrugged. "At least I didn't call the Network."

"I contacted your network for you," Gonzales said. "I was able to secure your release, but the local law-enforcement refuses to release your …"

"My boss," Rowan answered the unasked question. "She's the field producer and lead investigator for our show."

"I need to know exactly what happened."

"If we had our equipment, we could show you," Jean-René said. "They confiscated all our cameras."

Rowan blanched, swaying with exhaustion. "What about the digital recorders?"

"Those won't help our case any." Jean-René ran a hand over his closely cropped hair. "She did verbally threaten Señor Prieta."

"She didn't mean it."

"She threatened the government official?" Gonzales' brow furrowed. "Wait a minute. I need you to tell me everything."

"Let's go back to the hotel and get out of the cold," Jean-René said. "It's just down the street."

"We can't leave her here." Rowan protested.

"What choice do we have?"

———

Rowan didn't have the strength to argue. Back at the hotel, he sank into a chair in the lobby, yearning for a good night's rest, yet still jittery. A Peruvian jail was no place to sleep, and after a night in the back of a moving truck with a camera case for a pillow, his back ached.

He let Jean-René fill the embassy rep in on their expedition, and what had transpired between Lauren and the government escort. "And that is when she said something like, if you keep it up, it won't just be a headless chicken-man they find in a cavern in Peru."

"But she didn't mean it," Rowan interjected. "She gets really cranky when people get between her and her work."

The diplomat's assistant looked dubious. "It sure sounds like a threat."

"Look," Rowan said. "She's a scientist in a field that doesn't get a lot of respect. She is trying to be taken seriously, but she never seems to get a break. She was right. We needed the specimen to analyze, but Señor Prieta wouldn't let her have it, so we negotiated for a small sample."

"Oh?"

"She made nice. She did everything she could do to be polite after that."

"And did he accept her apology?"

"Well." Jean-René shrugged. "She didn't exactly apologize."

Consuela set one hand on her knee and leaned forward on the colorful loveseat. "Maybe that's what we need her to do."

———

Lauren lay with her head on the table, praying for some relief for the pain in her shoulders. Hours had passed since the police officer had shattered every camera in her bag. Her face was throbbing, and it was a toss-up what hurt worse, her face or her shoulders. She refused to cry. Tears would make her eyes swell even more and it wouldn't change her situation, so she held them at bay. While distraught over her own plight, she was just as terrified for Rowan, not to mention what the Network was going to say about this fiasco. A muscle in her back spasmed.

There was nothing to save them from simply disappearing from the face of the earth. She blinked rapidly then pressed her eyes closed tight. Maybe that was exactly the idea.

When the door opened again, a woman in a blue jacket and jeans entered. Lauren lifted her head. The woman sat down on the metal chair across from her, the only other seat in the room. "Miss Grayson?"

"It's *Doctor* Grayson." Lauren swallowed hard.

"Dr. Grayson, I'm Consuela Gonzales, with the US Embassy." Her eyes narrowed at Lauren's injured face. "I spoke to your network…"

"What?" Lauren snapped, adding under her breath, "Now we really are going to get cancelled."

"Look, Dr. Grayson. My assignment here is to negotiate your release, but it's very difficult. You threatened a government official."

Lauren heaved a sigh. "I did. But I wouldn't have hurt him … couldn't have."

"Oh?"

"Biggest knife I have in my kit is a scalpel. I could never cut off a man's head with a scalpel, even if I wanted to."

"You are a trained doctor," Consuela said with a hint of a smile.

"A biological anthropologist, not a surgeon; completely different skill set."

"Well, I'm not sure there's anything that would convince them otherwise, but I've brokered a pretty decent deal that could get you out of here. And with what they've done to you, we may have another bargaining chip."

Lauren sat up straighter. "Tell me."

"Initially, they offered to have the charges against you reduced to a misdemeanor if you pay a fine and leave the country immediately. You also have to apologize to Mr. Prieta."

Lauren looked at her blankly. "I will pay the fine. I will leave the country. But I will not apologize to that man."

"I was afraid you'd say that."

———

Consuela paced in the police chief's office that smelled of cigarette smoke and bad coffee, as did the police chief himself. She choked back her disdain as she made her argument in Spanish. "You assaulted an American citizen. You destroyed equipment, including video that could be evidence. Based on this, we will not agree to your offer."

"No one assaulted her," one of the officers offered tonelessly. "She fell."

Consuela did a double take at the comment but calmed herself. "I have been instructed to notify my superiors that if anything happens to this team, Ambassador Francisco will notify the State Department and begin the process of preparing our argument to take to the UN."

The police chief's face turned a beet shade. "You have some nerve."

"I also understand there was video of the confrontation between you and Dr. Pierce," she said. "Video that one of your goons may or may not have destroyed. I need to watch the video from the rest of the cameras, assuming you haven't destroyed those too."

The two men exchanged dubious glances. "May we have a moment to confer, Señora Gonzales?"

"Of course." She stood and walked out to the lobby where Rowan and Jean-René waited. Both of them popped up from the couch like clock springs.

"Did you see her?" Jean-René asked.

"You didn't tell me she'd been beaten."

"What?" Rowan paled, sinking back onto the chair.

Consuela crossed her arms. "We negotiated a deal, but I told them I wouldn't agree to anything until I spoke to Dr. Grayson. After I saw her, and she told me they destroyed some of her video equipment, I went back in with a few more bargaining chips."

"Was it just Lauren's cameras?"

"I don't know," she said. "But I asked to see your video, if it still exists."

"If they haven't ruined our equipment, we're going to need it back."

"I'll do what I can," she said. A wave of dusty smoke billowed out as the police officer stepped into the lobby and motioned her to return to the office.

———

Almost two hours later, Consuela returned. She avoided looking at Rowan and Jean-René. Rowan was running on no sleep, no coffee and no sign of Lauren's release; he felt completely empty.

"I got the charges against her dropped and they've agreed to return all your equipment on one condition."

"Which is?" Rowan asked.

Now Consuela turned and met his eyes. "She has to apologize."

"That's it?" Jean-René asked. "Well, what are we waiting for? Tell her to do it! We'll catch the first flight out of here."

"There's a problem," Consuela said.

A disgusted titter escaped the back of Rowan's throat. "She won't do it."

"You know her pretty well."

"Can I see her?" Rowan asked, feeling the heat of an embarrassing flush rising. "Maybe I can talk some sense into her."

Consuela shrugged. "Let me see what I can do."

———

The pieces of his shattered heart fell into his boots. Lauren sat with her head on the table, her hair coming loose from its plait. She lifted her head as he approached and sat down across from her. "You okay?"

"Do I look okay?"

Rowan shook his head. "Two words. That's all you have to say."

"You're asking me to lie."

Rowan shook his head. "No one said you have to mean it."

"I will not apologize to that hapless little fraction of a man." She enunciated each word, dripping with venom.

"A written apology would do. You wouldn't even have to see him."

"Then there'd be a record of my perjury?" Her voice escalated.

"We can be home in sixteen hours." He held up his hands to placate her. "You can sleep in your own bed tomorrow night. Or mine."

Her eyes narrowed. "Shhh. They're probably listening."

"So what? Just tell him you're sorry and we can go home."

She set her jaw, glaring at him. "I'm only going to say this one more time. I will not apologize, and you are more than welcome to go back to San Diego without me."

"Fine." He stood abruptly. His pulse pounded in his temples. He wanted to rub the headache with his fingertips, but he kept his arms pinned firmly to his sides. "Just fine."

———

Three days later, Lauren stood in front of the police chief's heavy oak desk as the escort himself unlocked the cuffs from her wrists. Lightning bolts shot through her joints, and her fingers tingled. Three days of miserable conditions, no food, barely any water, and constant harassment had finally broken her. She hung her head and stared at the tiles as she forced her dry tongue to make the words.

"I'm sorry."

It left her with a sharp feeling, like a needle through her insides. If anything, she was sorry she *hadn't* hit him. And now, seeing his lips curve in a superior smile, she wanted to even more.

The officer behind the desk returned her backpack and what was left of her equipment. She grabbed it and hugged it to her chest for a second. Fragmented camera pieces rattled in the bottom, but when she unzipped the flap she heaved a sigh of relief; the samples were still there. She only hoped the lab would be able to do something with them.

Then Rowan walked through the door and came over and wrapped her in his arms. She stood there with her head on his shoulder, backpack in one hand, unable to put her arms around him. She wanted to cry now more than ever. But she refused to let any of the policia see her fold. She hated for Rowan to see her like this, but she really needed him.

"You okay?" he asked.

"Other than needing some food, a shower and a handful of Motrin, I'm just freaking great."

"Come on," he took her backpack. "Let's go home."

He put an arm around her and led her out into the dark. She didn't even protest, evidence of how exhausted and beaten she felt. He paused to peel out of his jacket, laying it over her shoulders. He leaned down to kiss her cheek, but she leaned back and pressed her lips to his.

"What was that for?" he asked.

"That was a thank-you … for not leaving without me."

CHAPTER 2

"LET'S GET OUT OF HERE," ROWAN SAID, AT THE DOOR OF THE hotel room Lauren and Bahati had shared. It was almost noon, but Bahati was still in the clothes she'd slept in, looking rumpled and bleary. "Are you okay?"

"I think I had some bad tacos."

A twinkle sparked in his eye. "Are you sure it wasn't too many margaritas?"

She winced. "I only had one." She turned and disappeared behind the bathroom door.

"Got any Pepto?" Lauren asked as she walked over and put her own bags by the door.

Rowan shook his head.

"Some medic you are. Give me a minute and I'll help her get ready."

"It's probably the altitude." Rowan collected her bags to take down to the truck.

"Maybe," Lauren said.

The journey home was a rough one. Bahati spent most of it in the lavatory. The rest of the trip, she curled up in one of the empty rows near the back of the plane.

———

Whatever made Bahati sick, Lauren caught it too, only much worse. Lauren was still weak when they reconvened in a conference room six days later in San Diego. She sipped on bottled seltzer water and noshed on saltines. The bruises on her face had faded to yellow, giving her a jaundiced look.

"You look terrible," Jean-René said. He took a seat across from her, setting down his plate loaded with fruit and a bagel smeared with cream cheese. He had a large Styrofoam cup of coffee and a handful of creamer cups and sugar packages. He made a ritual of opening each cup, pouring the creamer into the coffee, stacking the cups, stuffing the scraps of the lids into the last cup, and then stacking the sugar packets. "You look like you need a rock to curl up under."

Normally, she would have flipped him off for a comment like that, but today she was in no mood. "I think I brought home a little souvenir from Peru," she groaned, glaring at his plate, her stomach churning at the thought of real food. The aroma of the skunky coffee hit her, and she could feel acid rising in her throat. Against her pitch-black hair, her skin looked sallow. Dark circles framed her coal-colored eyes.

"You didn't get malaria, did you?"

"I'm sure it was just something I ate. Too cold for malaria." She shrugged, closing her eyes. "Probably the same thing Bahati ate."

"You should go to the clinic and let them check you out."

"We've lost enough time. We need to work on the evidence. I just got the samples picked up by the courier this morning. They won't be back from the lab for at least ten days."

Jean-René crammed half a bagel in his mouth, chewing viciously. She envied his appetite, thinking about how gaunt she'd appeared that morning in the mirror. She needed calories, but right now, she just wanted to vomit … again.

Bahati came in, followed by Rowan. "Christ, Lauren. You look terrible," Bahati said. "And I thought I'd been sick in Peru."

"Just a stomach bug," Lauren assured them. "Grab some coffee and let's get started before I pass out."

"You should be at home in bed," Rowan scolded as he stowed his equipment in the corner. He needed to change batteries and do other maintenance tasks before their next assignment. His first aid supplies also had to be replenished, but right now, Lauren had his attention.

He sat beside her and put a hand on her forehead. She wasn't feverish, but her skin was moist. "You're clammy." He inspected her with a trained eye and checked her pulse. "Did you take the doxycycline while we were down there?"

Lauren shrugged in a way that told him she hadn't.

"You weren't this sick yesterday, were you? When did it get worse?"

"I don't know. It's all running together." She brushed him off, pushing him away weakly. "I'm fine. Please. Let's just get started. Where's the—"

Rowan caught her elbow as she swooned. He kept her from falling face first into the table, leaning her chair back to keep her from slumping out of it.

"That's it." Rowan stood and scooped her up. "You're going to the clinic."

The room spun about her and she felt a veil of blackness returning. "No. Wait. Put me down."

"You guys go ahead and get started on the after-action review," Rowan instructed them.

Jean-René stood. "I'll drive." He grabbed Rowan's medic kit. "Let's just take her straight to the ER. The clinic won't be able to do much for her."

———

The doctor stared down his nose over his glasses at the preliminary test results. "It doesn't appear to be tropical."

Lauren curled up in a ball, gripping her stomach, a fresh emesis basin close to her face in case she felt the need to vomit … again. An IV dripped into her veins and replenished her fluids and electrolytes. She was badly dehydrated.

"What did you eat while you were in Peru?"

"I really don't want to talk about food right now," she groaned.

"Did you eat anything while you were in jail?" Rowan asked.

"Jail?" The doctor's brows lifted.

"No." Lauren rolled over.

Rowan shook his head. "She ate pretty much the same things the rest of us ate. We followed all the rules, bottled water only, didn't eat any fruit we didn't peel ourselves. We avoided street vendors and stuck to pre-packaged rations as much as possible. No raw fish, no raw vegetables. Tacos and margaritas in Cusco, but nothing unusual."

"I'll run a few more tests, but it's definitely not malaria." He scratched his nose with his pinkie. "Any chance you might be pregnant?"

Rowan caught her eye.

"No," she said. "Absolutely not."

"I'll run a pregnancy test anyway, just to make sure."

"It's a waste of time."

"Probably. But you'd be surprised how often I hear that, only to have the test come back positive."

"It won't," she insisted. She rose to her elbow in time to vomit into the basin. Jean-René and Rowan blanched. Now the words came easily: "I'm sorry." Physical weakness embarrassed her.

The doctor collected his chart and rose. "I'll send the nurse in with something to help ease your nausea." He patted her shoulder. "Just hang tight until we figure this out. We'll get you admitted and find out what's going on."

———

Whatever the nurse gave her, it didn't ease her stomach, but it did make her loopy. She slept through the afternoon. When she finally came around, her stomach had settled enough that she didn't feel the need to barf immediately, though her body felt like lead and her head felt stuffed with cotton. The IV in her hand hurt, and the tape holding it in place tugged on the fine hairs of her arm.

Rowan stood by the window staring out over the wide San Diego bay. The water was dark; winter-stormy. The constant beep of monitors and the acrid smell of antiseptic filled the room, but he was a million miles away. He turned abruptly when she shifted, and he realized she was awake. "Welcome back," he said, smiling. "Feel better?"

"A little." She shrugged, pulling the blanket up over her shoulders. She was cold and she wasn't sure if it was the temperature or if she had chills.

"Well, it isn't salmonella, it's not botulism, and it's not any kind of waterborne illness, spirochete, or parasite," he said, leaning on the bedrail.

"I guess that's a good thing."

"We know what it isn't."

"What about the pregnancy test?"

"Negative."

"I told him so."

"What made you so certain?" He eyed her cautiously.

"A woman knows," she said, closing her eyes.

"Would you have been upset if you'd been wrong? I wouldn't."

"You know we can't do what we do if we're tied down with a kid."

"So, this is it? This is all we get?"

"What are you talking about?"

"You're almost thirty. I am thirty. How long are we going to bounce around the world? Can't we settle down? Stay home for a while? I want to marry you, Lauren. I want to think about a life with a home, with children. Don't you want children?"

"I used to," she said, rolling onto her back, fixing her eyes on the ceiling. "But I love what we do. I like our life the way it is now. I don't want to mess that up." She put her hand on his as it rested on the bedrail. She shifted uncomfortably but didn't withdraw her hand. The plastic mattress cover crinkled beneath her.

He placed his other hand on top of hers. "Will getting married mess that up?"

"Will *not* getting married mess that up?" She challenged. "It's just a piece of paper."

"It's not just a piece of paper. It's a commitment."

"I made that commitment the first time I kissed you, Rowan. I don't need some arcane mating ritual to prove that to you. Do you?"

"I wouldn't say I need it, but…I want it."

"I don't need it and to be honest, I really don't want it."

"Does that mean…you don't want me?"

"Of course it doesn't." She softened her stern façade. "I do love you. Really. You know that, right?"

"You won't even let the rest of the team see that we're together." He slumped. "We can't live together, and when I do stay over, you make us show up to work in separate cars. I don't know why it has to be such a secret."

"You know why. We both have a professional reputation at stake. Do we really have to discuss this now? Can we please change the subject?"

"You want something to eat?" he asked.

She sat up abruptly and puked into the basin. He withdrew his foot just in time to avoid the overflow. "We've been through this...before, Rowan." Lauren choked out the words, coughing as she reached for a cup of water to rinse her mouth out before collapsing back to the bed.

"Can you just drop it already?"

"Don't my feelings count in this equation? You've put me off and pushed me away every time this subject comes up. I'm not going to let it go. Dammit! Marry me."

Lauren set her jaw as she stared him down, her eyes as black as night, her expression just as cold.

He met her gaze with equal fortitude. "This is about getting cancelled isn't it?"

"What?" Lauren turned abruptly against her pillow. "No! God, no!"

"You're afraid if the show gets cancelled then you won't have any more excuses to not marry me. Fine! I hope they cancel the damn show!"

The words raised the color on Lauren's pale face to a red-hot glow. "That's got nothing to do with it. We needed that stupid alien in Peru to keep our jobs. Five years we've been at this, and in five years have we ever found anything? Unidentified hairs and one footprint in Nepal. That's it! Even the crew of *Ghost Adventures* has had better luck at finding ghosts than we have. The team looking for the Loch Ness Monster got some halfway decent footage."

"I'm not sure a grainy clip that looks like a giant eel counts as decent footage; not even halfway." Rowan sat on the foot of the narrow bed.

"We talked about this when you joined the team. The last thing I want is a show where all anyone does is scream at the squirrels rustling in the woods." Lauren softened. She snaked her hand into his. "Look. If we don't get these next six episodes produced, the Network won't have anything to show for their investments and we will get cancelled for sure. If we get cancelled then it's back to working as an EMT for you, and I have to go off to some university and beg for a job working as a stupid lab assistant. Then, neither of us will be happy."

Rowan remained stone-faced. "I'm not happy now, Lauren."

"But don't you love what we do?" She had never really seen this side of him before, and she felt the need to defuse his anger.

"I love everything we do, but I don't like who we are. I don't like *this*!" He snapped, and he liked that it seemed to faze her. "I don't like being held at arm's length in limbo. I don't know how much longer I can pretend I don't love you. Quite frankly, Lauren, I don't know how you do it."

The words were harsh, and they hurt. "But ..."

Rowan raised a finger in front of his determined face. "Stop. Don't say it."

"What?" Lauren lifted her empty hands in question.

"Don't say I love you," he said. "I don't need your empty words. I don't want to hear it."

Lauren felt as if the air had been knocked from her lungs. He bowed up like he had more to say, but abruptly turned and blustered out of the room, leaving her in the awkward dust cloud of his anger. She heard the crash of falling dishes in the hallway.

She understood how he felt. She just didn't get why he, of all people, felt the need for society's approval.

———

Rowan broke through the main doors at the San Diego General Hospital. He hesitated only a moment, caught off guard by the sudden change in the weather, the afternoon rain immediately buffeting his face. Resigned, he stormed down the sidewalk. He didn't stop until he was standing in the middle of the parking lot of the San Diego Zoo. The miles had passed along with his anger and the afternoon rain.

Although exhausted and spent, he paid and entered the zoo. He had it nearly to himself at this time of year. He hunched against the wind and trod through the pathways.

He loved Lauren more than life, but she obviously wasn't at the same place in their relationship. Their lives as well as their careers were intertwined. He loved the job as much as she did. He loved her as much as she loved the job. But for her everything else came second, himself included.

He just didn't know how to get her to see how important she was in his life, and how badly he wanted what other men had—a home with a wife and a family. Didn't he deserve happiness? Even the lions and wolves huddled snug in their dens. Her words resounded in his head as he replayed the whole argument until it threatened to drive him mad. Somewhere, in a distant cage, a monkey screeched.

Funny—Lauren could be so brave, standing with her fists clenched against a Peruvian government official, yet too chicken to admit her feelings.

He surprised himself by laughing out loud. What was he doing here, touring listless, caged animals in the winter, when he should be by her side?

———

Rowan's heart was still pounding from the hike. He heard his own pulse in his ears as he went down the long, quiet corridors toward Lauren's hospital room. He steeled himself before he opened the door. He entered quietly, finding the head of the bed had been raised. Lauren lay with her head back and her eyes closed. An untouched dinner tray sat on its mobile table, still covered, in front of her. Her red face and swollen eyes told him he wasn't the only one who'd had a good cry.

She started to say something, but he made a gesture that cut her off as he pulled up the rolling stool and sat beside her.

"Look, I don't want to fight right now," he said, leaning his arms on the rail of her bed. "I shouldn't have brought it up when you're so sick, and I'm sorry."

Lauren let her head fall back on the pillow, too weak to hold it up and glare at him. She shook her head and closed her eyes, turning away.

Rowan rolled his eyes, heaving a heavy sigh. "I'm sorry, Lauren. Can we just talk about work for a second?"

Lauren turned back toward him eagerly. "Really?"

"It figures, *that* would get you to perk up. Well, Bahati and Jean-René have poured over the data. They sent the pictures of that…thing… to the forensic anthropologist. He thinks it may be mammalian, but he doesn't know what it is. The anthropomorphic data has him stumped. The shape of the hip bones, and what look like feet, don't identify it as a bird—or anything else for that matter. Without the head, it's just hard to say. We'll probably have to wait for the lab results."

"Fine. What about the disc in the sky?"

"They've replayed that section of the tape hundreds of times. Even in slow motion, frame-by-frame, they can't get the image to clear."

"Did they enhance the video?"

"They're working on that now."

"Have we finished the post-production voiceovers for the last episode?"

"You've got some left to do. But you've got a couple more days before we need to worry about it."

"Can I get something to drink? Sprite or ginger ale or something?" The carton of milk and glass of iced tea had been untouched, along with everything else, except for a package of saltines.

A toothy grin spread across his face. "I thought you'd never ask," he said, feeling relieved that she needed him for something. "I'll get it."

———

She was sipping ginger ale from a plastic spoon and nibbling ice chips when the doctor came in with her chart.

"Miss Grayson?" He glanced up at her. "Have you undergone treatment for cancer recently?"

"No." She set the cup down, swallowing hard, nearly choking on the ice. Rowan got out of his chair and came to her bedside, paled.

"No radiation treatment?"

"No."

"Were you anywhere near a nuclear reactor while you were in Peru?"

"Not that I know of." Lauren felt nauseated again. "Why? What's going on?"

"Our tests show you've been exposed to some form of radiation. It appears to be mild, but you will need treatment to remove any residual contamination from your system and we'll need to watch you for signs of anemia."

"Radiation?" Lauren fumbled. "We passed through security x-rays several times during the trip. The airport here, the one in Cusco."

"The radiation from those are negligible. This would have been something significant." He took her hands and examined the skin on her arms. "We've got a specialist on call who's reviewing your chart to develop a treatment plan. Usually people with radiation exposure will have some kind of skin damage, anything from what looks like a sunburn to hair loss or a severe rash. But I don't see any marks at all."

"I went everywhere she went and I'm not sick," Rowan said. "How can that be?"

"You may have lesser exposure. But we should probably test you as well."

"We should test the whole team. Bahati got sick too, but we presumed it was altitude sickness," he said.

"That would be a good idea," the doctor agreed. "There are several treatment plans, and once the specialist goes over your test results, we'll be better prepared to discuss your options."

CHAPTER 3

ONE OF THE NURSES WALKED WITH LAUREN AS SHE LEANED ON the IV pole like a crutch. She'd spent the past few days taking walks like this between treatments, hoping to regain her strength. Today, it tired her out, and she said as much. They stopped at the nurses' station for her to rest. "Sit down," the nurse said. "I'll go get you some water."

Lauren complied, leaning her head against the wall. In the med room, two of the staff were having a raucous conversation. "I don't know why I even bother watching that stupid show," one of them said. "It's not like they ever find anything."

"I'll admit, I only watch it to see who's going to fall off a cliff or trip over a rock in the dark," the other retorted. "Not like I believe in little green men from Mars or el chupacabra. It's laughable at best."

"I know, it's all just a bunch of hokum."

Lauren stood and directed an evil eye at them both. One of the women saw her. Her face turned red. Lauren could feel the heat rising in her own cheeks. The other turned and gasped. The first tried to apologize, but as soon as she opened her mouth to speak, Lauren took a hold of the IV pole and used the last of her energy to rise stiffly and return to her room. Her anger fueled the effort and she made the decision right then and there that she was going home.

————

Lauren was fumbling with the clothes she'd worn to the hospital when Bahati came that afternoon. The IV was in the way. She picked at the corner of the tape, trying to save ripping it off, along with the hair on her arms.

"What are you doing, Boss?"

No one else had tested positive for radiation poisoning, and Lauren reached the limit of her patience. The incident at the nurses' station was the tipping point. She refused to take this lying down. She'd had enough.

"I'm going home," she snapped. "I don't have time for this."

"You're in no shape to go home."

Lauren's knees buckled; Bahati reached out and caught her arm. "Sit down before you fall down."

Lauren knew it was futile. She surrendered.

"Did the doctor say you could go home?"

"It's still a free country, isn't it?"

"Lauren," Bahati scolded. "You're just going to make yourself even sicker. Didn't you tell me the doctor said it would take a week to finish the treatments?"

"The treatments aren't working." Lauren lowered her voice an octave. "I'm not getting any better...and I sure as hell can't get any work done tethered to this ... this ..." She held up her hand, inspecting the IV line pathetically. The medication that flowed through it was designed to bind with the radioactive metals that were plaguing her, so they could be flushed from her system "I don't have time to be sick."

"You don't have the strength to waste fighting what must be done, Lauren," Bahati sat down beside her. She put her arm around her and ran a hand down Lauren's long braid. "What's really bothering you?"

Lauren hung her head. She choked back her emotion. "We're going to get cancelled, and it's all my fault."

"You don't believe that, do you? It's nothing more than gossip, you know. Right?"

"Most shows don't last as long as we have. It's inevitable. The Network is going to cut us." She ran a weary hand over her face. "I don't blame them. We never find anything. It's all just a bunch of ... *hokum*."

"We have over 800,000 followers on Twitter and Facebook."

"We used to have a million."

"Our Yeti episode was the number one most-watched reality show of all time."

"All we found was a footprint in the snow. And the cast broke in shipping!" She looked over her friend's shoulder and out the window, as completely devoid of emotion as the gray sky.

Bahati threw up her hands in disgust. "We had more people show up for our panel discussion at Comic-Con than the cast of *The Walking Dead*."

"So?"

"So, we're the anchor show for Friday night programming on the Exploration Channel. They'd be stupid to cancel our show. We make a lot of money for the Network."

"It's not enough. It's never enough." Lauren felt too weak to sit up anymore. She curled up against the head of the bed. "Ratings have been falling. Critics blast us at every turn. I needed that stupid little headless chicken man thing. I needed it to fix this." She gestured vaguely, sucked in a deep breath, then trembled as she let it out. "Stupid Peruvian government. Can you imagine what our ratings would be like if we could have proven that thing was extraterrestrial?"

Bahati straightened and narrowed her brow. "Shame on you,

Lauren Grayson." She shook her finger at her boss. "Since when has our job been about proving headless chicken things were aliens? You preach it to us all the time. We're doing this to find the *truth*. It's not about revealing aliens or ghosts or proving monsters exist. Hoax or myth, fact or fiction. Finding the answers is our mission, period. You've lost your focus, Lauren. Don't let them do that to you. Stick to the founding principle of our work—the truth."

Lauren's face twisted sarcastically. "The *truth* doesn't make for good television."

"If you're dead, you won't make for good television either. Now will you please forget about going home and stay where you belong? You don't look so hot."

Lauren wanted to put up a fight. She wasn't one to let an argument go so easily. At the moment, her strength was waning. She decided to bide her time, for now. When they left her alone long enough, she'd get dressed, sign out AMA and call for an Uber. At least, that was the plan.

CHAPTER 4

THE DOCTORS DECIDED THEIR TREATMENTS WEREN'T ENOUGH TO
cleanse her blood of the toxins. Although she wasn't getting
worse, she wasn't getting better, either.

"I think a blood transfusion or two are in order," the doctor
said the next afternoon. "We've tried adding a protein to
increase the production of white blood cells, but it would
appear your red blood cells are low too."

Lauren whimpered. "I can't keep going like this."

"Hold tight." He patted her arm. "We're going to get you
feeling better, but you have to do your part."

"What's that?" Lauren rolled her head towards him.

"Rest, eat well, drink lots of fluids …"

"If it gets me out of this lumpy bed faster, I'll do whatever
you tell me."

"Those are my orders."

Lauren raised a shaky hand toward her brow. "Aye, aye,
Captain."

———

As soon as Rowan picked her up from the hospital to take her home a week later, she insisted he stop by the studio so she could record her voiceover for the episode in post-production. He protested, but realized arguing would only make things worse, so he acquiesced. Fortunately, it didn't take long. Lauren was a pro.

Lauren's apartment on Ambrosia Drive featured floor-to-ceiling windows that brightened the rooms and provided spectacular views of the city surrounded by palm trees and hills. The pool outside her patio seemed to stretch to the horizon, meeting the ocean. She plopped down on the sofa as Rowan placed her suitcases by the bedroom door.

"Jean-René made soup and brought it over last night. I think there's some French bread too, if you're hungry."

"I'm tired," she admitted. "I thought after spending a week in bed that I'd be more anxious to do stuff, but all I can think of is a nap."

"So, take a nap."

Lauren didn't move to the bedroom. She sank more deeply into the sofa, staring out the window. "I can't keep going like this." Her shoulders slumped as she lay her head in her hand.

"You won't," he said. "This too shall pass."

"What are we doing with the show?"

He sat down across from her, running his hand through his mop of rusty-brown hair, tugging at it as he groaned. "We keep looking for the truth."

"What if we never find it?"

He turned and looked away, staring out the window rather than looking at her. "I don't know." He stood and paced to the kitchen. "I guess we find something else to do."

"I don't want to end up working for a university...it got me my PhD, but I hated being stuck in a lab all day."

Rowan came over and put his hand on her back. "We'll figure something out. I sure don't wanna be an EMT again, and

I sure ain't going to work at Burger King." That made Lauren laugh through her tears. "Now, go lie down and get some rest. This is the worst possible time to try and make any decision, when you're tired like this."

Lauren nodded, reaching for a tissue to dry her eyes.

"I'll come back by this evening and check on you."

"No," Lauren caught his hand as he started to leave. "Please. Don't go."

A little surprised, Rowan nodded and helped her to her feet. He took her to bed and lay down beside her, letting her use his shoulder for a pillow. Her leg snaked over his as she melted into him.

"What's our next investigation?"

"We were supposed to go to Washington State," he said, surprise ebbing away. "They've had some recent alleged Bigfoot activity."

"Wonder if Bigfoot will be as helpful as his cousins, the Yeti, were. Maybe they'll leave us better prints."

"You're not up to traveling yet, least of all a hike through the mountains at high elevations. You saw what the altitude did to Bahati. And she was healthy."

Lauren nodded against his chest. "We need to start planning, at least. We should be ready to go as soon as we can."

"Maybe in a couple of weeks." Rowan bit his tongue. For her, everything was job, job, job. "You need time to mend."

"I will do nothing but rest for the next few weeks." She yawned. "I promise. Will you get with the Network and make travel arrangements?"

Rowan stiffened, but as always, he gave in to her. "Sure."

———

Much to his surprise, Lauren did exactly what she had promised. She spent most of her time in bed, though with her iPad, reviewing the remaining video and photos from Peru from every camera and every angle. If she wasn't curled up in bed, she was stretched out on the sofa. Rowan brought all her meals and tidied the apartment. One afternoon he came in with Chinese food. She seemed more her old self, and that put a big grin on his face.

"When are we leaving for Spokane?" She fidgeted with the tassel on the sofa cushion.

"I'm still waiting for word from the Network. Maybe in three or four weeks. The weather should be better by then, though it's still early in the season. We'll see. Do you think you'll have a doctor's release by the end of the month?"

Lauren nodded. "I've got a follow-up appointment next week. I feel tons better and I'm getting restless." She joined him at the table. "There's just so much to be done here before we leave."

"It's being done," he insisted. "You don't have to worry about any of it. All the samples were sent off. We've reviewed all the film footage and other evidence, but we haven't come to any kind of a consensus yet. The team will handle the analysis."

"I've been looking at the video, but ... I'm just as stumped as you are."

"Maybe the lab will have better luck."

She inhaled the perfume that wafted from the plate, taking the chopsticks out of the paper wrappers, snapping them apart. "Mm I smell egg rolls."

Rowan placed one on the plate in front of her. "I'm glad to see you getting your appetite back."

His phone rang as he was about to sit down. He noted the number on the Caller ID. Odd that the lab would call so late. "Rowan Pierce." He left Lauren to her feast and took his phone call out to the patio, closing the door behind him.

"Hey, Rowan. It's Glenn. What the hell is this stuff y'all sent me to analyze?"

"We were hoping you'd tell us."

Rowan turned his back so Lauren couldn't see his reaction, just in case she was watching. He tried to be casual as he leaned on the railing overlooking the pool.

"I've got three lab technicians in the hospital with radiation poisoning and I've had to move the samples into containment. I can't even get them analyzed to find out what kind of radioactive materials they contain. I don't have the resources for that here."

Rowan tensed straight up. "That explains a lot. Lauren carried the samples. She did all the evidence collection."

"She's not sick, is she?"

"She spent a week in the hospital. We never put two and two together."

"Well, what do you think these samples are? Where did you get them?"

"A mummified corpse in a cave in the Peruvian desert. The anthropomorphic data has our scientists puzzled. They think it could be mammalian, but there's conflicting evidence."

Rowan pressed the phone hard to his ear, waiting apprehensively through the pause on the other end. "You've sent me lots of crazy stuff over the past few years, but this takes the cake," Glenn allowed. "Are you thinking it might be extraterrestrial?"

"That's the theory," Rowan said. "But without those samples, we have nothing."

"So, what do you want me to do with them?"

"Any chance they were contaminated after collection?"

"Knowing Lauren and her chain-of-evidence collection procedures? I'd have to say no. Why do you ask?"

Rowan didn't mention the incident with the police in Cusco. "Never mind. Are there any labs that can analyze them?"

"I've made a few phone calls. I found one in New Mexico that can."

"Ship it and send me the bill." *If it's not one thing it's another.*

The Network was gonna have kittens when they found out they'd made the lab folks sick too.

"How's Lauren doing?"

"She's resting at home and getting stronger all the time," Rowan said. "She's hoping we'll be able to leave for Spokane in three or four weeks."

"Well, don't bring me any other radiated samples, okay?"

"Just fuzzy brown hairs. At least, that's the plan."

"Going 'squatchin'?" Rowan could hear the grin. "Be sure to bottle any fecal samples in alcohol. That's the best way to preserve the DNA."

"Which is better, vodka or rum?"

"Isopropyl." And the line went dead.

CHAPTER 5

"Stories of the Wild-Man are found throughout the history of the indigenous tribes here in the Pacific Northwest," Lauren explained as they unloaded the truck at the trailhead. The crew included camera and audio specialists, assistant researchers, and *Sherpas* to haul the equipment. Everyone gathered around, inspecting equipment one last time to make sure it hadn't been damaged in shipping. "Members of the Lummi tribe told tales of the *Ts'emekwes* ... their name for Bigfoot."

"So, let's talk about some of the hazards we can expect to encounter." Rowan took a seat on one of the cases. A mission and safety briefing was routine before every expedition. "Over the course of the next week, we're going to be doing a lot of hiking on Mount Saint Helens. Most of it will be uphill, and we'll be gaining approximately 4,500 to 5,500 feet in elevation. I hope everyone ate their Wheaties this morning," he joked. "Human error is one of the leading causes of injury here in the National Park. Second is the climate. I checked the weather conditions, and it looks like we have a few good days ahead of us, but there's a chance of rain later in the week. Rain comes with the risk of lightning, alluvial flooding and mudslides."

Lauren took over. "This is a strenuous climb. Now, we're all in pretty good physical condition, but that doesn't mean we can let our guard down. So, check your gear, double knot your hiking boots, and let's load up. We have a long hike ahead of us."

———

"As if it's not bad enough worrying about the active volcano beneath our feet, we're hunting for a man-eating bigfoot," Rowan narrated to the camera as the team made its way up the damp mountain path—an animal trail, really. "Two days of hiking in the cold rain has been miserable, and everyone is near exhaustion, but we're getting closer to the lair of the legendary Bigfoot."

Jean-René flipped the camera off. "Clear."

"Man-eater?" Bahati gulped.

"Don't let him scare you. It's just an old folk tale," Lauren said. "The worst reports, of late, have just been some rock throwing."

"It is a wild creature," Rowan warned. "Just because it hasn't been violent doesn't mean it won't protect itself or its offspring if it feels threatened."

"I don't intend to threaten it." Bahati held her hands up.

Lauren shrugged the pack onto her shoulders to adjust it. Her back ached and her feet were cold and wet. "I just want to take its picture. Do you think it would pose with me for a selfie?"

Rowan rolled his eyes and stepped up to where the path opened onto a wide clearing. The sound of running water implied there was a stream nearby, a sorely needed source of fresh water.

"This looks like a good place to make camp for the night," Jean-René said.

"We've got two hours of daylight," Lauren said. "Let's go

ahead and break out the equipment. Jean-René and I will scout the area once we make camp and see if there are any signs of our target."

———

In no time, Jean-René had the camera equipment unpacked. Lauren checked her dart pistol before she returned it to her hip holster. It was loaded with a powerful tranquilizer, the only weapon they were allowed to have in the National Park. Guns were prohibited by Federal law. She'd had to use it once before when an aggressive black bear surprised her in the Alaskan back country. She hadn't been that lucky when she ran into a grizzly a few months before, and had narrowly escaped by slipping inside an abandoned cabin. She wouldn't go out without one now.

"Aren't you tired?" Jean-René asked, once they were alone.

"Yes," Lauren admitted. "But I have a job to do."

"You should lie down after dinner and rest. It could be a long night."

"I won't be able to sleep. Especially if we get any kind of activity. There's plenty of time for sleep tomorrow."

"Rowan said he wanted to get deeper into the forest." Jean-René shook his head. "We might have to hike … especially if we don't find anything here."

A rustling in the distance drew her eyes to the tree line. Jean-René looked at her, then turned, searching for what had caught her attention. He lifted his camera and switched it to infrared. "Did you see something?"

"Maybe." She held a finger to her lips as she paused to listen. "Got anything on camera?"

"Heat signature on that big fir tree, fading fast."

She moved to see the viewfinder. "Do bears leave hand-prints?" The fading mark on the tree looked almost human.

"Chance!" Jean-René shouted. "Rowan?" A distant crash echoed above them on the steep hillside. Something moved farther in the distance; a large shadow in the woods. "What was that?"

"Let's find out," she said, taking off after it.

"Lauren, wait." Jean-René rushed to catch up with her. "Are you sure it's a good idea to go chasing bears in the woods?"

She stopped abruptly, looking down at the loam in front of her. With a hint of caution in her voice she said, "I don't think it was a bear."

Jean-René followed her gaze to a large depression in the soft earth. "Oh, wow…"

The footprint was at least fifteen inches long, twice as long as an average human footprint. It was deep in the mud, but it looked as if it hadn't been there long, though the soil was lightening as it dried around the edges.

Lauren called Rowan to join them. He sat on his heels beside her. "Did you bring the casting kit?" she asked. Jean-René nodded. "Make sure the site is secure. We don't need whatever made that print sneaking up on us."

"Look, you can see the toes. Is that an imprint of hair?" Jean-René was still focused on the print. Lauren bent down on her hands and knees with a magnifying glass and flashlight, inspecting it.

"Sure enough," she said. "Great way to start the investigation! I didn't think we'd find anything for at least another day or two." She mixed the compound with water from her canteen. "It's a good location. Close to the water, off the beaten path. Looks like there's plenty of game and natural cover. If I were Bigfoot, I'd like it here."

Rowan gasped as he knelt beside her, inspecting the depression with his flashlight. He shook his head. "Impressive."

"Okay, I have the casting agent mixed. Ready to film?"

"Yeah. Let's get this one in the can on the first take, okay?"

Jean-René gave them the thumbs up as he switched on the camera.

Lauren narrated as she poured the plaster into the crater left by the unknown creature. "I'm using a product called *Dental Stone*. It's stronger and less likely to crumble than plaster. We'll want to make sure this cast is viable for researchers for many years to come." It would take thirty minutes for the cast to dry, but the viewing audience would see less than thirty seconds. The half-hour spent waiting for the cast to dry would be edited out in post-production.

———

"We better make sure the motion-activated trap-cams are set around the perimeter. I don't want this thing walking in on us unawares in the middle of the night," Lauren instructed, as they waited for the cast. "Jean-René, do we have a GPS ping on this location?"

"Yes, I've got it logged," he said. "I'll get the trap-cams set up. How long until dinner?"

"Always worried about your stomach." Lauren rolled her eyes at him, grinning.

"I think it's Lauren's night to cook, right?" Rowan winked at Jean-René. "I can pull the cast when it's dry. Why don't you go start dinner?"

Lauren's eyes flamed, as did her cheeks. "Do you think I'm your wife or chef or something?" She narrowed her eyes, staring them both down. She spoke intentionally to their Director of Photography and avoided looking at Rowan.

"It's only because you're such a good cook," Rowan said, clearly letting the comment go.

She softened. "Was someone going to start me a fire?"

"Bahati is in charge of setting up base camp, and that

includes getting a fire going," Rowan said. "I don't smell smoke yet."

"Why can't she cook dinner? Oh, right … she can't cook. My bad." Lauren rose, turning away from the casting. "What sounds good?"

"Red beans and rice," Jean-René and Rowen said in unison. It was always what they asked for when it was Lauren's turn to cook.

"Red beans and rice it is," she said, pulling on her backpack. "Make sure you bag it and fill out the chain of custody records," she called back.

"Do I look like a rookie to you?" Jean-René asked. She flipped him off over her shoulder as she headed back to base camp.

———

Bahati had set up the tents in a semi-circle around the fire. A pile of wood had been collected by the team and sat ready for a fire to be built.

"They sent you to camp to cook, didn't they?" Bahati asked. She swore under her breath, but all Lauren heard was, "Men."

"No kidding," Lauren said. "Where's the chow locker?"

"Over by Jean-René's tent. I found a tree stump that would make a nice stool or prep table. Looks like loggers have been through here before."

Lauren studied the stump and nodded. "It's been a while." She started building a fire. "Funny how some place so isolated from the world has ever seen man's touch … yet, here's proof."

"There's no wild planet left anymore," Bahati agreed, putting bed rolls out in each tent.

A blood-curdling cry broke the stillness of the afternoon and reverberated in the pines. The trembling of the branches made the needles fall like snow. They froze, wide eyes locked on one another. Bahati scrambled into the tent, spinning around on her hands and knees. Her eyes widened and her skin seemed darker against the white of her frightened gaze. Lauren rose, turning her head in the direction of the sound.

Jean-René appeared with the cameras rolling to catch her reaction as she searched for the source of the eerie cry. "You guys heard that?"

"What was it?" Bahati asked. "Wolves?"

"That was no wolf," Lauren said. She would know. She spent several years in Yellowstone studying the wolf population when she was doing her internship as researcher for PBS on the science program, *Nova*. She'd filmed wolf populations in Alaska as well. If there was one animal she knew better than any other, it was the wolf.

"What was it, then?" Bahati's voice trembled, and dwindled to a frightened squeak when the somber cry broke the trees again. Birds scattered and the woods went quiet.

Lauren reached for the dart pistol on her belt, loosened the clasp, but kept it holstered. Her eye went to the locker she knew contained a can of bear mace. The dart gun should be enough, but she only had two shots before she would have to reload. The mace would be easy to reach, but would it be as effective on a cryptid as it was on a bear?

"That was closer." Jean-René's voice was strong, but Lauren recognized his growing concern by his thickening accent. He moved in, still keeping the camera on the women. Bahati huddled in her tent, while Lauren stood fixed, ready for battle.

"Where are the digital recorders?" Lauren asked. Bahati scrambled out of the tent to one of the piles of packs that had been hauled up the mountain on the backs of the technicians and *Sherpas* who accompanied the team. They established a base camp where most of the support crew would remain while the production team continued on, carrying only what they needed on their backs. It kept unnecessary parties from ending up in a camera shot but left them close enough to provide additional support if needed.

Bahati brought her one. Lauren clicked it on. "We're in the Cascade Mountains in central Washington State on the lower fringes of Mount Saint Helens." She hesitated when the howling reverberated again, this time to her left. Still distant, the creature was obviously on the move…or there was more than one.

"Camera rolling," Jean-René said. Lauren nodded and set the voice recorder on the stump.

"Is it possible," she asked, still watching the tree line cautiously, "that a giant, hairy creature called Bigfoot could inhabit the forested lands of our planet? Many people think so. This reclusive, unpredictable animal is the subject of much debate, and though often called a hoax, the legend of Bigfoot continues to be perpetuated by eyewitness encounters, scratchy audio, and grainy photographic evidence.

"The name Bigfoot," she continued, "is often interchangeable with Sasquatch, a word derived from the Salish language meaning hairy man—a bipedal creature, rarely seen, yet often discussed. Many disbelievers claim that ample evidence does not exist to substantiate the existence of Bigfoot. *The Veritas Codex* team is here in the mountains of the northern United States on the trail of the elusive Bigfoot. If there's evidence out there, we intend to find it."

"Good," Jean-René lowered the camera while Lauren returned her attention to the trees, searching for any sign of movement or eyes watching them.

"Where's Rowan?"

Jean-René sat the camera down, rubbing his shoulder. "He was collecting the cast. When we heard that noise, he sent me to you."

"We need to stay together until we figure out what that was and where that was." Lauren's hair stood up on the back of her neck. A sense of dread washed over her. She wasn't prone to such flights of discontent, but when she felt this way, she knew it was important to act on it. "We need to find him."

"I sent Chance to take over the camera when I passed him on the trail," Jean-René said. "So, it's not like he's alone."

Lauren reached for the walkie-talkie on her belt. "Base camp to Rowan."

There was a long pause. "Rowan here." The audio crackled and he sounded winded.

"We've got audio set up. Where are you?"

"We had rocks thrown at us about the time all the howling started. We followed something into the woods across the river, but we seem to have lost whatever it was."

"Did you see anything?"

"No. But Chance is going to have one hell of a shiner. Whatever it was, it's a good shot. They really do throw rocks."

"We need everyone back to base camp to set up the perimeter and get ready for sunset. If anything else is going to happen, it's more likely after twilight."

"We're on our way back now," he said. "I'm gonna need my medic bag."

CHAPTER 6

A SOMBER HOWL ECHOED OVER THE MOUNTAIN. HEART-SHAPED aspen leaves trembled. Pine needles fell like rain on the team's heads as the deep timber reverberated through their branches. For a time, the forest grew quiet, and only the thundering clamor of his pulse echoed in Rowan's ears. The hike was hard enough in the higher elevations without the fear of a monster lurking in the woods. Another round of howls seemed to follow from the other side of the valley as Rowan and Chance returned to base camp. This time it was farther away, a comforting distance that allowed the team to breathe a sigh of relief.

Chance looked a bit peeked, and true to Rowan's prediction, a growing bruise spread around his eye, accented with a goose-egg forming just above his temple. There was blood running down his brow and along the side of his face where it was beginning to dry, the stain on his gray t-shirt turning dark.

Rowan put on gloves and got out some sterile gauze while Lauren sat Chance on the tree stump for a closer look. She handed him a bottle of water and he drank from it greedily. Lauren put a reassuring hand on his shoulder as Rowan knelt at his knee. He tore open a blister pack and handed him two pills.

Chance took them and swallowed hard, washing them down with the last of the water. He handed the empty bottle back to Lauren. "What was that?" His voice trembled as much as his hands.

"It's Tylenol for the headache you're sure to get. That's the best I have," Rowan said.

Chance nodded, taking a deep breath as Rowan came at him with an antiseptic wipe. It stung and he swore loudly. Rowan steadied him with a hand on the top of his head. "Hold on buddy, this is the worst part. I want to see if you're going to need stitches."

"No wonder you dropped out of med school. Your bedside manner leaves a lot to be desired," Chance muttered as the wound was cleansed. "At this rate, I'm going to need something stronger than Tylenol. Got any whiskey?"

"I'll buy you a beer when we get back to town." Rowan set aside the antiseptic. "It doesn't look too bad," he said. "I'm going to butterfly it. I don't think you'll need stitches."

"Is it going to leave a scar?"

"Chicks dig scars," Lauren said, patting his shoulder.

———

The rest of the team set up perimeter barriers and strategically placed night-vision cameras along the trail by where the footprint was found, as well as other parts of camp. Once the work was done, they reported to Lauren at base camp.

They discussed their evening's plans over tin plates of spicy red beans and rice. "We have barrier monitors set up around base camp. If anything comes in, it will set off the alarm. We've also got trail cameras set up with night- vision lenses and all our gear is ready to go," Jean-René said.

"After dinner, we'll break up into teams. Team One will follow the trail Rowan and Chance were on earlier. Team Two will go to the west and see if they can find anything along the trail to the mountain, where hikers reported seeing the creature a few months back. We need to determine where the creature might take shelter, find out what it's eating, where it hunts."

"We'll follow standard protocol," Rowan announced. "Everyone checks in with base camp on the half hour. If you're more than five minutes late reporting, we come looking for you. Keep your transponders on, and don't turn off audio or video."

"I want each of the teams to carry the dart guns. We've already had one attack today. If we need to tranq the damned thing to take its picture, we will."

"Imagine the press we'd get if we brought in a live specimen." Jean-René rubbed his hands together maniacally.

"That's not why we're here," Rowan grinned, knowing he wasn't serious. "We use the tranquilizers only to save our lives. Bringing one in live would be nice, but our primary mission is to gather evidence. This isn't a monster hunt."

But really, it was.

———

Lauren kept everyone in line, but it was dark by the time everyone completed their final AV tests. All the shoulder mounted stedi-cams were pointed back at the faces of their carriers, equipped with night-vision capabilities and audio. A good portion of their production budget was dedicated to electronic equipment, another chunk went to travel, while the rest went to insurance, just in case something went horribly wrong.

They'd had mishaps before. Bahati and Lauren taking ill in Peru had been only one among the many illnesses and injuries they'd seen in their adventures. Jean-René had been bitten by a barracuda and lost part of his big toe while filming in the Bermuda Triangle. Rowan had broken his ankle in Nepal looking for the Yeti. Their former production director, Gerald, had gotten West Nile virus searching for *el chupacabra* in Mexico. Malaria, altitude sickness, dysentery, water-borne parasites—they'd been through it all.

"Remember, stay together. Don't let this thing sneak up on us. Base camp, call if you need anything," Lauren gave final instructions. "Let's go out there and see what we find."

———

"Ape Canyon had a sordid history." Lauren penned the words in her journal. "In 1924, a group of miners were attacked by what they described as hairy apes, but the legends were much more ancient. An American missionary named Elkanah Walker retold the stories of the local Spokane natives in his journal in 1840."

Even before leaving San Diego, Lauren interviewed a number of the local residents she'd been referred to by the local Bigfoot Field Researchers Organization, or BRFO. She'd found their contact information online and they had been keen to help her with her research. One member she'd interviewed claimed to have been the descendant of one of the men who'd claimed to have captured a young Sasquatch in British Colombia in 1884. "The captors called him Jacko and described him as being *half man, half beast, four feet, seven inches tall and weighing 127 pounds.*" She added in the current *codex* she kept documenting their travels.

She'd also talked to geologists and National Park staffers who told her about the 1980, Mt. Saint Helens. One of the rangers told her about his own personal encounter near Ape Canyon that had been heavily impacted by the blast. He said, "I was on patrol when something I still can't explain crossed the path in front of my ATV. It'd moved so fast and crossed the path in two strides. To this day, I still get goosebumps just thinking about it."

Sitting on the side of a mountain, looking out over the

valley, she could only imagine how barren the moonscape might have appeared. Today, it had returned to a verdant wilderness. There was much debate as to whether the local Sasquatch population would have been able to survive such an eruption, or if they fled in advance of the cataclysm.

She continued writing. "It could be no coincidence that there has been a long dry spell of sightings after the volcano went ballistic and ejected more than 2.4 million cubic yards of ash and pyroclastic flow over twenty-three square miles. In some places, the ash cover layered the landscape thirty feet deep." She felt like at least half that was in her shoe. She set her pen and journal aside and kicked off her hiking boot, dumping the fine grains out. Sliding out of her sock, more grains fell away. She brushed her foot off and redressed it before taking up the codex again.

"Five more eruptions between May and October of that same year sealed the area's fate. But the fate of the indigenous legendary Bigfoot remains unknown."

Not so long ago, a young boy crayfishing on a nearby river looked up and noticed a white Sasquatch peering at him from the opposite bank. He said the creature stood well over six feet tall, with a potbelly, bloodshot blue eyes, and a pink complexion. The boy had been so frightened, he threw down his belongings before scrambling onto his dirt bike and peeling out of there. He later returned with his father, too afraid to return alone. They found footprints which suggested the creature had a crippled foot.

Sometime later, two more sightings of the white Bigfoot were reported. In all three cases, witnesses reported the white Bigfoot had a pronounced limp. Ten years passed since the white beast's appearance. Lauren wondered if, even after all these years, the white Bigfoot could still be alive. The reports they received, the ones that summoned them to the volcano, involved reports of frightened hikers, chased from the trails —

sightings of a dark hairy beast dashing across valleys in broad daylight; howls in the night.

One of the interviews Lauren had done was with a local man who'd run into the beast while spelunking through one of the caves. The eyewitness had been so shaken up that he still had a hard time talking about it, even though it happened many years before. He claimed the beast grabbed him and roughed him up before he managed to escape the cave, certain the beast would have eaten him alive, if he hadn't gotten away.

Who'd want to eat that?

———

Lauren and Jean-René were assigned to survey the area east of base camp. The terrain was rugged and grew more so as they gained elevation. Trees were thick and lush. Pine needles littered the forest floor. Birds and bugs sang a raucous cacophony all around. The night air was cool, and the distant gurgle of water could be heard from a nearby stream. Lauren found a narrow trail and blazed her way beneath the massive pines and diminutive aspens. The going was slow, and it took more time than either expected to reach a spot where they could stop and rest.

Just as Lauren tipped back her canteen for a much-needed drink, a distant growl in the trees off to their left startled them both. Lauren turned, wiping her chin on her sleeve. She caught the flash of movement in the distant trees out of the corner of her eye. A dark shadow moved between two trees, as if hiding, or watching. She could feel eyes piercing her soul and it chilled her to the core.

Holding out a hand to signal her camera operator, she raised a finger to her lips to silence him. She gestured toward the sound. He turned his camera on and pointed it that way. Lauren realized the forest had suddenly gone quiet.

She screwed the lid shut on her canteen and tucked it back in the pocket of her backpack, setting it aside, as she watched for the shadow in the trees to move again. There was a heavy crash of footfalls as something lumbered through the trees. The decrescendo of footfalls told her whatever made the noise was moving away. She froze and her heart raced, thumping so loudly in her chest she was sure her mic would pick it up.

Jean-René gasped. "Did you see it?" she said, just above a whisper.

"What?" His eyes shifted, the whites glowing in the almost nonexistent moonlight. "It's so dark, how can you see anything out here?"

"Shhh." she ordered over her shoulder. "Anything on night vision?"

Jean-René turned his camera in the direction she nodded, changing the setting with the flick of his thumb. The telltale figure, really more of a nondescript blob, was hunkered down in the brush. It could have been an elk or a bear, but it was hard to say. On the FLIR, it glowed in shades of blue, yellow and red, based on the infrared signature of the form. Suddenly she was aware of a low deep grumble, like a large dog growling deep in its chest.

Lauren squeaked, cupping her hand over her mouth. "I see it," she whispered. "Don't move."

"Team One to Team Two." The walkie-talkie squawked loudly. Jean-René and Lauren both gasped. A crash in the thicket thundered in their direction. A dark flash of something large barreled at them. Jean-René turned to run, falling flat on his face, the camera tumbling wildly down the hill. He let out a yelp of pain and fear.

"Team Two, we heard yelling. Lauren? Was that you?" There was a long pause. "Come in, Team Two. Team Two? Report! Report!"

Jean-René saw the red light of the walkie-talkie in the fallen leaves and scrambled for it. "Team One! Team One! Mayday! We're about two miles east from base camp near Ape Cave. We've just seen … something … I don't know what it was!" He panted, breathlessly dropping to his knees, looking around. He froze. "Rowan … we need you here, now!" He threw the walkie-talkie down and leapt to the form laying halfway down the slope in a heap, unmoving.

"Team Two! What's wrong? Come in Team Two! Come in Team Two!" The radio squelched. "We're coming!"

CHAPTER 7

"LAUREN?" JEAN-RENÉ PULLED AT HER JACKET, TRYING TO GET her to stir. "Come on, Boss. Wake up." He rolled her limp body over. "Lauren?" he repeated, this time more loudly. "Come on, dammit! Don't do this." His French-Canadian accent was more pronounced when he was agitated, and at the moment it was thick and brisk. "*Tabernaque!*" He genuflected, half-heartedly, his eyes briefly going towards the heavens; a silent plea for divine aid. He used the light to inspect her and froze when he realized she was bleeding from a gash behind her ear. "Dammit."

He fumbled through his backpack, for the small first aid kit they all carried. He found a pack of gauze, using it to apply pressure to the gash, holding her head between his hands. It wasn't enough.

———

Rowan, Chance and Bahati were breathless when they arrived. Bahati recoiled at the odor that could only be described as a sickening blend of kitty litter and beast. Rowan didn't seem to notice. "What happened?" Rowan dropped beside his cameraman. Jean-René knelt holding a limp form in his lap, he held his hand clamped over a wound. Blood oozed from between his fingers. The tang of iron found its way to the back of Rowan's tongue as he switched on his flashlight. He confirmed what he'd suspected when he heard his friend's panicked cry for help. It was bad.

"I don't know … this thing … maybe it was a bear … I didn't see it. It was so dark … it charged us." He started babbling in French.

Rowan narrowed his eyes at him. "Calm down." He turned his attention to Lauren, assessing her injuries. Rowan reached for his walkie-talkie. Jean-René held her head between his hands, his bandana pressed to the side of her skull. She had a deep gash behind her ear. Blood seeped from between his fingers. "Team One to Base Camp."

"Base Camp, over. What's going on out there?"

"There's been an attack. Lauren's hurt. I'm bringing her into camp. Get my triage kit ready, set up the light towers. We'll be there as soon as we can."

"You're going to move her?" Chance asked.

"I don't see that we have any choice," Rowan said. "Bahati, help me get her out of this camera rig."

Bahati jumped into action. She loosened the clasps and peeled off the straps of the steady cam. Rowan fumbled through his field kit and found the collapsible c-collar. He used it to stabilize her neck. "Get me some more gauze," he said. Chance found more in his kit and handed it over. Rowan placed it over the wound behind her ear, securing it with an elastic bandage until he could tend to it properly. It was the best he could do, given the circumstances.

Rowan watched the trees nervously.

"Bring the camera rig." Rowan scooped her up. "Maybe we can see what happened to her."

Jean-René realized he'd lost his camera when the thing

darted out of the trees. He searched in the dark until he found it. He fell in with the others, pushing past Chance so as not to be last in line as they filed through the stands of aspen and pines.

———

Lauren stirred as Rowan lay her down on the sleeping bag laid by the fire. She moaned and pinched her eyes shut, blinded by the light-stands that flooded the area. Rowan got his first good look at her injuries. An angry red scratch spread across her face from the corner of her mouth across her nose, to the outside corner of the opposite eyebrow. He turned to the bandaging, lifting it to inspect the wound in better lighting.

"Ow!" She flinched. Rowan put a gentle hand on her chest, holding her down.

"Don't move," he said, soothingly.

"Oh man …" she groaned, reaching for her throbbing head. Rowan took her hands in his. He was glad now he'd put the neck brace on her.

"Lauren," he said. "Lay still. Let me take a look. I need to see how bad it is."

"It feels like my scalp's been peeled off my skull and taken my ear with it." She drew her knees up. He removed the bandages and used fresh gauze to blot away the drying blood. She bit her lip. He could tell the laceration was deep. He also knew she wouldn't be able to hold still long enough for him to stitch it up. Lauren was a horrible patient. He'd seen her kick a doctor in the groin once. He didn't want her to do that to him.

"It's not anywhere near that bad," he lied. "I'm going to get you something for the pain."

"Please." She was shivering. It was a common pain-response. He needed to stabilize her.

"How's your neck?" He asked.

"Everything hurts," she whimpered. "Please ... do something. Hurry."

"That's what all the ladies say." He mused. He patted her on the shoulder. "Give me just a second to get everything I need."

"How bad is it?" Jean-René waited until he'd moved away to ask.

Rowan lowered his head. "The laceration is deep. She's in a lot of pain but I don't have anything stronger than Tylenol. It's not going to be enough."

"No whiskey?" Jean-René asked.

"I drank the bottle I got on the airplane," Rowan said.

"Anyone else take anything for pain, maybe have brought some with them?" Jean René looked around.

"Wait." Rowan hesitated, his hand resting on the dart pistol on his hip. He turned his gaze to his patient. "I have an idea."

"No! Rowan, you can't be serious!" Jean-René caught his wrist as Rowan unsnapped the holster to his tranq gun.

"It's all I've got."

"Don't do it," Jean-René insisted. "You could kill her."

"Rowan." Bahati called. "You have to see this." She brought the camera over where Rowan could see it as he knelt beside her. The team huddled around. Bahati replayed the video from the attack. The FLIR camera aimed at her face showed a kaleidoscope of colors congealing over her shoulder into a bipedal form as it charged her. Lauren's blurred form was sent crashing to the ground, tumbling down the mountain. Violently, her skull struck a tree with a hollow *thwack*. The camera went dark.

Bahati set it to loop, decreasing in speed until they had frame by frame images. The images were haunting, but inconclusive.

Lauren groaned but tried to sit up so she could see. Rowan tried to sooth her, holding her down with a gentle hand. "Don't move," he cautioned.

"What happened? Where am I?"

"You got hit by something that knocked you down," he said. "We're still not sure what it was," Rowan explained. "Lauren, you're going to need stitches and I only have one option for pain."

"I'll take it. Whatever you have."

"Whatever?"

"Anything."

"Okay." He shrugged. "You asked for it."

CHAPTER 8

"WHAT THE …? ROWAN!" JEAN-RENÉ GASPED. EVERYONE LEAPT to their feet as Rowan holstered the dart gun.

"You got a better idea?" Rowan yanked the dart out of her thigh.

Jean-René clenched his jaw, judgment written on his features.

"What? It's a sedative," he said in his own defense. "I can't treat her while she's awake and in pain. What else was I going to do?" He went to work on his patient, peeling her out of the bloody jacket, before tending the wound.

"That stuff will put a full-grown grizzly bear down for an hour."

"Well she's going to be as mad as a grizzly bear when she wakes up. You better hope I'm done stitching her up before she does," he said.

"I don't think I'm the one that needs to be afraid," Jean-René said.

———

Lauren woke, flat on her back, unable to move for the pain in her head and shoulders. She reached out, realizing Rowan was sleeping beside her. She wrapped his shirt in her hand, tugging on him as firmly as possible.

"What?" He was suddenly wide awake.

"Did you shoot me with a tranquilizer dart?" The words came through her clenched teeth, laced with impending wrath.

"Why would I do a fool thing like that?" He grumbled, sitting up and rubbing a weary hand over his head and face.

"What the hell did you give me?"

"A Benadryl injection. It's all I had." The lie came easily. He didn't even blink. "Why would you think I'd shoot you with a tranquilizer dart?"

"I don't know," she let go of his shirt, finally. "I guess the Benadryl gave me bizarre dreams."

"It always does," he said. "How're you feeling?"

"I can't move," she said. "I feel like I got hit broadside by a Mack truck"

"Close," he said.

"What was it?" She asked, squinting as if to see into him.

"Wish to hell we could tell," he said. "The thermal images are inconclusive."

"Great. Just great." She clenched her jaw in frustration, wincing at the pain it caused. "What was it the critic in TV Guide said? *No one's better at not finding the truth than we are?*" she asked. "Leave it to me to get hit broadside by a Bigfoot and not get it on camera."

"You think it was a Bigfoot?" Rowan arched a brow. He wanted it to be a Bigfoot, but the video was no help. It could have been a bear.

"It made a run at me. Not Jean-René. It was after *me*."

"Why would you think that?" Rowan asked, reaching for the bandage and peeking beneath it.

"I'm not sure. Call it intuition."

"I think you're just being paranoid," Rowan said.

"Maybe." She closed her eyes.

———

The rest of the evening remained quiet. Lauren slept by the fire where Rowan could monitor her. He diagnosed her with a concussion and whiplash. It wasn't life-threatening, but their expedition was in jeopardy.

It was near dark when the smell of food and wood-smoke woke her again. She was finally able to roll up to one elbow, still unable to turn her head. She groaned as she pushed herself up to a seated position slowly, with great effort. Bahati was at her elbow with a bottle of water and a pack of Tylenol caplets that Rowan had instructed her to give to Lauren.

"Where is everyone?"

"Rowan took Jean-René to collect the camera traps for analysis so they can reset them before it gets dark."

Bahati returned to the fire. "I bet you're hungry."

"Starving."

———

Lauren was eating a plate of fried eggs, potatoes, and biscuits when they returned.

"It's alive," Jean-René razzed.

She raised her hand, flipping him off. "I'm still not sure if that's a good thing," she grumbled.

"Looks like good grub." Rowan glanced at her plate, taking a seat beside her, laying the cameras out around him.

"Want some?" She asked.

"I'll get some once I download the film from the trail cams," he pulled his laptop out of his pack, setting it up on the tree stump he used for a worktable. He connected each one to the computer, downloading the files from the cameras.

"Chance and I will go reset those when you're done," Jean-René said as he took a seat with his dinner plate. Jean-René turned to Lauren. "Feeling better?"

"Yeah," she said. "My head is pounding, but that's actually an improvement."

"Did you give her the Tylenol?" Rowan asked Bahati.

"I did," she said, and handed Rowan a plate.

"Thanks." He set the cameras and computer aside in favor of a hot meal. As night came, the night air chilled and the sky was chalky gray. A warm meal, even if it was Bahati's cooking, would carry him through a long cold night of Bigfoot hunting.

Rowan had reservations about continuing. The safety of the team was his utmost concern. Lauren's especially. He'd been mulling it over all day. On the one hand, they'd hiked all this way, specifically for an encounter with the elusive Bigfoot. On the other hand, two members of the team had now fallen victim to the unknown. Safety on an expedition like this was a gamble. Everything was safe enough, until it wasn't.

———

"So, here's the plan for tonight. We're going to stay together; one team. No one goes off alone. Lauren, Bahati and Rob will stay at base camp. Jean-René, Chance and I will go back toward Ape Cave. I want transponders on everyone, and I mean *everyone*." Normally, this would be Lauren's job. It amused her when he took charge. He was good at it. "We're not having any more sneak attacks like the other night. Everyone stays on their toes."

Lauren turned her whole upper body to glare at Jean-René. "What happened the other night?"

"You don't remember?" He asked. When Lauren looked at

him blankly, he told her the whole story. His voice trembled as he recounted the harrowing ordeal. Lauren seemed to sway. Her cheeks paled. "It was probably a bear or maybe a large wolf."

"Or a Bigfoot," Bahati said, dropping her tone. A distant howl broke the silence of the forest. "Speak of the devil …"

"That's no wolf," Lauren said. "Where is my digital recorder?"

A grin dimpled in the corner of Rowan's cheeks. "There she is. Welcome back, Lauren," he rose. "Let's get to work. The sooner we get this one in the can, the better."

CHAPTER 9

IT WAS A BUSY NIGHT. THE TEAM CHASED TRAP CAMS AND howling noises through the trees for hours. Lauren sat by the fire, her laptop on the stump as she sat cross-legged on her sleeping bag. Rob and Bahati hovered around watching the camera feed over her shoulder.

"Dang it. One of the perimeter cameras went down," she snapped. "We're completely blind without that camera."

"Did something break the beam?" Rob asked.

"The alarm would have sounded if it had. It just went dead," she said. A second quadrant of her screen went blank. "Shoot! There went #2."

"What the hell?" Rob moved in. "I'll go check them."

"You can't go alone," Lauren said. "Bahati, go with him."

"What about you?" she asked. "I can't leave you alone."

"I'll be fine," she waved them off. "Nothing will come near so large a fire," she added.

Bahati and Rob stood looking at one another, not sure what to do. "You know Rowan would kill us if we left you here alone," Bahati objected.

"I'm armed," she, said setting the dart pistol up on the stump by her laptop. "Please. Go fix that camera."

"Team One to Base Camp," the walkie-talkie interrupted the argument, and she shooed them off as she reached for it. "We found a deer stand in one of the trees; we're going to send Jean-René up with the night-vision and see if we can see anything."

"Sounds good. There's a problem with the perimeter cam, but we're going to get it reset. Hopefully it's just a dead battery."

"I checked those batteries myself," Rowan said. "They were fine a few hours ago."

"We'll keep you posted."

"Over and out, Base Camp."

———

"What happened here?" Rob found the perimeter sensor on the ground by the tree where he'd secured it a few hours before. The bark on the tree was damaged. He picked up the remains of the alarm and held it up to the light for Bahati to see that it was nothing but a bunch of broken plastic and dangling wires. "What the hell?"

"I don't have a good feeling about this." Bahati shook her head. "Let's fix it and get back to base camp. The longer we're out here, the more likely we are to end up like Lauren."

"Or worse," Rob agreed. "Did you bring a replacement?"

"Yeah," she said.

———

It took less than an hour to fix both damaged sensors and return to camp. Neither could explain what had happened to them.

Lauren's laptop screen shone brightly, and the fire had died down to glowing coals, twinkling red beneath the char and ash.

Nothing seemed out of place, but someone was obviously missing. Lauren's coffee cup lay on the ground next to the tree stump upended in the dirt. The sleeping bag she'd been sitting on was disheveled. The lantern lay on its side a few feet away near the edge of camp.

"Lauren?" Bahati called.

"Surely she didn't go off into the woods to pee," Rob said. "Look, her tranq gun is still here. She wouldn't leave without it, would she?"

"Surely not." Bahati agreed. "Lauren!" She yelled even louder. "Lauren?"

There was no response. "Where is she?" Rob paced, searching the tree line for her, his flashlight swinging wildly in the darkness.

"Check her transponder."

Bahati sat down at her computer and pulled up the tracker. "I'm not getting anything on her." Bahati picked up the walkie-talkie. "Base Camp to Team One."

"Team One here." The response came a moment later.

"Have you talk to Lauren recently?"

"It's been a while," Chance answered. "Why? We thought she was with you."

"We went to fix the perimeter alarms. When we got back, she was gone."

"Well maybe she went to pee," Chance suggested.

"Bahati…" Rob called out, his voice cracking. Bahati walked over to see what Rob was looking at by the edge of the clearing.

"Team One … you better get back here."

————

The footprint was nearly 20 inches long. It was deep, too. The ground wasn't particularly muddy, but whatever had made the print was big … and heavy.

"There's no sign of a struggle. No other prints," Rowan rose from his examination of the depression. It was twice the size of his hand.

"Do you think she took off after it?" Jean-René asked. "Or away from it? Maybe she was scared, and she ran."

"I've never seen her run from anything," Rowan said. "Never."

CHAPTER 10

"OUR MISSION IS TO SEARCH FOR THE TRUTH, NOT CREATE speculation," Rowan stood at the trailhead in front of a slew of reporters. Word had gotten out, and it was interfering with his efforts to find her. The U.S. Forestry Service had taken over the search. Meanwhile, the Network had insisted he personally address the media. "We are concerned for Lauren's well-being and we will not rest until she's returned safely." He stepped away from the mic. He did not take any questions.

Rowan knew there was plenty of speculation that their Field Producer had been abducted by Bigfoot. Everyone from CNN to TMZ had put the theory out there, and everyone was beginning to believe it. Tabloid headlines declared *"Adventure Show Host Abducted by Bigfoot."* Lauren was going to be furious. If they found her. And if… He didn't allow himself to even think the rest of that sentence.

"Mr. Pierce. This way. The chopper is waiting." The park rangers arranged for him to ride in one of the helicopters flying over the area, looking for any sign of Lauren. They surveyed the area in an intentional grid pattern, combing the trees, straining their eyes to see a flash of metal from her signal mirror, or a whiff of smoke from a fire.

Rowan took a great deal of comfort in knowing that Lauren was trained to survive in the wilderness, but her recent injuries troubled him. She had suffered a concussion in the first attack. Head trauma could do strange things to people. When he'd been a medic in Afghanistan, he had seen soldiers suffer traumatic brain injuries and turn on their own troops. One of his comrades took shrapnel from a mortar blast, then asked him if he'd tried their mother's apple pie yet. Ten minutes later, he was dead. He'd suffered a massive aneurysm. Concussive trauma effects were not always immediate, and delayed reactions were not uncommon. She could have run off chasing rabbits or become disoriented. The thought that someone or something had taken her was more than he could bear.

Rowan wasn't buying the theory that she'd gone to the bathroom and lost her way. That wasn't the Lauren he knew. She had an impeccable bump of direction. He had gone with her on more than one occasion when she led a team through the darkest jungles and come out the other side within 50 yards of where she was supposed to be, without any navigational aids.

She knew how to keep herself alive. She could catch a fish with her bare hands, bite its head off, and eat it raw. She could build a fire without flint or matches, and she could find water in the middle of the desert.

In her college days, she spent her summers in Alaska working for National Geographic when an aggressive grizzly attacked her tent. She managed to flee, wounded, but undaunted. She escaped from the bear, who decided her pack of military rations were far more interesting than a lean researcher. It was a rookie mistake; leaving food in her tent. She had a locker, but she didn't think the sealed pouch would attract any attention. She had been wrong.

With a mangled arm and numerous bite and claw wounds,

she had managed to get back to civilization. Once mended, she headed right back up to her camp. She salvaged what was left, collected her data, and continued her research.

It had taken her three days, then. She'd been gone now for six. Each passing hour made them worry more. Bahati hadn't eaten in two days, and when Jean-René tried to force her to eat, she threw up. She spent the rest of the afternoon crying in her tent.

The team tracked down Lauren's transponder and found it just down the hillside from where she and Jean-René had been attacked. Without it, they had no way to track her.

Jean-René, Rob and Chance went out every few hours, calling her name while scouting the animal trails around their camp. The park service captain, Ranger Kent Derry, took a team into the nearby caves to look for her, but came back empty-handed, several hours later.

"It's just one big lava tube. It's about 14,000 feet long and there are too many twists and turns. It's open to hikers year-round, and we've never lost anyone in there yet. It's not likely she's there, but I can't give you a 100% guarantee. We'll send a team over to Smith Creek and Lava Canyon, tomorrow, if the weather permits."

"What's the forecast?" Rowan asked.

"It's not good. Conditions on the mountain can change at a moment's notice. Could have freezing rain, maybe snow," he said. "We need to be ready for anything if you're not willing to evacuate."

"We're not leaving." Rowan remained stoic.

"Well, I can't say as I blame you, but you best be ready to hunker down and wait out a big storm."

"We've done it before," Jean-René said to the ranger. "Remember Nepal?" He turned to Rowan.

"Yeah." Rowan blanched, his ankle throbbing in response. "I

remember Nepal." There was a long pause. "Let's hope it's not as bad as Nepal."

Before this, Rowan hadn't thought anything could be worse than Nepal. They'd been making the trek towards basecamp on Everest when an unexpected storm came over the great mountain. They'd been so excited when they found the suspected Yeti-track. They were anxious to get back to civilization and get the cast to their experts back in the States. Their enthusiasm carried them for a time, but as the storm grew worse, Rowan knew they needed to hunker down and ride it out. Instead, he chose to push through, believing base camp was within reach. It was a mistake he paid for in pain. Crossing a crevice on snow ladders, Rowan lost his grip and slipped through. In a desperate attempt to save himself, he tried to turn and catch the ladder on one side as he fell. It worked, but the ladder flipped with his ankle still between the rungs. The gut-wrenching breaking of bone had been audible, and the sound of his own pained cry echoing in the crevice still lingered with him. The ache in his bones was a constant reminder of how close he came to death.

This time, he made the decision to hunker down. He wouldn't leave without Lauren. He hoped she knew it—wherever she was.

CHAPTER 11

ROWAN SAT UNDER THE CANOPY THAT COVERED THE CENTER OF camp. He poked at the fire, staring into the flame. His face was a reflection of the desperate panic in his heart.

Jean-René watched him for a moment before sitting down across from him. "Let's hope this is the worst of it." Thunder answered him, and lightning cast a brilliant glow on his equally troubled face.

"Probably not." Rowan's voice was heavy with exhaustion. Everyone else had retired to their tents. They were too tired to do much else. Since Lauren disappeared, there had been no mournful calls from the trees, no new footprints, no rock-throwing. It was as if the monster had disappeared with her.

"She tries so hard to hide it, but … we all know." Jean-René lowered his voice. "You realize that, right?"

Rowan blanched. "She wouldn't let me say anything." He managed a dour laugh. He hung his head, fighting back tears.

"You never had to." Jean-René studied his boss. He looked exhausted. "Her eyes say it all. Every time she looks at you—even how she gets mad at you—how she tries not to let the rest of us see how she smiles at you." There was a long silence between them. "When I saw that, I envied you. Did you know that?"

"Really?" Rowan ran his hand over his face.

"Well, I am French. Eh, French-Canadian. Whatever." He chuckled. "A beautiful woman like her? How could you blame me? But then I realized she wouldn't even give me a moment's consideration. She didn't see me. She saw only you."

"I asked her to marry me." Rowan managed a small laugh, but his brow knit and his smile faltered, his voice cracking. "More than once but ... she said no." He pursed his lips. "She said she didn't need it ... didn't want it."

Jean-René shook his head sadly, empathetically putting a hand on Rowan's arm. "She's an independent woman. She's afraid to admit she might need a partner to rely on. She doesn't realize that there's more to marriage."

"And you're the expert?"

"I was married for twelve years."

"You were?" Rowan sat up straight. He had never known about this side of his co-worker.

"Catherine died in a car crash," he said. "It was a long time ago."

"I'm sorry to hear that." Rowan looked up at him. There was a long pause. "You must have married young."

"We did. I was twenty, she was eighteen."

"That's too bad," Rowan said. "I can see you miss her."

"I do. Some days, I am still very sad."

"Is that why you've never re-married?"

"No. I just haven't found another woman who captured my soul like Catherine did. She was everything to me."

"That's how I feel about Lauren, but ... I just don't think she sees it."

Jean-René chuckled. "Believe me, she sees it."

"I just hope we can find her. So I can tell her."

"We'll find her."

———

The weather continued to deteriorate through the night. The temperature dropped even more. Rain turned to sleet, tapping on the top of the tent where Rowan lay fretting. Sleep eluded him.

When he crawled out of his tent the next morning, there was an inch of ice on the tents and the tarps over the center of the camp. The trees bent under the strain. The tents bowed under the weight. Only the heat from the bodies inside had kept them from collapsing.

The team milled around camp, distraught and helpless. Rowan rummaged through the equipment, finding the walkie-talkie. He radioed the Park Service team in charge of the search, only to learn it had been called off until the weather passed and it was safe to resume.

"I'm going out." Rowan stood abruptly; swaying with exhaustion.

Jean-René put a hand in the middle of his chest to steady him. "You can't," he said. "It's too dangerous. The ground is slick, and you'll freeze to death."

Rowan hesitated. He glowered at Jean-René when one of the camera crew reached for a camera, as if this were the time to get some footage for the episode. One icy look from Rowan, was enough to prompt the tech to retract his hand.

"I have a coat." Rowan turned back to Jean-René. "Lauren doesn't. She's going to freeze to death if I don't find her."

Bahati caught his elbow and put herself between him and the trail. "Look, you are no good to Lauren like this. You need to rest. I know you haven't been sleeping. It's affecting your judgment. You know you can't go out in this."

"I have to find her," he said.

"Look at me," she said, softly. She took him by the shoulder and turned him. "You can't do anything for Lauren now. You know that. Rest now. When the weather breaks, we will go find her."

Rowan nodded. "You're right," he said. He clenched his jaw. Turning, he ducked into his tent and zipped it up behind him.

———

The rain turned to snow just after noon. It was heavy, large wet flakes that clung to the branches of trees and drifted high against their tents. No one had expected it to get so cold so late in the spring. But the weather in the Pacific Northwest was unpredictable, especially at these elevations. At least the volcano was sleeping peacefully … for now.

Rowan glanced up at the peak of Mount Saint Helens that loomed over the horizon. It was barely visible for the snow that swirled around him. It had been quiet for most of the past 20 or so years. In the last six months, there had been signs of recurrent activity in the mountain, and researchers were monitoring it closely to see if it was going to erupt again. Several times over the last year, USGS reported an eruption was imminent, but the data hadn't been proven, yet. Volcanic eruptions had never been predicted with any kind of accuracy. Not yet, anyway. His emergency evacuation plan for the expedition took possible eruptions into account. He'd trained the team on terrain traps, to avoid the canyons and riverbeds like the ones that had been flooded by pyroclastic flows back in 1980. His plan assumed they'd be together if something happened. He'd never expected them to be separated. No one could have anticipated a scenario like this. He could only pray the mountain would sleep for many more years before it woke.

———

The mood among the searchers remained overcast as hope for finding Lauren waned. Temperatures now hovered just above freezing as the sun began to undo all the work Mother Nature had put into the past few days. With the Park Service team taking the lead, the search party blazed a trail along the northern path toward Climbers' Bivouac. It was an area they had slated to investigate, but search teams hadn't been able to get to before the weather had gone foul.

"How much farther?" Rowan asked. The trail was muddy and icy even where the sun was nearing its zenith as they topped the ridge. Rowan was anxious to get there.

"Maybe thirty minutes that way, if we keep at this pace," the ranger said.

A broad meadow lay ahead. Rowan stopped. He scanned the scene, noticing that a large briar trembled, and a shadow moved behind it. The figure rose slowly, turning in their direction before calmly moving off into the trees.

Rowan looked at the rest of the team. Their aghast expressions told him they saw it too.

"What was that?" Bahati asked. "Who got that on film?"

Jean-René seemed to turn to marble, his features locked. The camera on his shoulder drooped at an angle. Rowan turned and slugged him in the shoulder, snapping him out of the stupor. "What?" Jean-René demanded. He fumbled with the camera, righting it on his shoulder.

"Did you see it?" Rowan turned to the ranger.

"I saw something," he said. "Was it a bear?"

"That was no bear," Rowan said. Turning back to Jean-René who was fumbling with the replay on the camera. "Did you get it?"

Jean-René gulped. "I got something."

While they were standing around the camera, trying to get a good look at the replay, Bahati glanced up. "Lauren?"

Rowan looked up. His heart quavered in his chest when he

realized it was her. She staggered awkwardly towards them in the same direction in which they saw the figure. He tossed down his gear and dashed across the expanse towards her. Halfway across the clearing, he skidded on a patch of ice. He righted himself. Sprinting across the wide meadow he reached her. She looked like a zombie, her hair wild about her head. Her clothes were torn, her face bruised. He caught her by the arms as she stumbled toward him.

A gut-wrenching yelp echoed across the valley. *"A'yo!"* Her gaze went down to her right arm. She looked back at him, then her eyes rolled back, and she went limp in his arms.

CHAPTER 12

THE HELICOPTER LANDED IN THE MEADOW. PARAMEDICS RUSHED in. Rowan had already triaged her. She was alive, battered and bruised, but in poor condition. Her pulse was thready. She was in shock. Rowan helped them get her into the Stokes basket, falling in behind them. "Sorry. No civilians."

Rowan protested. "I'm a medic. Was a medic … in the twenty-third med-evac. Three tours in Iraq and Afghanistan. Please, she's my girlfriend. You have to let me go."

He wasn't sure what part had been his ticket, but it worked. One of the flight crew handed him a set of headphones as he took the jump seat behind the pilot. When asked, he did his best to explain what had happened, without mentioning the creature he was certain he had seen. As the chopper lifted off, he found his gaze returning to the spot in the meadow where he'd seen it. Nothing but blank snow remained.

———

"Welcome to the Madigan Army Medical Center," a voice over said the com an hour later. "This is the top trauma center in the region."

"Why didn't we go to Seattle?"

"We had orders," a voice squawked in his headphones.

Rowan was reminded of his days as a paramedic in Estes Park, Colorado, when he found it common to get strange calls from the Stanley Hotel. The hotel had inspired Steven King to write *The Shining*. Rumor was, the hotel was haunted. It always gave him the creeps.

One time, a group of paranormal researchers filming a television show at the Stanley ran into some trouble. Someone was hurt.

His partner laughed when they got the call but the look on everyone's faces when they arrived told him they'd experienced something that none of them could explain. For them, it was very real.

Their lead investigator had been pushed down the narrow staircase and had landed at an awkward angle, her leg broken badly. It was so bad no one had dared move her.

"I'm going to go ahead and start an IV and get you some morphine." Rowan spoke in a soft voice. He was trying to calm her. She was in tears as he cut up the leg of her jeans, finding a compound fracture where the bone stuck out. Her color was sallow. "I won't move you until the morphine kicks in. Then I'm going to stabilize your leg and get you onto a back board. I'll have to put you in a collar, just until we're sure your neck isn't injured."

"Please." Lauren shivered, her teeth chattering. "Just hurry …"

"That's what all the ladies say," he flashed a smile. She laughed, then winced in pain. "You've still got your sense of humor. That's a good sign. You're going to be all right."

"Promise?" She looked at him with those piercing dark eyes.

"I promise." He took her hand and folded it over his.

"That's what all the men say." Lauren winced, a pained cry escaping her lips.

"I'm not most men," he said. "Let's see about getting you out of here."

Lauren later told him it wasn't his dimples, his bright smile, or even his charming bedside manner that had won her heart that night, but those deep-set green eyes. He had made her feel safe, and not quite so scared anymore.

Now he felt helpless, and he hated it. Despite his medical training, he could do nothing but sit and watch as the ER team worked on her. They had confirmed that her shoulder was dislocated and were studying the x-rays on a light board as he watched through the window. He knew they were discussing their strategy for resetting it, until they noticed the spiral fracture in her humerus.

He'd only seen a fracture like that once in his career. When he was in basic training, his unit had a couple of recruits that had played college baseball. They challenged another unit to a friendly game one hot afternoon outside of Bagdad. His buddy had a mean pitching arm and had thrown a wild screwball with such force that he'd broken the bone in his upper arm, just like Lauren's was broken now.

One of the doctors glanced up from the chart and looked at Rowan. He looked familiar and the same sense of recognition passed over his face. He came out into the hallway.

"Pierce?" He asked. "Lt. Bennett McGuinness. Do you remember me?"

"Ben?" Rowan recognized the man from basic training. "Ben McGuinness! God! Yeah! It's been a long time."

"Yeah it has," he said, shaking his hand vigorously. "I watch your show. What kind of trouble have you gotten yourself into now?"

"How's Lauren?"

Ben glanced over his shoulder, his friendly countenance turning sober. "Someone's beaten the hell out of her," he said. "She has a couple of bruised ribs and her arm nearly got ripped off. Other than that, she's lucky to be alive. Who sewed her head up anyway?"

"That was me," Rowen said. "Is she going to make it?" He blanched, and Ben caught his arm, steadying him.

"She's in bad shape, but she's not that bad off," he said. "I didn't mean to frighten you like that." Ben studied him for a moment. "Come here, I want to show you something."

Rowan followed the doctor into the exam room, his fingers brushing along the old scar on Lauren's bared leg as he passed. Ben turned to his patient. He lifted her arm and turned it enough for Rowan to see the bruise that spread from elbow to wrist. It was dark, angry and the exact shape of a massively large hand.

"This is a classic example of an injury we see in abused children."

Rowan wasn't sure if he was going to pass out. He forced himself to stay conscious as he studied the bruises on her arm and face.

"Whatever happened, she put up one hell of a fight."

Rowan rubbed his face.

"I need to know who did this. I have to file a report. It's standard procedure when we see signs of abuse."

"Not who," Rowan said. His eyes were fixed on her. "What."

"What do you mean?" Ben knitted his brow.

"You're never going to believe it, even if I tell you."

Ben locked eyes with him. "Is there something I need to know? Are you and this woman involved? Did you …?"

"No. Ben, I would never!" Rowan realized what he was implying. "I guess you haven't been watching the news the past week or so."

"I've been on call for the past week."

"We better get a cup of coffee. It's a long story."

"Condense it for me." Ben folded his arms over his chest.

"It wasn't *someone* who did that to Lauren," Rowan said. He laughed, tears welling in his eyes at the same moment. "I'm still not so sure what it was. I can tell you what I *think* it was."

"What the hell was it then, Rowan?"

"Bigfoot," he said. "It was a Bigfoot. Okay?"

"Oh Jeez, Rowan! Is that the best you can do?" Ben scoffed, his brow furrowing even deeper.

"You have to believe me. You said you watched my show."

"I don't get to watch it all that much." Ben softened his gaze. "But I know you, Rowan. I know your character. I'm just having a hard time buying into the whole Sasquatch business."

"At the moment, so am I."

———

While Lauren was in surgery they sat down and Rowan told Ben the whole story, from start to finish. He was finally able to convince the doctor he hadn't gone completely insane. Their search for the truth had led them to an even greater mystery, one only Lauren could answer now. *Where had she been for the past ten days?*

"This has to be a hoax. Someone's playing you, at her expense," Ben said. "Her injuries could just as easily have been caused by a man. The Bigfoot legend has persisted for centuries, but there have been more documented hoaxes than rational explanation. Everyone likes a good monster story."

"I saw *something* I can't explain. Without further proof, I'm inclined to believe it was a hoax, provisionally," Rowan said.

"You just said it yourself though. You don't have any proof."

"Not yet," Rowan said. "But the truth is out there, and I intend to find it."

"Oh, now you sound like Mulder on the X-Files." Ben shook his head.

"That's not the first time someone's said that to me." Rowan sniffed. "Meanwhile, Lauren's upstairs fighting for her life. I can't let this all be in vain." He crushed his empty coffee cup in his trembling hand. "I owe her that much."

CHAPTER 13

ROWAN WAS GIVEN THE BAG CONTAINING LAUREN'S PERSONAL effects after Ben left him in the waiting room. He sat going through it. He inspected the pair of flannel lined blue jeans, the silk undershirt, and the navy-blue flannel shirt he'd bought her for Christmas last year. The vest she'd gotten from REI was tattered, the fluffy insulation ripped to shreds. She also had a pair of thick wool socks, and her black hiking boots. He examined the damaged seam on the shoulder of the flannel shirt. The pocket was ripped, and several buttons were missing. Her bra was damaged too, one strap completely torn away from the cup, and the center clasp had been broken. Her underwear was torn, and the jeans were ripped on the right knee. The left hip pocket was gone, leaving the denim frayed beneath it.

Blood stained the shoulder of the silk shirt. He found the corresponding spot on the flannel shirt. Bloodstains spattered on her jeans were consistent with the bleeding he'd seen. He buried his face in the silk top, inhaling the unnatural smell of her clothes as he sat back and completely fell apart.

———

The team arrived a few hours later. They found Rowan pacing in the waiting room. He was a mess, but having the team together again seemed to fortify him. "The doctors say her prognosis is good." He tried to remain positive. "She should be out of surgery any time now." Bahati wrapped her arms around him and held on tightly.

Jean-René reached down and took her arm. "Come sit down over here," he said. He took her to a chair, and she complied numbly. "I'll get us some tea." She nodded, drying her eyes on a tissue.

"She's been inconsolable," Jean-René said to Rowan. "We had to wait for a snowplow to get through before we could drive here. I thought she was going to have a nervous breakdown in the Jeep."

"We're all on pins and needles." Rowan nodded. "But Lauren's safe. That's what we were praying for."

"Is it as bad as it looked?" Jean-René asked.

"It's pretty bad," Rowan said. He recapped the doctor's report. "She's going to need at least twelve weeks to mend. Lots of physical therapy. It looks like the damned thing beat the daylights out of her."

Jean-René put a hand on his arm. "She's a strong woman. If anyone can survive this, Lauren can."

———

Normally, Rowan would have agreed with Jean-René, but he wasn't sure. She didn't seem so strong now. In fact, she looked almost childlike in that hospital bed. Her dark, tangled hair fanned out over the white pillowcase. Her pallor had gone from copper to ashen. Ben explained they were keeping her sedated.

He took a seat on a stool, gently taking her uninjured hand, running a thumb over the finger where he'd planned to put his ring. He drew it from his pocket and slid it on, pleased it still fit. It seemed so small against her bruised knuckles.

He turned her hand over to study her palm and noticed it was bruised where her fingernails had dug into it, as if she'd made a fist and hit something hard, the force of her own nails damaging her flesh in the process.

A mottling of bruises colored her arm from where he held her hand, until they disappeared beneath the gown that was loosely draped over her shoulders. He could only imagine what she'd been through. His imagination was quite vivid.

He realized she was trembling. She stirred slightly, rolling her head away from him, a low moan reverberating from the back of her throat.

A nurse came in to check on her, resting a hand on her leg, "Are you in any pain?" The moan repeated itself. "I'll get you something, okay? Just give me a second." He quickly retrieved the ring and put it back in his pocket.

The nurse nodded in greeting but went about her business of drawing the medication into a syringe before injecting it into the IV line. "Okay, Lauren," she said, raising her voice. "You should start to feel that in just a few seconds. Just keep breathing for me, okay? Deep breaths." Lauren didn't answer, but Rowan could feel the trembling ebb away. She seemed to melt back into a relaxed state of oblivion.

Only when she had been moved from ICU did Rowan leave and get checked into the nearby hotel. He showered and changed into clean clothes Jean-René had brought him. Lauren was still sleeping when he returned.

Bahati sat with her, filing the broken nails on her uninjured hand.

"She stirred a few minutes ago, muttered something I couldn't understand and then went back to sleep," she said.

"I know she needs her rest, but … I have so many questions."

"We all do," Bahati said, standing. "But mine can wait. I need a shower."

He handed her a card key. "Room 247 at the Holiday Inn. The address is programmed into the GPS on your rental car," he said. "I figured I'd be here most of the time, so I only got one room. I put your bags in the corner by the television."

"Makes sense to me," she said. "I'm going to grab a few hours of sleep in a real bed after my shower. Call if you need anything?"

"I will."

"Let me know if she wakes up?" Bahati's dark eyebrows arched hopefully.

"I will," he said, putting an arm around her. "She'll want you here, I'm sure of it."

Bahati nodded and took the key, collecting her jacket and purse from the chair in the corner. Her hand brushed along Lauren's leg as a fond farewell.

Rowan sat in the chair beside her bed, his mind racing. He had done everything he could think of to get through to her. He needed her to understand how much he loved her. She made him feel like he was nothing more than a *friend with benefits,* and he wanted to be so much more.

Lauren didn't let her emotions show. That was one of the reasons she was such a good paranormal researcher. She was objective. She didn't give into flights of fancy and she didn't need anyone to do the field work for her. She was stoic and strong, yet open to new ideas.

He liked all those things about her, but it also made her headstrong and stubborn. Once she set a goal, she didn't quit until she achieved it. She'd attack with a bulldog's tenacity and tear into a challenge without fear of the repercussions.

Usually, they weren't this severe. They might find evidence of a hoax or leave with more questions than answers. So far, this year, they were on a roll. The last three expeditions had put someone in the hospital, and it wasn't a record Rowan was especially happy about. One of the camera technicians tripped over a loose cobblestone and hit his head in China on the search for the ghosts of Tiananmen Square. Then the whole affair in Peru, and now this.

He didn't even want to think about what this was going to do to their production schedule. Initially, the Exploration Channel held them to a contract for ten episodes this season and they'd only finished six. They might not be able to do four more before the end of the production year.

Rowan was startled out of his thoughts when Lauren bolted up in bed and let out a blood-curdling cry. He caught her, eliciting another yelp as he removed his hand and put it on her chest to calm her and keep her from flailing out of bed. *"A-gi...hna...sv..."* she panted, her voice raspy and desperate. He recognized a bad dream when he saw one. *"A-ga...yv-li... ge...gi no..."*

Rowan searched her wild eyes for the fire he knew should be there. Her gaze was distant and empty. "Shhh … just relax. Tell me what you need."

"U-ni … hna … lv'..." she panted, grasping his sleeve with her free hand. *"E qua … tsu na … tsv-s-gi-no."*

Rowan had a flash of inspiration, reaching into his coat pocket, he withdrew his digital recorder. As a paranormal investigator, it was a habit to keep one handy. He clicked it on. "Lauren, it's Rowan…tell me what happened."

"U-ni … hna … lv'..." She melted back into the bed, gasping for breath, wincing at the pain in her arm and body. *"E qua … tsu na … tsv-s-gi-no."*

The nurse rushed in and looked her over. "What happened?"

"She bolted up in bed and started babbling," he said, as the nurse prepared a sedative.

"A-ga-yv-li-ge a-yo-hu-hi-s-di….a-ya…a-ya u-na-sti-sgi…" She panted weakly as the medicine ran down the IV tube to her arm.

"Sounds like Russian," the nurse said. "Or Inuit. We get a lot of the indigenous peoples from Alaska here for treatment."

"Do you think there's someone here that could translate that?" Rowan asked, holding up the tape recorder.

"*A-tsa s-gi-li* …" Lauren's voice trailed off as the medication did its job. "*Tsul'Kalu* …"

CHAPTER 14

Several hours later, the nurse met Rowan in the lobby with a frail old man in a wheelchair. He might have been 100. A toothless grin brightened his face as the nurse brought him in.

"Rowan, this is John Seawolf." A little more loudly, she spoke to the old man. "Mr. Seawolf, Mr. Pierce has some questions for you."

"I understand you can speak Inuit, Mr. Seawolf." Rowan raised his voice too.

"Yes. Yes, of course." His voice was deep and hoarse. His thin, white hair floated around his head like wisps of smoke. "I was a Code Talker once, when I was a younger man. I speak many languages."

"If I played a tape for you, could you try to make it out? We're not sure what language it is. Maybe you could point us in the right direction."

"Yes, I will try. You must play it loud. I'm an old man and my ears are not as good as they used to be."

Rowan did just that. The old man leaned closer, listening to the ranting of a delirious woman. Rowan played it a second time, and then a third. "Not Inuit," he said. "Iroquoian, perhaps."

He nodded. "Play it again?" he asked, leaning even closer. He furrowed his brow as he folded his hands in his lap. Rowan set it to loop. He let him listen to it over and over.

Finally, the old man perked up. "Cherokee, maybe. Yes, Cherokee ... western dialect."

"Lauren's family is Cherokee," Rowan said, more to himself. "Do you know what she is saying?"

"Some of it," he nodded. "There are many words here that I cannot remember," he said. "Ancient ... evil ... devil ... witch..." he said. "I am crazy."

"You're not crazy, Mr. Seawolf." Rowan said, trying to make sense of it.

"No. That is what this woman says. *I am gone crazy...*" He tapped a gnarled finger on the recorder.

"Ancient evil?" Rowan scratched his head.

"*Tall man.* I think she says something about a tall man," said the translator. "Her words are not clear, like a baby who doesn't know syntax. She speaks as a child speaks. Frightened words, as if wakening from a nightmare."

"Thank you, Mister Seawolf," Rowan said. "This has been very helpful."

———

Rowan paced, listening to the digital recorder over and over again. He had even more questions now than answers. "Ancient evil ... devil ... witch ...a tall man." *What was she trying to tell him?* He struggled to put the pieces together. He read over the Iroquoian legends of the Bigfoot online, disappointed that none of them referred to the creature as ancient evil, devil or witch. Some of the Cherokee legends called him *Ot-ne-yar-hed ... Stonish Giant.* Yet in those legends, the creature was small, about 4-foot tall and more man-like than ape. The Algonquin called him *Yeahoh* ... the Aztec-Ianoan called him *Tse'nahaha* but

Lauren wasn't from an Algonquin tribe or Aztec-Ianoan. Some tribes called him a *Mountain Protector,* or *Tree Man, Char Man* … others called him *Hidden Spirit.*

"It is said the creature moves silently and swiftly through the undergrowth, towering over everything it passes. It strides in the woods as little more than a shadow. It has exceptionally large shoulders and moves like a heavily muscled beast, leaving just its massive footprints." Rowan read from a webpage on his iPhone, holding the recorder near his mouth, collecting his thoughts and documenting his research. "Over the last two centuries, there have been thousands of people who have claimed to see a giant hairy beast lurking in the forests of North America. The phantom creature has been known by many names, *Hairy Ghost, Indian Devil.*" He lingered on this one a moment. "*Sasquatch* …. *Bigfoot.*" He breathed heavily. "And now, our own investigator, Lauren Grayson, may be among those who have not only encountered the beast, but possibly been its prisoner. Was she held captive for ten days in the lair of the beast? At this point, it's too soon to know exactly what Lauren experienced. We can only wait until she can tell us for herself."

CHAPTER 15

LAUREN'S EYES HOVERED JUST SLIGHTLY OPEN; LETHARGIC, AND barely conscious. Rowan tried to coax her into talking, but she said nothing. Instead, she peered out from beneath the veil of her eyelashes, her gaze seemed distant, transfixed.

"You should try to eat something." He looked over the tray of food. There was little more than broth, gelatin and some crackers, as well as a cup of iced tea and apple juice.

She seemed oblivious to his suggestion, still lost in the world halfway between awakening and sleep. He took her hand, sitting gingerly on the edge of the bed. "Lauren?" He said it more forcefully. Her gaze lifted up to his, but there was still that emptiness in her eyes.

"She won't eat anything?" Bahati came in, looking refreshed. She now wore a pair of jeans and a form-fitting long-sleeved t-shirt, seeming at ease as she inspected the tray.

"Well, now, Lauren." She clicked her tongue. "It's not much, but you have to start somewhere." She opened the wrapping around the plasticware and unfolded the napkin and lay it over Lauren's chest. "My mother always said red Jell-O would cure anything. Green is for sore throats, and yellow is for upset stomachs." She chattered as she spooned up a bite and held it to Lauren's lips. Lauren didn't turn away, but didn't lean into the spoon either. Bahati was undaunted and pushed the spoon toward her. Instinctively or purposefully, whichever the case was, she opened her mouth and swallowed the Jell-O.

Bahati smiled brightly at Rowan. Rowan half-heartedly mirrored her expression, taking a seat. He watched as she repeated the feat until the bowl was empty. "There we go," Bahati patted her leg. "How about some soup?"

Lauren managed a bit, finally turning her head away, yawning, her eyelids heavy as the morphine pump automatically fed her pain medication, and she drifted back to sleep. Bahati cleaned up, pulling the blanket up over Lauren's arm.

"She's been terribly quiet." Bahati came over to the chair beside Rowan. She lowered her voice so Lauren could sleep.

"She hasn't said anything since she first woke up," he said. "And then it was only in Cherokee."

"Cherokee?"

"I didn't even know she spoke Cherokee."

"Me neither." Bahati shook her head. "But then again, I learn more about her with every assignment. She's a bit of a mystery. She hasn't ever really opened up to me."

Rowan stared down into his hands. "It's not just you."

"It's hard to get close to her," she said. "She's been hurt by someone close to her, I would guess."

"She told me once that her whole family was like that. Her father left when she was little, and her mother wasn't very affectionate. She speaks highly of her brothers, well, most of them ... but they aren't close."

"She once mentioned her older brother got a full football scholarship."

"That's Michael," Rowan said. "He works as a contractor at NASA. I think she told me he was working on the spatial

sensors and other monitoring systems for the newest genera-
tion of space shuttles."

"Impressive. I'm surprised she never mentioned that."

"She and Michael have some ... professional disagreements.
They've always been competitive, and he keeps telling her he's
going to find aliens before she does." Rowan rubbed his eyes.
"He's teasing, but I think it hurts her feelings. You know her,
though. She'd never admit it."

The conversation was interrupted when the orthopedic
surgeon came in for rounds. "Good afternoon." He introduced
himself, and Rowan stood to shake his hand. He glanced over
Lauren's chart. "She came through surgery well. We were able to
reset her shoulder and install some internal stabilizers on her
arm. There's a steel plate and four screws that are holding it
together. Is she right-handed?"

"Yes," Rowan said.

"Hmm. That will be a challenge, but I'm sure she'll get
through it just fine. Most people do."

"How long will she have her arm like that?"

"We'll re-evaluate in four weeks. If it is mending well, we'll
move her to a sling and start her on physical therapy. Within
twelve to sixteen weeks, she should be mostly healed if all goes
well."

"So long?"

"It's up to her. It could take less," he said. "It was a pretty bad
break, and we don't want to rush it." He glanced at the monitors
that tracked her vitals, then examined the morphine pump. "Has
she been awake much?"

"Just long enough to eat some Jell-O and some soup."

"That's encouraging. She needs to eat. We'll back off a little
bit on the medication and work towards some non-narcotics
for pain management. If she does well, we can talk about
sending her home in the next few days."

"It's a long flight back to San Diego," Rowan said. "Will she be up to the trip?"

"We can keep her comfortable enough. I have a friend who's an orthopedic surgeon in San Diego. I can make you a referral, if you like."

"We'll take you up on that."

Before Rowan could even sit back down, two men in dark suits walked in. "Rowan Pierce?"

"Can I help you?"

"I'm Agent Andrew Miller, this is Agent Joshua Morrison. We're with the FBI. We've been assigned to investigate the kidnapping and attack on Miss Grayson. Can we talk?"

Bahati furrowed her brow as she rose from her chair. "Why is the FBI investigating?"

"Miss Grayson's attack occurred on Federal land. The National Park Service referred her case to us for follow up."

"It's *Doctor* Grayson, and she was kidnapped by a Bigfoot. Are you prepared to consider that option? Or are you going to tell me I'm a nut job too?" Rowan asked bluntly.

"A Bigfoot?" Morrison asked, stoically. "*The* Bigfoot?"

"You say it like there's only one," Rowan said.

"You say it like it's real," Morrison retorted.

Rowan pursed his lips and shook his head. "It's still just a theory, but so far, it's the only one we have. We're paranormal researchers. We came to Washington to look into reports of recent Bigfoot sightings around Mount Saint Helens. Thirteen days ago, Lauren was attacked by something we couldn't identify. She was slightly injured in that incident. Twenty-four hours later, she went missing. We didn't find her for ten days. It was freezing out there. I don't think a random hiker grabbed her."

"Did she tell you she was abducted by a Bigfoot?"

"She hasn't said anything that we could understand." Rowan

pulled the digital recorder out of his pocket. "Just this," he played it for them.

"I'm told it's Cherokee. A linguist here was able to translate a few words. Ancient … evil … witch … tall man."

"Tallman?" Bahati asked. "Native tribes have referred to the Bigfoot as Tallman."

"That's all we have," Rowan said. "We've got video and audio data from our investigation that we'll have to review to see if we have anything that'll provide us any more information."

"Provocative theory, Mr. Pierce," Agent Miller said. "We'll need copies."

"Of course," Rowan said. "I'll contact my team and have them burn you a disc."

Morrison handed him a business card. "Contact me here when it's ready," he said. "I'll send a courier to pick it up."

"You believe me?" Rowan stood, flabbergasted.

The two agents looked at one another briefly. "We don't have enough evidence to believe anything at this point," Morrison said.

"But you're willing to consider that she might have been abducted by a Bigfoot?"

"Our job is to collect the evidence. Then we'll consider all possibilities," Miller said.

"Lauren is going to like you two." Rowan grinned, feeling a bit relieved himself.

CHAPTER 16

THE CONSTANT TATTOO OF THE PULSE MONITOR WAS hypnotizing. Rowan finally fell asleep. He was exhausted from pacing and worrying. He was comfortable enough in the recliner. Still, he was aware of the nurses' comings and goings in the night. He was restless, sleeping in short spurts, stirring at any change in the ambient noise.

He awakened when the nurse came in to do the morning vitals before the shift change. She seemed oblivious to his presence. He watched her work and was surprised when he realized Lauren was staring at him. The head of her bed had been slightly elevated. Her thousand-mile stare aimed in his direction. He waited until the nurse was gone before he rose.

He felt his countenance lighten with relief, but she turned her head away. It was almost as if she still was not there. "Hey," he leaned in and kissed her forehead. "It's just me." He brushed her hair back off her brow. She didn't protest, but there was still no response. He sat on the edge of the bed and took her hand, gingerly. "It's okay. You're safe now."

Lauren's hand wrapped itself in his. He found her eyes meeting his. The light came on and it was as if the morning sun had just broken over the Rocky Mountains. Rowan's heart seemed to swell in his chest at the beauty of it. "How are you feeling?"

It took a moment for her to answer. "I have a headache." She swallowed hard. Her voice cracked.

"I can have the nurse get you something for that."

"Where am I?"

"You're in a hospital," he said, intentionally omitting details. "Do you remember what happened to you?"

"Did I fall down?"

"It was a little more than that," he said. "Don't you remember?"

"Tell me," she said.

"We don't know what happened, Lauren. We were hoping you could tell us."

"Did I fall down?" She repeated. She gazed at him as if he had all the answers in the universe. Her eyes looked as innocent as a child. His heart broke.

He gazed at her swollen fingers. "Not that we know of," he said. He decided there was no need to push her any farther. This was more than they'd gotten so far, and he was grateful that she was back with them...for the most part. "Can I get you something to drink? You must be hungry."

"Bahati fed me," Lauren said.

"That was yesterday," he said. "It's almost time for breakfast. You need to eat to get your strength back."

"Can I have a cookie?" she asked. Rowan couldn't help but smile.

"I'll see if I can find you one. Want milk with that?"

"Sure," she said, glancing down at her arm, wincing when she realized she couldn't move it.

"What happened?" She glanced back up at Rowan.

He rolled his eyes. "Don't you remember?"

"Did I fall down?"

She was obviously still very loopy. There was no point in going through this with her over and over again. "I'll go find you a cookie."

"I love cookies. Can I have some milk with it?" She let out a breath dreamily, her eyelids dropping as her head rolled to the side.

"Sure."

———

Rowan returned a few minutes later with a carton of milk and a package of graham crackers. He'd hoped for Oreos, knowing they were her favorite, but they didn't have any and one of the nurses suggested they might upset her stomach.

"I hope you like these," he said, unwrapping the package.

She didn't stir at first, and when she did, she gazed at him blankly. "Rowan?" Her voice was gruff, different than it had been just a few moments earlier. She winced, trying to move her shoulder, her face twisting in pain. "Where am I?"

He furrowed his brow, taking her hand. "Don't you remember?"

"My head is killing me." She pulled her hand away and put it to the side of her face. "I feel like I got hit broadside by a truck."

"You were hurt very badly. But we don't know what happened. We hoped you could tell us."

"Where's Bahati?"

"She went back to the hotel to sleep," he said, glancing at his watch. "It's just after six in the morning."

"I have the feeling I'm supposed to be somewhere," she said, putting her hand back in his. "What day is it?"

"It's Friday," he said. "You've missed a few days."

"I have?" She arched her brow. "My shoulder." A deep moan escaped her throat. "It hurts."

"Your arm was nearly ripped out of the socket," he said. "The bone was broken too. Doctors had to do surgery."

"Oh wow," she leaned her head back on the pillow, squeezing her eyes closed.

"Do you need something for pain?" he asked.

"Yeah," she said. "It really hurts."

"Okay. Hold on. I'll get help." He rose and stepped out to the nurses' station. He returned a moment later with the nurse in tow.

"Welcome back," she said, watching her patient cautiously, as she checked the IV. "How's your pain?"

"It's bad," Lauren said through clenched teeth.

"On a scale of one to ten?"

"Two-hundred-ninety-four," she said. "Maybe three hundred."

"That bad, huh?" The nurse mused. "I just switched the morphine pump to manual. You just press this button as you need it." She tucked the control in Lauren's hand. "You can have a small dose every fifteen minutes, but there's a limit, so go easy. This should be more than enough to take the edge off."

Rowan could tell the pain medicine was reaching her. She seemed to melt, her jaw relaxing. She inhaled deeply. "Mmm," Lauren managed. "Are those for me?" She saw the graham crackers on the tray.

Rowan nodded at the nurse as she departed, returning to his spot on the foot of the bed. "Yeah. If you're up to it." He handed her one.

She nibbled on it, letting her hand fall back to her lap as she chewed the bite, then lay the cracker back down. "Maybe not yet."

"How about some tea or maybe some ginger ale?" Rowan suggested.

She shook her head. "Maybe just some water,"

As if in answer, the nurse came in with a pitcher of ice water and a cup and straw. "How are you doing?" she asked.

"I'm kind of queasy," Lauren said.

"I'll get you some ice chips," the nurse said. "It'll help. I promise."

———

Bahati arrived in time to help with breakfast. Rowan sat in the corner, feeling helpless. He resigned himself to the fact that he wasn't needed and announced his intentions to go and get a cup of coffee.

The ice had helped. Lauren was actually able to keep down some toast and tea. Bahati coaxed her into eating some tapioca pudding but the eggs and oatmeal went untouched.

"I don't think anyone's done anything with your hair since you got here," Bahati said, running a long hand over her raven tresses. "Want me to brush it?"

"No," she said. "I'm just going to close my eyes for a little bit." She yawned.

"You've earned it," Bahati said.

———

Bahati and Rowan paced the halls the rest of the morning. Jean-René stopped by with the disc and stayed only long enough to talk logistics before the crew left on the next flight back to San Diego. They would start analyzing the evidence they had collected. After all, there wasn't anything else they could do. There wasn't much Bahati and Rowan could do either, but they needed each other, and when Lauren was feeling better, she would need them too.

"I can't believe she doesn't remember anything." Bahati said.

"It might be more merciful this way."

"What do you mean?"

"I can't imagine what she's been through." He ran a weary hand over his scalp. "I just think it might be better that she doesn't remember."

"In the long run, she'll need to know," Bahati said. "It'll drive her crazy. You know how she is."

Rowan nodded. "I do."

———

Lauren was sitting up and trying to get out of bed when Rowan returned from the cafeteria. "What are you doing?" he asked, rushing over to stop her.

"I have to go to the bathroom," she said. She was groggy and moved slowly.

"No, you don't," he said. "Lie back down."

"I do," she insisted.

"Lauren, you've got a catheter and you're hooked up to wires and an IV. You don't need to go anywhere. You have to stay in bed. You're going to hurt yourself." He took her arm blocking her from getting up. She surrendered.

Lauren lay back, gazing at him. Her face was void of emotion. "Where'd you go? I missed you."

"Pacing the halls," he said.

"Why?" she asked, her brow furrowing.

"I've been worried. You were gone for 10 days," he said. "I thought I'd lost you forever."

"I was just sleeping," she said, looking confused.

"Lauren?" he hesitated. "Do you remember anything that happened to you in the last, say … two weeks?"

"I ate some Jell-O," she said. "It was green … or was it red?"

"That's it?" He arched his brow.

"We went…" She hesitated. "We went camping."

"Why?" he asked. He was testing her.

"Because. Because …we like camping?" He shook his head. Lauren furrowed her brow. "We were looking for something," she said. "But … I don't remember what it was."

Rowan's breath came out in a ragged gasp, his knees no longer holding him as he sat down hard. "It might be for the best," he said, softly.

Lauren looked at him blankly. "What do you mean? What happened? Did I hit my head?"

"I wished to God I knew. But … I'm glad you don't. I just want to take you home and put this trip behind us." He leaned on the rail and her hand came to rest on his head. He took it and pressed it to his lips, looking at her fiercely.

"You said I was going to be okay," she managed to smile. "I will be. So will you."

CHAPTER 17

A NURSE CAME IN LATER THAT AFTERNOON WHILE LAUREN WAS napping. She had a wheelchair ready, but hesitated.

Lauren stirred, lifting her head. "What?"

"The doctor wants me to take you down for a CAT scan," she said.

"Why? What happened?"

"You had a little accident," the nurse said. "The doctor is worried about your memory loss and he wants a scan to see what's going on."

"Oh. Okay."

The nurse sent Rowan out for a few minutes while she took care of a few things and he could only assume she was removing the catheter and disconnecting the monitors. He could hear running water and washing hands, and the ringing of a washcloth.

———

When he was allowed back in, Lauren had been cleaned up a little and had her hair combed and pulled back in a low ponytail. Her eyes brightened as she gazed up at him. He helped get her into the wheelchair and fell in beside her as the nurse wheeled her to the elevator. He'd mentioned to the doctor his concern for her lack of recollection, not just of the events in the forest, but her inability to remember conversations that had only occurred a few minutes before.

"You'll have to wait out here," the nurse said to Rowan when they reached the imaging lab.

He leaned down and kissed Lauren. "I'll be here when you come back."

———

An hour later, the orderly brought her back out. "Hi, honey," she said faintly. She looked exhausted.

He stood and forced a smile. "Hi," he said. He couldn't remember her ever calling him *honey*. "Ready to go back to bed?"

"Do I have to?"

Rowan tilted his head at the orderly, who nodded.

"It's been raining on and off for days," Rowan said as they walked down a long hall of windows. "Mostly on. I miss San Diego. If it rains there, it's usually just a short cloud burst. Here, it never seems to stop."

"Where are we?"

"Washington State," he said. He wasn't surprised she didn't remember.

"Oh. Bigfoot country," she said. "We should do some Bigfoot hunting while we're here."

At least she remembered that much. "Maybe next time."

———

Once Lauren slept again, Rowan tried to watch television, but he was restless. His iPhone chirped. The text message was the welcome diversion he needed.

Sending video clip for you to watch — emailing to your laptop. Watch carefully.

It was from Jean-René. Rowan got up quickly and went to his bag over in the corner and pulled out the small laptop. It took a painfully long time for it to boot up, and even then, he didn't have internet access. "Dang it," he snapped, folding it shut, tucking it under his arm.

———

Rowan sat in the coffee shop across the street from the hospital, staring, transfixed to the video loop Jean-René had sent him. He turned up the audio clutching his noise-cancelling headphones to his ears as it replayed. In the video, Lauren had turned on her laptop's webcam to record a video blog entry that would eventually go up on their website. Halfway through her introduction, a loud noise echoed in the brush behind her. She gazed over her right shoulder, reaching for something just out of the camera's view to her left. She froze, glancing at her screen with eyes wide. "Did you hear that?" she said. The camera image showed her knees. A moment later there was a frantic rustling, followed by heavy footfalls that shook the camera and the sound of something making a ragged breath as it approached quickly. The camera got smacked around hard, as Lauren screamed, and a monstrous roar made the image tremble. A flash of something dark whipped past the frame, and a cacophony of cries and roars were followed by a sudden silence. Then Lauren wasn't there anymore.

It all happened so fast. There was hardly time for him to comprehend what must have occurred in those scant moments that looped before him. He felt the blood rise to his face. His hands were trembling as they fell from his ears to the table. He nearly knocked his coffee over.

He was used to analyzing video clips like this. He was accustomed to the bizarre and even the frightening. But this was too much to take. He'd witnessed the exact moment of attack, and there was no doubt Lauren was the target. He sat wondering, as he tried to compose himself, folding his arms over his chest, leaning back gazing at the still of the dark flash across the screen.

This was not the first time she'd been attacked. Something or someone had jumped her in the bushes, and he had to think that there was more than just happenstance at play. But why Lauren?

Was it her native blood? Perhaps her Cherokee heart beat in a rhythm the creature recognized. Perhaps it was something in her eyes as she gazed into the darkened forest, seeking answers. Maybe it was her hair, or the smell of her skin. A thought came to him and chilled his soul. Maybe it was because she was a woman. What if that thing was looking for a mate? No! That couldn't be it. Lauren wasn't the only woman on the expedition. Bahati. Who else? Did Abby come? No. Her mother had passed away a week before and she'd stayed behind. Carmen hadn't gone with them since Tibet. Monique had a baby six months ago.

Lauren and Bahati were the only women on the expedition. Perhaps the creature hadn't recognized Bahati as female. She was a beautiful woman, but long and slender, with subtle curves that might not have been obvious beneath the cold weather gear. No, Lauren was a more obvious choice. She was curvy with her long raven hair, which she wore in braids for easy care during their investigation. What had that thing done to her?

No wonder she didn't want to remember anything. He rose abruptly and slammed the computer shut, tucking it under his arm as he dashed back to the ER.

———

"A *what?*"

Ben had been in the middle of his rounds in the ER when Rowan caught him pausing at the nurses' station to chart orders for a patient.

"Did you perform a rape exam on Lauren?" Rowan trembled, gagging on the words. He struggled to keep the contents of his stomach down.

Ben stared at him blankly. "Why?"

"She was missing for ten days. She has no memory of where she was. Suppressed memories. What if there's something she doesn't want to remember. If she was … *raped* … that would explain a lot."

"Aren't you the one who told me she'd been abducted by a Bigfoot?"

"I know." Rowan was shaken and could no longer hide it. "I know. I know. But look at the evidence. Lauren was attacked twice. She was the intended target both times. This creature, or whatever it is … *who*ever it is, baited the team away—lured them from her. It must have circled back to get to her. It wasn't attacking at random. What if … what if it was looking for a mate?"

"You talk about this thing as if it were a rational being."

"Animals are never rational when it comes to mating," he said. "They lose their damned minds. Nothing matters more. Some animals go days, even weeks without eating while they're in rut. They're like most men. They'll do anything to get … to get lucky."

"I'll order the test," Ben said without changing expression.

"It terrifies me to think of what someone … or something might have done …" Rowan's voice faltered.

Ben's hand went to his shoulder. "We'll do everything we can for her."

"Wait." Rowan caught Ben's arm. "Does she have to give consent for the test?"

"Of course," Ben said.

"I was hoping to spare her of the trauma of being violated a second time."

"Presuming she'd been violated the first."

"Her clothes were torn … her jeans … her underwear. I didn't even think about it that way until now," he said. "I can't imagine the thought of some animal … that thing touching her."

"Rowan." Ben took his arm. "You're going to give yourself a stroke." He steadied his friend. "Look, you don't need to go through this either. I can take care of it."

"No. I should be with her."

"Suit yourself," Ben said. "But I need you to calm down. You're no good to her like this."

Rowan took a deep breath. "Just help her."

Ben eyed him warily. "I'll do what I can."

Rowan followed him upstairs. Ben leaned on the nurses' station and asked for Lauren's chart. "When was her last dose of morphine?"

"The computer shows she hit the trigger about ten minutes ago," she said.

"I need a favor," Ben said. "One without a lot of questions."

The nurse furrowed her brow. "Of course, Dr. McGuiness," she said. She had no idea what she was agreeing too.

"I need an OB-GYN exam room, and a rape kit," he said. "And a chaperone."

The nurse stood fast for a moment. He could see her hesitation. Ben pulled her aside. "I'm not doing anything illegal or unethical, if that's what you're thinking. Dr. Grayson's privacy is my only concern.

"I can set you up in exam room six," she said.

"Thank you."

Once she walked away, he calmly went behind the station to the meds room, looking until he found a particular bottle and a syringe. He made an entry in the log, as required, before he tucked them into the pocket of his white coat. Doctors made obscure entries all the time. Chances of anyone questioning his medical decision were slim to none.

Rowan watched, wondering how much the nursing staff had been told. He didn't know if Lauren was just a lost hiker to them. Being on television they were often recognized, but not always.

Ben nodded, drawing Rowan back, and then went into Lauren's room, finding her napping. "Good afternoon Miss Grayson," he said, leaning on the bedrail. "Do you remember me?"

She stirred. "You're the cute doctor who's taking care of me." Lauren yawned.

"You do remember." He laughed. "Look, we need to run a few more tests to find out what's going on with you. Is it okay if we let you sleep and take you down the hall for the tests?"

"Sure," she said, dreamily. Rowan didn't like her flirting with another man but blamed it on the head injury. "Yeah, that would be okay."

"That's my girl." Ben glanced cautiously at Rowan but reached for the medication in his pocket. He added it to her IV.

"What was that?"

"Don't ask questions," Ben said, softly. "It won't hurt her, but she will sleep for several hours and have no memory of most of the day. It's a powerful medicine, but by the time of her next blood draw, it should be out of her system, and it isn't routinely tested for."

"She's already having enough trouble with her memory."

"This won't make it any worse … or better," Ben said.

CHAPTER 18

"THERE DON'T APPEAR TO BE ANY SIGNS OF TRAUMA," BEN SAID when he came back out from the exam room. "We'll know for sure in about 24 hours." Rowan hadn't realized he was holding his breath. He let it out slowly, relieved that this was over.

He stood numbly as she was wheeled back toward her room. "Why do I get the feeling we just broke every rule in the book?"

"*Management and Care of Victim* protocols require us to care for the patient in accordance with her needs and in her best interest. That's what we did." Ben justified it. "We did what was best for Lauren."

"God, I hope so." Rowan rubbed his red eyes.

Lauren slept all day. Even Bahati couldn't wake her up for dinner. He hadn't mentioned his fears — or their earlier escapade — to her. He didn't plan to. This was his worry to bear alone. Rowan paced all evening until he was ready to drop.

He watched the video clip over and over for hours on end. He couldn't look away, and he couldn't make sense of it. He felt helpless and afraid. It wasn't something he was accustomed to. He had always been able to maintain his cool, even when everyone around him lost theirs. It was his military training that carried him through.

Serving in the Middle East had tested him to his limits.

On one reconnoiter, his unit went into a small town in Al Anbar province one cold morning. A chemical manufacturing facility had been found a few days before. Their unit was there to determine if it was still in use. As they rolled into town, the normal morning life in a rural farming community was all but silent. "Pierce." His buddy had nudged him. "All the livestock is dead." He gazed at the corpses of a fallen flock of sheep. The faint odor of wet hay lingered in the air — the tell-tale sign of phosgene gas. No one in the village had survived.

The feeling that washed through him then was the same one he had now. It was that gut-twisting fear of knowing something was wrong, but not knowing what.

———

"Rowan?"

He sat up with a start. He was not in Al Anbar anymore. He hadn't had flashbacks in years. It frightened him.

"Rowan?"

Lauren reached out her good hand to him. "Are you okay?"

"Yeah. I'm fine." He shook off the ghosts that haunted him. He rose to take her hand. Sitting on the edge of her bed, he brushed her hair away from her eyes and kissed her knuckles. "How are you?"

"I hit my head," she said. "I think."

He had to smile. That seemed to be all she could remember. "Yes," he said. "You did."

"What's for dinner?" she asked.

He glanced at his watch. "It's three a.m. I think you missed dinner."

"I did?" She furrowed her brow. "I've been so sleepy. I can't seem to stay awake."

"It's the pain medicine." He wasn't lying. "It'll wear off when you're not in so much pain."

"I'm hungry," she said.

That was encouraging and Rowan said as much. "Tell me what you want. I'll go find it."

"It's three a.m.," she said. "I'll take whatever you can find."

"There's a coffee shop across the street, and a Taco Bell not too far away." She wrinkled her nose at that.

"A bagel with cream cheese would be good if you could find one." She remembered watching Jean-René eat one after they got home from Peru.

He rose, smiling. "I'll be back as soon as I can," he said. Finally, something he could do.

————

He came back with a dozen donuts of every kind, and a bag full of bagels with cream cheese. He had two large coffees. One was spiked with cream and sugar to her taste. He slathered cream cheese on one of the bagels. Lauren made short work of a chocolate-frosted cake donut while he did.

He watched her eat. It gave him the first real glimmer of hope he'd felt in days. It was good to see her appetite had returned. He was amazed that she could each that much. In truth it was half a bagel and a donut. When she was done, she gazed at him dreamily as she leaned back on her pillow.

"Better?" he asked.

"Yeah," she said. Her eyelids grew heavy in the euphoria of the feast. "Thank you."

"Can I get you anything else?" he asked.

"No." She shifted in her bed to make herself more comfortable. Rowan was envious of having a bed. "Come here." She lifted the blanket, making room for him.

He hesitated a moment, but she insisted. Wearily, he made himself comfortable in bed beside her. She curled up in the crook of his arm and lay her head on his shoulder, yawning. "Wonder if there's anything on TV?"

"Let's see," he said. He kissed her head and found the remote beneath her pillow.

He groaned, finding that the only thing on at four in the morning was *The Veritas Codex*. It was the episode at Eastern State Penitentiary. No one had gotten hurt on that trip, though they'd all gotten the piss scared out of them by the shadow of a dark form that passed between Lauren and Rowan. It was captured on film passing through Jean-René. It frightened him so bad he dropped his camera.

They'd managed to salvage the footage right up until the black shadow consumed the shot and the camera fell. That episode earned them their first Emmy nomination for Best Reality Television Series. Unfortunately, it hadn't won. Still, it was one of their favorite episodes.

"*The Veritas Codex*," Lauren perked up. "I love this show."

Rowan answered with a heavy snore.

CHAPTER 19

THE NEWS WAS ON WHEN BEN CAME IN TO CHECK ON HIS PATIENT. She was awake. Rowan was still sound asleep. "He's exhausted," she whispered.

"Yes, but you need your rest too." Ben scolded.

"Just leave him be. I am fine."

The doctor didn't argue. "You look a bit more alert this morning," he said. He noticed the half-empty box of donuts. "How's your headache?"

"Better," she said. "My arm still hurts, though."

"That's to be expected. I'm going to try switching your pain meds a bit. We need to wean you off the opioids. Just let the nurse know if your pain isn't well-controlled."

"I will," she said.

He crossed his arms, considering her. "So, do you remember any of what happened to you?"

She thought for a moment. "I hit my head," she said. "But I'm not sure how. I think we went camping."

"Why would you go camping?" He was testing her. "It's still early in the season and the weather on the mountain can be unpredictable."

Lauren furrowed her brow. "We do it all the time," she said.

"What do you do for a living, Miss Grayson?" he asked.

"I'm a research assistant," she said, without missing a beat. "For Cal Tech. I'm working on my PhD."

"And what do you do as a research assistant?"

"I go out and I research stuff," she said. The strain of trying to recall details showed on her face. "Wolves primarily," she added, smiling as the information came to her. "I also do some work in television." Now Rowan was awake and watching her cautiously. His brow furrowed. "Ever heard of the show Nova? It's on PBS. Maybe you've seen it?"

"Lauren, you haven't done that for almost ten years, not since you were a grad student. That was before you got your PhD," Rowan said.

"I got my PhD?" she looked at him as if that surprised her.

"So, where do I work now?"

"For the past five years you've been working with me on our show *The Veritas Codex*. We watched it last night. Don't you remember?"

"Oh yeah." She nodded. "What was I thinking?"

"Do you remember what we were doing here?" Rowan asked. "When you hit your head?"

Ben watched her, noting her eyes darting from side to side. "No," she said. "No. Maybe. We were researching stuff. It's all a blur."

"We were researching the area ... looking for Bigfoot," he said.

"Did we find him?" she asked.

Ben made some notes in her chart.

"Well, no one's better at not finding the truth than we are." Rowan snarked.

"You've got a very bad concussion," Ben supplied. He recognized Rowan's distress. "We've run some tests, but there's nothing conclusive. With these kinds of injuries, it's hard to predict the outcome. You may remember. You may not. We will just have to wait and see."

———

Rowan followed Ben out into the hallway. "Isn't there something we can do?"

"I can get you in to a psychologist. There may be some therapies they can recommend. But I can't make any promises."

"Do you think if we showed her the video? Tell her everything?"

"She may not accept the information. She may reject it. Or it could put her into a panic, and it might be devastating to her. Is it really so bad that she doesn't remember?"

"It's what we do, Ben. We go out there and we find the truth. If it's a hoax or if it's real, we accept it. We don't judge. We collect evidence and analyze it. That's all I want for Lauren ...to find the truth."

"She may not be ready for it. Give her some time. Talk to the psychologist, let them guide you through this process." He put a hand on Rowan's shoulder. "I know this is frustrating. Remember the class in basic training on caring for victims of trauma? We don't want to make it any worse for her. She's been through enough."

Rowan hesitated for a moment. "The test results came back. Didn't they?"

"Everything was negative," he said. "She wasn't raped."

"Thank God." Rowan's posture bowed and his hand went to the middle of his chest.

"She needs time, Rowan. Give her that. The memories will come soon enough."

———

Rowan noticed the men in black suits coming down the hall as Ben went to the nurses' station. Agents Miller and Morrison looked like men on a mission. "Mr. Pierce," Miller said.

"Have you found anything?"

"That's why we're here," he said. "There's been another reported sighting near Ape Cave. A hiker on the trail where Lauren was found reported seeing a giant monkey."

"Primate, yes. Monkey, no."

"We're still working to determine exactly what he saw. We think it might have been a bear, but after what happened to Miss Grayson, we can't rule out anything."

"We were hoping we could talk with her," Miller said.

"She doesn't remember anything," Ben said, crossing his arms as he moved in front of the door to her room. "Post traumatic amnesia."

"She doesn't remember anything?"

"She remembers that she hit her head," Rowan scoffed, feigning a laugh.

"May we speak with her anyway?" Morrison asked.

Ben looked like he might not allow it, but he knew these men had the authority here. He stepped aside. "Only for a few minutes."

"Lauren?" Rowan led them into the room. "These gentlemen are trying to help us figure out what happened to you. Will you talk to them?"

Lauren looked confused, but nodded. Miller approached her, but Morrison spoke first. "Miss Grayson, we understand you had some trouble in camp a few days ago and we'd like to help find out who did this to you. Can you tell us what happened?"

"I hit my head," she said.

"Yes ma'am." The two agents glanced at one another. "That's what your doctor told us. We are trying to figure out how you hit your head and who might have tried to hurt you."

"Why would someone want to hurt me?" She protested. "Did you know I am on a TV show?"

"Yes, ma'am," Miller said. "We've seen the video from ..." Ben shook his head, making a growling noise in the back of his throat. He discouraged the man's line of questioning with his eyes. "Err ... from your show. We wanted to know if you saw who hit you."

"I don't know what you mean." Her eyes narrowed. She looked to Rowan. "Do you know what he means?"

"I tried to explain to these gentlemen that you don't remember anything that happened to you."

"Do *you* know what happened to me?" she asked Rowan, point-blank.

"We think ..." he started, glancing at, then ignoring, Ben's warning glare. "We think you were attacked by ... a ... Bigfoot." He spit it out, despite his better judgement.

Lauren pursed her lips and wrinkled her brow. "A Bigfoot?" An impish smile graced her bruised face. "You think a Bigfoot did this?"

"You don't?" Miller asked, analytically.

Lauren puzzled over this for a moment, the smile quickly fading. "I don't know," she said. "I've seen a lot of strange things in my life ... but I've learned to base my reality on facts." She turned to Rowan again. "Do we have any proof of any of this?"

"Nothing conclusive," he admitted. "It's all circumstantial at this point."

"Well, you know what that means," she said. "We need more data."

"We aren't going back out there," Rowan stated flatly, knowing exactly what she had in mind. Still, this was the Lauren he knew. The spark was back.

"There's no proof that Bigfoot exists," Ben said gently. "Researchers, both amateur and expert, have been trying for decades, if not centuries."

"Absence of evidence is not evidence of absence," Lauren said, curtly. "You know the rules, Rowan. We cannot come to any conclusions without sufficient evidence."

"I won't take you back out there," Rowan protested. "You're in no condition to go traipsing off into the woods."

"I have to agree with Rowan," Ben stated flatly.

"Ma'am. We have taken over your investigation," Morrison said. "Your job now is just to focus on your recovery. If we find any further evidence, we'll be in touch."

CHAPTER 20

"I want to see the evidence." Lauren refused to eat until he produced the video.

"I don't have it with me." It was a lie. Still, he held the spoon out to her. "Please? Just eat."

"I'm not buying it, Rowan." She took a bite with a glare, as if she were doing it just to spite him. "Where's your laptop?" she asked. "Where's Jean-René? He has it, doesn't he?"

"The team went back to San Diego. Bahati and I stayed behind to take care of you."

"Well, thank you for that," she snarled, snatching the spoon impatiently out of his hand. "I can feed myself."

He huffed at her for a moment, his ire rising as well, slamming down the almost-empty cup of pudding, slopping some of it on the table. Pacing, he cooled before he turned back. "Look, I'm taking you home tomorrow, Lauren." He took a deep breath. "I'm asking you, one more time, for the love of God. Please. Marry me? I love you. I want to be your husband. I want to stop living in this … this half-life, this limbo that you've been holding me in. I can't take this anymore!"

"Rowan." She started to speak but he cut her off before she could say *no*.

"You were gone for ten days, and I died every single time I woke up and didn't know where you were." He tore at his hair, leaving it disheveled. "I couldn't eat, not knowing if you were hungry. I couldn't gaze up at the sky without wondering if you could see it. Every time I thought of your cold dead eyes staring into the darkness ..." He choked back tears. "I love you. Why won't you let me in?"

"Rowan." Lauren put a hand on his shoulder.

He lifted his head. "Everyone knows about us, it's not a secret," he said.

Her eyes narrowed. "Who did you tell?"

"I didn't tell anyone. I didn't have to. Jean-René said he's known for a long time. So, please. Please, Lauren. Marry me!"

Lauren sat speechless. His veins throbbed in his temples and he felt the fury burning in his face. His eyes radiated with it. He held his breath as she gazed at him.

She took a deep breath and he could see her walls collapse around her. "Okay," she said, without any further protest. "Okay," she stated a little more surely. "You're right."

He couldn't believe what he was hearing. He'd asked her to marry him nearly a dozen times and she always had an argument for him. Never had she resigned herself to him, and he wasn't sure he'd heard her right. "Was that ... a yes?"

She nodded and lifted her brows. "Yes."

He thought his knees were going to buckle again, but he managed to steady himself, and reached into his pocket for the diamond ring he'd carried for years. He picked the pocket lint out of the setting, polishing it against his shirt before he held it out, reaching for her left hand. He hesitated a moment considering that she might not be in any condition to make such a decision. "Are you sure?"

"I've been a fool, Rowan. I realize that. I know I have a head injury, but I also know I love you and I want to be with you. If it's that important to you, then let's do it. Let's get married."

Rowan felt his heart swell. He'd waited so long to hear her say that. Without words, he slid it onto her finger. He inspected it, straightening it before looking up at her. His eyes were damp, and a tear ran down his cheek when he gazed into her dark eyes.

She fixed her eyes on him. He leaned in to kiss her, tenderly. She ran her fingers through the short mop of his already disheveled hair, caressing his cheek, pulling him into her. He withdrew a scant few inches.

"Thank you," she said, softly.

"For what?" he asked, confused.

"For saving me from the Bigfoot," she said.

CHAPTER 21

Back in San Diego, Lauren slept off and on for days. Rowan made sure she ate, and helped her bathe when she asked him to. He tried to work while she rested. He found it hard to focus. He had so many things running through his mind. There were so many unanswered questions. He did manage to find one way to distract himself. He perused the travel website that they so often used to book their trips, looking for ideas of where to take her for their honeymoon.

Of course, they'd never gotten around to talking about wedding plans, but he had placed the ring on her finger at long last. He was content with that — for now. It was so hard trying to find somewhere to vacation, one of the curses of traveling for a living. They hadn't taken a vacation in all the years they'd been doing the show, and no one in the crew did either. They would make time for side trips when they found themselves in someplace interesting, but traveling for personal pleasure was practically unheard of.

Where on earth could we go that there wasn't some mystery to solve? Did Scooby Doo and the Gang have this much trouble planning a vacation? He thought to himself.

The Paris underground had been a great investigation, but it took some of the romanticism out of the City of Lights. The Castles of Scotland, Tower of London, the Pyramids of Giza, Ghosts of Cape Horn, the list could go on and on. From one continent to the other they'd traveled time and time again.

Rowan was too tired to think. *Maybe we could just go to Vegas*, he considered. *That would be weirder than all the ghosts and Bigfoot combined.*

"What time is it?" Lauren came in and found him in front of the computer.

He glanced at his watch. "About time for dinner," he smiled. She was wearing a pair of shorts and a tank top and he longed to peel her out of them and celebrate their engagement, but he knew she was in no shape for a good romp.

"What are you doing?"

"Looking over itineraries for our next few destinations. I haven't made reservations, and I'm kind of glad now that I didn't." It was only a half-lie.

"Why?"

"Well, it might be a while before you're ready to travel."

"Probably for the best anyway." She turned his chair and sat in his lap. He snaked his arms around her, mindful of her healing arm.

She suddenly had his full attention. "Why do you say that?"

"We're not done with this investigation," she said. "You know, this could turn out to be the best episode of *The Veritas Codex* ever. We could get another Emmy nomination."

He blinked in rapid succession. "Have you lost your ever-lovin' mind?"

"Wait just a second," she said. "Hear me out on this." She took a deep breath. "Whatever happened to me, I survived. Sure, I'm busted and bruised, but I survived. But the mystery remains. Is Bigfoot real? To compound that, we have to find out the truth. Did I get kidnapped by Bigfoot?"

He bit his lip, certain she'd lost her mind along with her memory. "You know what they're saying about you? What's all over the tabloids, don't you?" He mimicked quotation marks over his head with one hand. "*I Was Kidnapped By Bigfoot.*' Might as well tell them you've been impregnated by aliens."

"Stop it, Rowan." She stood and took a few steps. She turned sharply. "Don't you get it? It's our job to find the answers to mysteries. To find the truth!"

"You keep talking about the truth, like ... like it'll change something."

"It's our job." Her voice raised sharply.

"It's your life, Lauren. That's what worries me. You nearly died. Doesn't that frighten you? 'Cause it sure scares the hell out of me."

Lauren's dark eyes turned tender. "I'm never afraid when you're with me, Rowan. That's why we make such a great team. We always have each other's back. We always will." She laughed so she wouldn't cry. "I need you at my back on this one. I have to know ... I just have to."

———

It went against his better judgment, but he called the team and scheduled a meeting, asking each of them to bring their data on the Bigfoot investigation. Bahati and Jean-René had been leading the efforts to analyze the data and were in charge of the project while Lauren and Rowan were occupied with her recovery. He hadn't told them he was bringing Lauren with him.

The conference room table was covered in computers, video and audio equipment. The team, more than a dozen people, were engaged in a heated discussion when he came in, his body shielding Lauren behind him.

"Hey, Boss," Chance said. The room went silent as Lauren stepped out from behind Rowan.

"Good to see you too." Lauren managed a smile. Everyone rose and gathered around to welcome her back. "Where are the bagels?"

———

"Okay, guys. Let's get started. We have a lot of work to do. Lauren's energy level isn't back to 100 percent, so we need to do everything we can before she gets worn out," Rowan took over, and helped Lauren to her chair. Without asking, he poured her a cup of coffee and went to work doctoring it for her. "Lauren has asked that we assemble the team to look over the evidence from Washington State. We're going to piece everything together to see what we can do to help restore her memory of the events there. It's the mystery we have to answer before we can start our next project. I need everyone on point here. Let's do this in chronological order, okay?"

"Okay." A collective response answered him.

"Jean-René?" He handed the cup of coffee to Lauren. "Let's start with the first evidence from our trip."

"Right." Jean-René produced the plaster cast of the first footprint. "Here's the cast we took on the trail near the river." He put it under the document cam so everyone in the room could see it on the big screen. "Jess?"

Jess Bynum was the team's assistant research anthropologist. Rowan had put her in charge of the cast analysis. She stood, taking over the discussion. "I consulted with my colleague, the preeminent expert on Bigfoot, Dr. Menlo in Idaho. According to Dr. Menlo, this print was made by a bipedal mammal of unknown origin. As you can see, the toes are clearly visible, five on each foot. The doctor provided me with this overview where he's drawn in the probable skeletal form of the creator's foot." The diagram appeared on the screen. "Notice the tarsal bones are more pronounced than a human foot, but it is more like a human foot than the foot of a gorilla." She put a cast of a gorilla footprint on the screen. "You can also see this was obviously not the track of a bear." She put up a bear track for comparison. "Let me zoom in on the cast again." It took a second to get the image to come into focus. "This cast shows remarkable details. Your team was lucky to arrive upon it so soon after it was made. The indentions around the edge are indicative of hair, and you can even make out the dermal ridges of the toes. It is my professional opinion, shared by Dr. Menlo, that this is a biologically significant sample."

"So, you are saying it's not a fake?" Rowan asked.

"That is what I'm saying," she said. "There's no way your every-day hoax-monger would know where to put the heel bone ... in humans, it would be much farther back than it is in this cast."

"What about the audio we caught?" Rowan turned to Bahati.

"There were other casts for comparison," Jess interrupted.

"I know. We'll come back to you. I'm trying to follow the chronology of the data collection," he said curtly, and she sat back down. If she was upset for being cut off, she didn't show it.

———

Bahati spent twenty-five minutes discussing the howls they'd captured on both audio and video tape, replaying them for the team. She put the video on the big screen and dimmed the lights. Rowan watched Lauren for any sign of a reaction and was amazed at how placid her face remained, even as she watched her own image respond to the cry—more like a baying moan in the black of night. She didn't even wince. It was as if she didn't associate herself with the woman on the screen.

When Jean-René began to discuss the events of the night before her disappearance, she turned her attention patiently to him. She listened to the discussions and watched the video clips, showing no emotion. Each of the team members told their side of the story. When Bahati began to recount the events from the night of the disappearance, Lauren seemed strangely disinterested, tugging at a string on the sleeve of her shirt. She watched the video from her web cam but again, it was almost as if she didn't realize all that actually happened to her. Rowan tugged at the whiskers on his chin as he watched her.

Finally, everyone stopped, just looking at each other. "Is that it?" Lauren asked.

"That's everything I have," Jean-René said, glancing at Bahati, who shrugged.

"Well I'm not done." Jess finally spoke up.

"What else do you have?" Rowan asked, remembering he'd cut her off before.

"Well, Rob and Bahati had the presence of mind to get a cast of the footprint they found at the edge of base camp after Lauren was abducted. In my opinion, this is one of the most telling pieces of evidence you brought back from the mountain," she said. She stood, taking up the second cast. "This print is approximately 20" long and 6" wide. The cast you took from the riverbank was only about 15" long and 5" wide." Jess put the two next to each other under the document cam, projecting the image onto the screen. One was obviously bigger than the other.

"So, we have a larger specimen?" Rowan asked.

"One would think," she said, curtly. "My calculations from the first cast, which my peers have confirmed, suggest we have a creature approximately seven feet tall, approximately 370 pounds. This cast is different. You'll notice the ball of the foot sunk in quite a bit deeper, not the toes. There's no evidence of dermal ridges, though we do have some hair imprint. The skeletal structure is significantly different. I managed to salvage a fiber from the plaster. I sent it to the lab for analysis. It came back as a synthetic polyester, most commonly used in fake fur.

This footprint is a hoax. A hoax-monger in a monkey suit ran through your camp, and abducted Lauren right in front of your own camera. This print is made by a 250-pound human, carrying your 120-pound field producer."

She appeared to feel vindicated for having to wait, and she stood smugly over the chaos she'd created. A flood of questions came at her like a hurricane. Lauren remained in her chair, while Rowan stood up, pounding his fists on the conference table to silence the room.

"But the first print was genuine. Right?"

"Yes," she said. "It appears to be genuine. There are databases of hundreds of these things. I compared it to every single one. We've got more fakes then genuine ones, but this one shares many of the common traits of those believed to be real." She held up the larger print. "This one matches every hoax we've ever seen," she dropped the fake cast on the table, and it shattered. "Hoax-monger in a monkey suit."

CHAPTER 22

Jess' words resounded in Rowan's head for hours. *Hoax-monger in a monkey suit.* He pounded his fist in the counter. Lauren flinched. Rowan wasn't prone to fits of rage, but his dander was definitely up.

"Well, at least we know one thing," she said, pushing her food around on her plate.

"What's that?" He paced a few more moments before coming to sit down at the table across from her. "What?"

"I wasn't kidnapped by Bigfoot."

He buried his eyes in his hands "Jeez," he snarled. "It was a lot easier for me to stomach the thought that a Bigfoot did this to you." He put his hand over hers, his thumb brushing over the small, cool diamond. It softened his anger just a bit.

"You know what this means, don't you?" she asked. It took a moment for him to respond.

"What?"

"We have to go back."

"We can't go back."

"We have to," she said. "You know I'm right."

"We are not going back. Dammit," he snapped.

"We don't have any other choice. We have to get more data, Rowan. We have to. *The truth*, remember?"

"Jess sent her report to the FBI. It's in their hands to investigate now."

"We have to go back," Lauren repeated.

"We are not going back!" he snapped. "You still have your arm in a sling. You could have died."

"But I didn't."

"You could have."

"You know I am right."

"We're not going back," he stated flatly. He set his jaw, but his lip quivered. "We're not."

"We have to."

"No. We don't."

———

Lauren was miffed. She was tired of being confined to bed, tired of trying to make herself comfortable on the sofa. She thought the recliner was slightly better. Her mood was brooding and restless. Rowan wasn't any better off. The lack of sleep wore on him and he often went on long runs to try and clear his mind. It didn't seem to be helping.

Limited to watching television and surfing the internet Lauren had no such opportunity to ease her stress. She was too bored to really pay attention, least of all to the television. She'd already made three tours through the ninety-some channels before she got fed up. She slung the remote across the room and nearly hit Rowan's head with it.

He glanced up from the computer. "What?"

"I'm bored," she moaned. "I'm tired of sitting around."

"What do you want me to do?"

"Take me to Washington," she insisted.

"Where do you want to go on our honeymoon?" He returned his attention to the work.

"Washington."

"I'm serious. I'm not taking you on another investigation until we decide where we're going on our honeymoon. And we aren't honeymooning anywhere where there's something to investigate."

"Like there's anywhere like that." She leaned back the recliner.

"Lauren," he pleaded. "Help me here."

"Where have we not been?"

"So far, we've missed Antarctica and Alaska," he said. "There's a reason for that. I don't like to be cold."

"Then we'll go to the beach," she said.

"Bermuda?" He smiled. He thought of their investigation in the Bermuda triangle.

"No way," she scolded. "I liked Bermuda, but you drank two pitchers of rum swizzles and nearly fell off the cliff by the hotel. You scared the daylights out of me."

"That's the only time you ever saw me drunk."

"For a reason." She laughed.

"What about Mexico?" he changed the subject, smiling at her. It was the first time they'd laughed since — well, for a long time.

"Aztec and Mayan ruins," she said, hooking a leg over the arm of the chair, kicking her foot like an impatient teenager.

"Florida?"

"Creature of the Okeefenokee Swamp."

"North Carolina?"

"The mystery hound of Randolph County."

"Galveston, Texas."

"Ghosts of the Great Hurricane of 1900."

"Greece?"

"Rosetta Stone," she replied. "Vesuvius, the Coliseum, mysteries of the Lost Gardens of Babylon. Do you need me to keep going?"

"So much for Rome, Alexandria, and Venice too."

"There's only one place where there's no mystery," she said. He came over, sitting on the sofa beside her. She turned and hooked a long, tanned leg over his.

"Where?" He surrendered as she wormed her way over and straddled him.

"Right here," she said, snuggling into him, resting her head on his chest, making herself comfortable.

"Oh, I'm sure there's a few mysteries left to solve," he grinned.

"Maybe."

He ran his hand through her hair, twisting it between his fingers.

"I know one thing that's no mystery."

"What's that?" he asked.

"How much I love you," she said, sitting back to look at him.

"The only mystery left is what made you finally say yes."

Her smile became shadowed. "I'm terrified, Rowan," she admitted, leaning back into him. He'd seen her frightened, maybe even afraid. But he'd never seen her terrified, not until the day they found her on the mountain.

"Not knowing what happened ... thinking about what could have happened. Wondering what you'd have done if you hadn't found me. I can't ... I won't leave things unsettled," she said. "You're right. You've always been right. I have been stubborn and stupid. I should have said yes sooner."

His thumb brushed the tear from her cheek, and he leaned down and kissed her. "I'm glad you said yes now," he said. He kissed her again.

"Me too." She agreed.

———

Days passed with no improvement in her mood. One afternoon, she was sitting cross-legged in the recliner, brooding. In her hands she held one of her old journals. The cover was dyed leather— a deep green — aged and cracked. The yellowing pages were full of all the things she had learned early in her academic career. Her thumb ran over the rough gold embossing that spelled out the school's motto. Her mind swirled thinking about the knowledge contained in these pages. It paled in comparison with the knowledge that swirled in her mind now.

Veritas. Truth.

"Penny for your thoughts?" Rowan asked as he came in. He glanced over her shoulder at the book.

She held up the journal. "Cost you a dollar."

He took it and studied the pages, thumbing through them with care. "If I didn't know better, I'd think this was Indiana Jones' diary," he said. He sat down beside her. The book was filled with notes, sketches, formulae, diagrams — ramblings on every subject. Some pages were covered from corner to corner. Every usable square inch of paper had been covered in blue felt-tip ink.

"What do you know of truth?" Lauren asked.

"Was it Plato that said, *the only thing I know, is that I know nothing?*" Rowan asked.

"It was," she closed her eyes and sat back. "I took a philosophy class once. We had this crusty old professor who was fond of mixing plaids. He wore these old polyester leisure suits that were two sizes too big. Awful shades of green and brown, clashed with yellow and orange. On Fridays though, he always came to class in a toga. He wore a crown of olive branches in his white hair. He looked like one of the old men in the balcony on the Muppet Show," she laughed. She remembered he always smelled of moth balls, Old Spice and cigar smoke. "He would stand on his desk and tell hippie jokes."

"Hippie jokes?" Rowan chuckled. He'd never heard this story before. It made him feel better that her memory was returning with such clarity.

A faint smile crossed her weary face. She clutched the journal to her heart. Fond memories were contained within.

"Remember any of them?"

She chuckled. "A few," she said. They were written down, along with all her class notes. She always expected one of them to show up on a quiz. "Why couldn't the lifeguard save the hippie from drowning?"

"I don't know," Rowan smiled.

"He was too *far out, man.*" She waited for a reaction. He groaned. That was the joke that had turned up in her final exam. It was an essay question asking them to pontificate on the meaning of the phrase *far out, man.* Lauren had gotten an A on that test. "When the Network first approached me about doing our show, I wanted to call it simply *Veritas,*" she said. "But they were dead set against it. They said it was too cerebral. We came to a consensus. It was this journal that made us arrive at *The Veritas Codex.*"

"It does have a certain ring to it," Rowan said.

Lauren looked at him with concern written in her features. "Have you ever studied philosophy?"

"Only at the bar in Estes Park on poetry night," he said. "There was usually a lot more drinking than thinking."

"What is truth?" She asked rhetorically. "Philosophers spend a lot of time contemplating the concept of *Veritas.* In the Graeco-Roman world, the goddess Veritas was the personification of all that was understood as truth. Every Roman citizen was expected to dedicate their lives to the journey of seeking truth." Lauren said. "Dr. Philpott taught me a lot about how we think and what we know of truth. But ..." She struggled to find

the right words. To find a way to make him understand something she couldn't even understand herself. "There are some
who say truth is timeless ... eternal. Some say truths are
omnitemporal entities."

"Omni what?" Rowan blurted. "Look, this is all ... obviously
... way over my head. What does it matter?"

Lauren debated how to say what she needed to say. "Rowan,
something happened while I was ... *gone*. I don't know how to
explain it." He looked afraid as she considered how to tell him.
"I see this word, *Veritas*, in a whole new way now." She turned
back to the cover. "I know it means truth ... but now, I get it. I
really get it. It means so much ... *more* ..."

"More?"

"Anselm of Canterbury wrote, *I do not recall ever having found
a definition of truth; but if you wish, let us inquire as to what truth is
by going through the various things in which we say there is truth.*
There's more to truth than most can comprehend. Where there
is balance in the universe, there is truth. There's a breadth of
meaning that human language cannot adequately express. It's
more than we can grasp. Truth pales in the shadow of all it
encompasses." Her voice took on a misty tone. "It was more
than I ever comprehended until now. There's a goodness and
comfort that comes with truth. I didn't get it before. I see it
now."

"What's different now, Lauren?" Rowan asked.

Her expression remained neutral as she spoke. "Me. I'm
different."

The heavy arch of his brow came down into a flat line over
his face.

"Something happened to me." She thumbed to the back of
the journal and read from the pages. *"Many of you have already
found out and others will find out in the course of their lives that
truth eludes us if we do not concentrate with total attention on its
pursuit,"* she quoted. "Gulag Archipelago. What happened to

me? Well now my full attention is on the truth, whether I want it or not."

"Lauren." Rowan started, but she cut him off.

"He also said, *Truth is seldom pleasant; it is almost invariably bitter.* I know it's not going to be easy. But I know what I need to do."

"Bitter is one thing," he reached over and took her hand. "Deadly is another." She turned to him. "You could have died out there. I thought you had." His voice trembled. "I couldn't bear to lose you, Lauren. That is a truth of which I am quite sure."

A stolid expression overtook her countenance. "Truth is a story," she said as she reached for his cheek. She caressed it. He melted into her palm. "Our story is far from over, but … I can't let it end like this. I need truth. I need balance. I'm afraid I'm going mad. There's so much swirling around in my head. I can't focus. Can't concentrate. I need to know what happened. If I don't, I will go insane."

"You're not going insane, Lauren," Rowan said. "You had a head injury and you suffered a traumatic attack. It's going to take some time. You need to see a counselor or a psychiatrist. You don't need to go back to Washington."

She took a deep breath and let it out slowly. She forced a smile in his direction. *"The truth … is a beautiful and terrible thing, and should therefore be treated with great caution."*

"Who said that? Plato?"

She shook her head. "Professor Dumbledore. *Harry Potter and the Sorcerer's Stone.*" Her expression went distant. The shine of tears formed in the corners of her eyes. Her lip trembled. Her knuckles went white as she clutched the book in her hand. "You have no idea," her voice dropped an octave. "No idea what's racing around in my brain. There are words I shouldn't know. They run like a news ticker behind my eyes when I try to sleep.

Letters and symbols of ancient text … words no one else can read. Words few can comprehend."

"Like Cherokee?" Rowan puzzled.

"Cherokee, Latin, Greek, Arabic, Toltec, Egyptian …" she closed her eyes and took a deep breath. "I keep thinking, maybe I'm hallucinating. I have to know what happened to me, Rowan. It's like a cancer that gnaws on my brain." She stood and paced, running her hand through her hair. Her finger found the scar behind her ear. The skin tingled beneath her touch. "Maybe the head injury took more of a toll than I remembered."

"Maybe you're tired," he said. He took her hand and pulled her into him. She buried her face in his chest. She let him wrap his arms around her. He kissed her head and brushed her hair back from her face. "Come on," he kissed her softly. Her lips responded. "I'll tuck you in."

————

She let him put her to bed but refused to let him sleep. She insisted she was up to a bit of lovemaking, as long as he was gentle with her. He made love to her slowly, attentively, molding his body to hers, warming her from the inside out and reminding her of all the reasons he was happy to be with her. He showed her how relieved he was to have her safely beneath him.

She fell asleep in the afterglow, wrapped in his arms. He held her long into the night, watching her sleep, dreading the thought of what she was insisting had to be done. There had to be a better way to help her remember. There just had to be.

————

A frantic scream broke the quiet dawn. Rowan bolted up from a dead slumber. Lauren thrashed about in the bed. He grabbed her uninjured arm and pulled her into him to stop her from striking out.

"Lauren!" He shook her gently. "Wake up! It's okay. You're safe."

"No!" she cried. "No!" Her screams faded into sobs.

He held her until the tears passed. He dried her cheek with his thumb and wrapped her in the circle of his arms. He lay her down, tucking her head under his chin. She smelled of rosemary and mint and all things feminine. He breathed her in and tried to lend her some of his warmth. She shivered and he stroked her head, tenderly. His hand found the bare line of healing flesh where her hair seemed to part naturally over her ear. He realized she was trembling, not just shivering.

"You want to talk about it?" he asked softly.

"Not really."

"When you're ready, I'm here."

"I just need sleep." She closed her eyes. He lay listening to her breathe, wanting to say a million different things. His mind raced with questions that remained unanswerable. He didn't go back to sleep until he realized she had stopped trembling.

———

The nightmares became more frequent and their intensity more severe. One afternoon, Lauren had just sat down to eat lunch, and Rowan found her with a far-off look in her eye. She'd hardly touched her food and her fork hung limp in her hand. It crashed to the plate. Her breathing became labored as she gasped for air. He caught her hand in his, and pulled her to him, as if his arms could protect her from the demons.

She screamed suddenly, a blood-chilling scream, that tore through him and he felt his heart shatter as he clung to her. "Lauren, what is it? Tell me what you see?" he said, knowing she would never talk about it when she was coherent. "What is it?"

"*A-gi ... hna ... sv ...*" she trembled.

He had those words memorized. "*Ancient evil ... witch.*"

Rowan trembled, himself, burying his face in her hair. Something had to be done. He got up and went to the computer and started looking at flights — for Washington State — against his heart and his better judgement.

CHAPTER 23

"How are you feeling?" Rowan asked when he picked her up from her last physical therapy appointment. He helped her with her seatbelt. It had become a habit after twelve weeks.

"Better," she said. She lifted her shoulder and flexed her muscle for him. She winced a little bit, but she had made great strides. "97 percent ... maybe 98."

"Think that will be enough?"

"The therapist says it'll only improve." She shrugged. It was something she hadn't been able to do twelve weeks before.

"Do you need to go by the apartment before we go to work?"

"I think I'm good," she smiled. "I could use some lunch."

"We have time to grab something," he said. "What sounds good?"

"Food," she grinned.

Rowan put the car in gear. "My favorite."

They had lunch at a beach-front deli before heading back up to the studio. The team was assembling, and Jean-René met them in the lobby at the elevator. "Problem," he said. He knitted his brows together as the elevator doors closed.

"What sort of problem?"

"Insurance problem," he said. "The execs came down this morning and said the insurance company dropped our coverage."

"Because of what happened in Washington?" Lauren asked.

"Or Peru?" Rowan added.

"Both. Partially," Jean-René said, as the elevator doors opened on the sixth floor. "Something about a problem at the lab."

Rowan blanched. "The lab? What?" Lauren gasped. He moved past his fiancée on the pretense of getting coffee. He signaled Jean-René to drop it.

"I know, right? So anyway, they dropped our insurance and we can't go anywhere until we get it renewed." Jean-René swallowed hard.

"It's not likely you'll find anyone who'll insure a high-risk expedition," Jacob came in behind them, closing the door as he did. "Your e-mod is a 2.75. I've never seen one that high."

"E-mod?" Rowan puzzled.

"Experience modifier," Lauren said.

"Fine. Everyone, let's work this out." Ordinarily Rowan might have flown off the handle, but this was not the time. If they couldn't get insurance, that might be just the thing to convince Lauren to abandon this folly and move on.

Without the insurance company's backing, Jacob wouldn't release funds to support their efforts, and without the financial backing of the Network, the team wasn't going anywhere.

"How are we supposed to produce a television show if we can't go out on location?" Jean-René grumped.

"Let's go start making phone calls," Lauren said. "I'll get State Farm or GEICO to insure us if I have too."

———

It wasn't that easy. The word of Lauren's abduction hadn't been any secret. Rowan tried going through channels, over people's heads, but at the end of the day, he hadn't gotten anywhere. He finally hung up the phone and walked out onto the balcony, leaning on the rail. He ran a weary hand over his face, but he wanted to scream. He was relieved and frustrated at the same time. He didn't want to go back. He also knew if he didn't make a fair attempt at securing coverage, Lauren would blame him for not trying.

"No luck, huh?" Lauren asked. She held a basket of laundry. He carried it into the bedroom for her.

"No."

"We'll figure something out." She took a small towel to fold.

"I'm going for a run."

"Want company?"

"I don't think I'd be very good company right now," he said, reaching into the basket for his running shorts. "I need to clear my head."

"Is there anything I can do to help?" She put a tentative hand on his shoulder.

He hesitated. "Be naked when I get home?"

"Not until after you've had a shower." She raised her brows, but leaned in to kiss him.

He drew back, grinning. "Maybe I'll just have you now, before I'm all sweaty,"

He tossed the shorts aside and pushed her back gently. He climbed on top of her, brushing her bangs off her face, letting his thumb trace the edge of her strong jaw.

She snaked an arm around him and drew him to her, kissing him again. "That's a better idea."

———

He awoke late the next morning, to the smell of coffee and pancakes. He found Lauren at the table on the phone. She got up as she continued her conversation. She fixed him a plate; poured him a cup of coffee, all with the phone in the crook of her neck. She sat it in front of him as he inspected the feast.

"So, we'll have the certificate of coverage how soon?" she asked. She couldn't help but notice the puzzled look that crossed his face. "Of course. I understand. Can you fax that to my attention? That'd be great." She sat down and picked up her coffee cup. "I appreciate your help, Greg. Thank you." She hung up the phone and glanced up at Rowan. "We'll have our certificate of coverage Monday."

"What? Who? How?" He cut off each word, dumbfounded. He'd made thirty calls at least, and she'd gotten it done in one day — one phone call?

"I had to insure myself when I got my research grant from the University," she said. "I know people."

"But ..."

"Just let me handle the insurance part. I need you to handle the travel arrangements."

"If anything happens to you I just ... I couldn't go on. We have to be especially careful on this trip. I won't lose you again."

"Nothing's going to happen to me, Rowan," she said. "I made a couple other phone calls too. I called that FBI agent. I found his business card in your backpack while I was doing laundry. He tried to talk me out of it too, but he said if I was determined to come, the FBI would lead the team."

"I still think we should leave it to them, Lauren," Rowan said.

"They've had three, almost four months to do something. The trail has gone cold. We are the experts here. We know our quarry better than they do. We can let them worry about the charlatans."

CHAPTER 24

WITH MT. SAINT HELENS IN THE BACKGROUND, LAUREN FILMED her first piece in months. "It has been over sixteen weeks since I was abducted by an unknown person or persons. Despite what the tabloids would have you believe, we are certain that my abductors were hoax-mongers in a Bigfoot suit. We don't know what their motives were or why they targeted our team. This is why we are working with the FBI on the investigation. We're joined by Special Agent Andrew Miller and Special Agent Joshua Morrison."

Rowan picked up the narration there. "We also have National Park Service Rangers Katie Jonas and Derry Kent. They are with us to aid in the investigation and provide security for the team. We've restricted our crew to four members: Lauren, myself, our Director of Photography, Jean-René Toussaint and assistant researcher, Bahati Yseri. No other camera or audio techs are with us. We are also joined by local Bigfoot researcher Pauline Jamison, who works for the National Park Service. She will be our guide."

"After a couple of months of rehabilitation, I am ready to

find the truth about what happened to me, and the truth about the legendary Bigfoot."

Rowan took over the narration. "Since our initial visit to the area, there have been numerous sightings of an unidentified creature raiding camp sites, smashing trash bins. It can be heard howling in the night. At least one witness reports seeing a large bipedal animal crossing the road in front of his car." He wasn't surprised how easily they fell back into their routine of playing off each other in their narrations. None of this had been scripted in advance. They each knew what to say. "Based on the evidence we found during our last visit, we believe that while there may well be some hoax-mongers at play in the area, we cannot discount the evidence that suggests we may have found proof of a real Bigfoot living in these mountains. Our goal is to expose the hoax, find the beast, and answer the question—*What happened to Lauren?*"

———

"Okay, perimeter alarms are set." Bahati came into camp as Jean-René clicked off the recorder. "I've set trap cams and we're ready to go dark."

Lauren yawned. She stretched gingerly. Travel days were always exhausting, but more so today than ever. They'd left the house and caught a red-eye flight to SEA-TAC the night before, renting an SUV for the team, their equipment and supplies.

The heavy load on her back was made even more difficult in the thin mountain air. The team had hiked until near dark, finally making it to a place to set up base camp for the night. Now that camp was set, all that was left to do was have dinner and then hit the sack.

They had the cameras and alarms set up as a passive control. If they caught anything, it would be a bonus. Tonight, they would take turns on watch and use the opportunity to rest.

Tomorrow they had another long hike into an area where few hikers dared venture, and even the logging crews hadn't been there in the past twenty years. It was closer to the clearing where Lauren had been found, and an area where several of the recent sightings had been reported.

Chores had been decided by lottery. Derry and Katie were in charge of dinner, Rowan and Bahati had first watch, and Jean-René and Pauline had the second. Miller and Morrison had drawn the last watch of the night and would also be responsible for breakfast. Lauren would be allowed to rest tonight and she couldn't wait for dinner to be over with so she could go lie down. The first day's hike had been hard on her, and she was exhausted. With three rotations, each team would only have to sit watch for a few hours.

"How's the shoulder?" Morrison came over and sat down beside her. She had her laptop open and was checking on weather conditions, just in case. Earlier, rain and thunderstorms had passed through the area and a humid pallor hung over the mountain; the air was still. The skies were starting to clear, and it was starting to cool off just a bit.

"A little sore," Lauren admitted. "Not used to carrying a backpack."

"I can imagine. You look better than you did the last time we talked."

"Oh, believe me. I feel better."

"Still no memories of what happened?"

"No," she admitted. "Rowan says I've been having nightmares, but I don't remember those either."

"He mentioned that," he said. "It's not uncommon, you know?"

"What's that?"

"The mind is an amazing thing. It's programmed to protect its owner. It can remember certain things with such vivid clarity… the taste of chocolate, the smell of your grandmother's perfume, the day you get married, your first born child, the smell of baby shampoo and powder, but not the smell of the diapers," he leaned back on one of the cases. He wore a plaid shirt and cargo pants — a distant departure from the black suit and Ray Ban sunglasses. "How easily we forget the pain of a scraped knee, the pain of childbirth, the heartbreak of our first love."

Lauren crossed her ankles and hugged her knees. "It's more frustrating than anything to me."

"I can imagine."

"I am a scientist. I'm trained to collect and analyze data. I thrive on data. Yet, this time I feel like the data is there, but somehow... corrupted."

An amused expression crossed his chiseled face. "You would have made a great FBI agent," he chuckled.

"Why do you say that?"

"We collect data too," he said. "Once we have the evidence, we analyze it, and work to come to conclusions."

"There's one difference between a researcher and an FBI agent."

"What's that?"

"You arrest your subject once you analyze them. Me, I just take video and turn it into good television."

"Good point, but there are those out there who think what I do is good entertainment."

"My second favorite show is *Criminal Minds*," she grinned. "So, maybe we're not so different after all."

"I like that one too," he admitted, blushing.

———

Lauren sat with her face on her palm, her elbow resting on her knee. She'd been writing in her journal but had nodded off, waiting for dinner. She nearly bolted out of her skin when

Rowan sat down beside her. His leg bumped hers, unseating her elbow from her knee. "Here." He handed her a tin plate of food. It was some kind of Mexican hot dish. It smelled spicy and her mouth watered as she took the warm plate in her hand.

"You look tired," he commented. He dug into his own food.

"Yeah, I'm beat," she said. "I'm sorry I didn't draw watch tonight, but I could sure use the sleep."

"Yeah, you're probably right." She didn't need to know he hadn't even put her name in the hat.

"Besides, I like to watch the stars in the mountains at night. I kind of like the midnight watch."

"I'd worry about you," Rowan said.

"I'd have my dart gun." She put a hand reassuringly on the dart gun on her belt.

"Damned lot of good the dart guns did us last time. The only thing that even makes me feel halfway safe is the presence of all these trained federal agents."

The Park Service rangers and the FBI agents packed real guns with real bullets. Regulations restricted anyone else from discharging a firearm in the National Park. Rowan had to nego-tiate a deal for the dart guns. He didn't mention they'd brought them with them before. If Rowan had known it was against the rules, he wouldn't say.

"Does it look like the weather's going to hold?" Rowan changed the subject.

"Yeah," she said, between bites. She still had the radar pulled up on her laptop. "There's some rain to the north, but it's moving to the east."

He nodded, taking up his plate. "Good. It'll be a beautiful night then."

"I've missed the stars," she glanced up at the sky, the last rays of daylight slipping below the timberline and behind the mountains.

"Sure to be plenty of them tonight," he said.

She yawned. As soon as her plate was mostly empty, she set it aside, and rested her head in her hand again. Rowan nudged her. "You have to eat it all."

"I'm too tired."

"Sooner it's done, the sooner you can go lie down."

CHAPTER 25

LAUREN WOKE TO THE SMELL OF BACON FRYING; HER MOUTH watered. She breathed in the damp morning and curled herself into Rowan's body, dreamily unaware of the passing of time. Rowan took a deep breath and wrapped an arm around her. He snored loudly in her ear. The magic of the moment was suddenly gone. Now fully awake, Lauren was aware the sky was almost the same muted pink it had been before she'd drifted off.

She lifted his arm to peel herself out of Rowan's grasp. She pulled on her jacket and then her hiking boots. She crawled out of their tent.

"Chow's almost ready," Jean-René said. The bemusement that curled the corners of his mouth did not escape her notice as she emerged from Rowan's tent. Now that their secret was out, they gave up any pretenses. The ring on her finger gave her authority to sleep wherever she wanted.

"I'm starving," she said, running a weary hand through her hair. "Anything happen overnight?"

Bahati brought her a cup of coffee. "You didn't miss anything, Boss. It was quiet all night. At least until Rowan went to bed."

Lauren laughed. "Rowan could wake the dead"

"Yes, but the real question is, can you wake him? We need to get moving."

Bahati was right. Daylight was burning and they had another arduous hike ahead.

Lauren looked back at the tent. "I'll see what I can do." She offered. She went to her equipment trunk and found one of the digital recorders. She kept the volume turned down until she found the segment she wanted, then she stood behind the tent, and turned the sound all the way up. A grainy recording of an unexplained yowl filled the meadow. Once it ebbed, there was a moment of silence followed by a second. Before that cry faded, the tent began to shake violently and the zipper was thrown back, Rowan all but fell over the threshold as he hopped out trying to get a shoe on. Clearly, he wasn't fully awake but when he froze and realized the whole camp was staring at him, he stood with his foot half out of the hiking boot, looking around, dazed.

A roar of laughter filled the camp. Lauren came around the tent holding the digital recorder. A devilish grin brightened her usually sober face. Rowan realized he'd become the victim of a classic prank in the world of paranormal research. "Good morning, Sunshine," she beamed, awaiting his reaction.

He straightened and he shook his finger at her. "Ha! Ha!" He gave her a toothy grin. "You got me."

She pulled him in, kissing him. "Come on. Let's get breakfast and pack it up. We've got a lot to accomplish today."

"Yes, ma'am," he kissed her again, then went to do her bidding.

CHAPTER 26

"So, which trail are we taking?" Lauren asked Pauline. The ranger had a map and GPS out and was plotting their course.

"That's what I was trying to decide. I know you and your team went up to Ape Canyon last time, but this is the height of our tourist season and it's twice as crowded as it was when you were here. I had thought perhaps a hike up to Spirit Lake, but now I'm debating hitting some of the areas less traveled. This area is still barren since the 1980 eruption." She pointed toward the volcano.

Lauren's eye found Bahati who was, fortunately, busy packing up her tent. "Where do you suggest?"

"Well, when we get near Windy Ridge Viewpoint, which is a high activity area for tourists this time of year, we can cross over the valley, across to Badger Lake," she said. "We've had some reports of strange things going on up in that area. I've been meaning to get out there to check it out. Now's as good a time as any."

"What kind of things?" Lauren asked.

"Reports of strange howls in the night. Some campers scared

out of their tents. Camp gear raided; food boxes ransacked. One of the picnic areas was trashed big time. Things like that."

"Sounds right up our alley," Lauren commented. She stood as Rowan approached.

"Looks like we're ready."

"We best get started," Pauline said. "I hope you folks brought sunscreen. There's parts of the trail where there's absolutely no shade, and it looks to be pretty hot today."

Lauren pulled on her large brimmed hat and smiled. "We came prepared for anything."

———

"The Loowit trail goes all the way around the volcano," Pauline explained as they trekked. "It's 26 miles if you were to hike the whole thing. You hiked part of it when you were here in the spring, according to Jean-René."

"I can't believe there's still so much damage from the 1980 eruption." Bahati was breathing hard. Lauren was too.

The trail had turned to the northeast, but they were still hiking uphill. Lauren was ready to get to the valley where she hoped the going would be easier. Her pack was putting strain on her shoulder. She suffered in silence and led the charge up the slope.

"This whole park took heavy damage in the eruption. It'll take decades more before it will return to pristine condition. Of course, by then, the volcano could erupt again," Pauline continued.

"Again?" Bahati swallowed hard. Pauline turned and looked at her.

"Bahati doesn't like volcanos," Lauren said. "She worked in the Philippines in 1991 when Pinatubo erupted."

"I barely got on a helicopter before the ash cloud made travel impossible," Bahati said. "I don't know how you can work on an active volcano."

"It's just part of the job," Katie said. "We hardly even notice it most of the time."

"That wasn't your only experience with volcanoes." Jean-René nudged her. "But that was a good one." Her nostrils flared as she glowered at him.

"There's no such thing as a good experience with a volcano," she snapped.

"What happened?" Derry asked.

Bahati shook her head and stared daggers again at Jean-René for bringing it up. "Fine," she said. "I'll tell you about it."

As they hiked, she told them the whole story. She'd been working in the Philippines as an assistant to famed nature documentary producer Arturo Jimenez. An earthquake measuring 7.7 in magnitude hit in the area of central Luzon. While not a photographer by trade, she'd captured some of the earliest pictures of the devastation.

By March the following year, there were more quakes in one of the villages she was visiting, on the northwest side of the island. They continued for two more weeks. The first warning of a potential eruption was finally issued.

"A few months later, we were working near one of the larger villages at the volcano's base. I was taking pictures and inter-viewing the villagers. I was surprised to find they had no fear of the potential threat. Even with the ash clouds. It looked like nuclear winter all around them but they remained calm." She stopped to take a deep breath. The rest of the team did the same. "An elder told me, *we've had many warnings in the past. This is our home. We do not fear our home. The warnings come every day, saying, this is it! The volcano will erupt today. But night comes and then the dawn. There is no explosion. No eruption. We think they are foolish for saying such things when they obviously are not true.*"

"We were evacuated later that week, only to be permitted to

return a few days later. This was repeated several more times. I began to think the villagers must be right. Perhaps they knew something the scientists did not. But now, I know the scientists were right."

"What was the VEI of the Mt. Saint Helens eruption?" Bahati asked.

"VEI?" Derry piped up.

"Volcanic Explosivity Index," Lauren explained.

"Mount Saint Helens was approximately a five. Pinatubo was a six."

"Has there ever been a ten?"

"Well, the VEI wasn't invented till 1982, so there's no way to be sure, but they estimate even Krakatoa was about a six," Lauren commented. "The highest was estimated to be an eight. Lake Taupo in the North Island of New Zealand. But that was over 26,000 years ago. The Icelandic eruptions back in February were about a four."

Bahati bit her lip. A visible shiver ran down her spine, despite the afternoon heat. "I was there for Pinatubo. I respect the power of the earth beneath our feet."

———

An afternoon thunderstorm developed quickly, and they had to hunker down in the meadow as lightning crashed around them, striking the taller trees. Rowan held his rain tarp over himself and Lauren. They crouched as low as they could. It was the best they could do, all things considered.

"How are you feeling?" he asked.

A shriek escaped her throat as the earth trembled beneath their feet, not sure if it was thunder or the ground itself. "Other than being terrified?" she grimaced. "I'm great."

"I love how honest you are," he grinned, and leaned in to kiss her.

"Hopefully, this will pass as quickly as it started." A hail stone bounced off her head. They were pelted with the small ice balls that bounced like popcorn off the green grass around them.

"Holy crap!" Rowan drew her into him to protect her. He put his other arm up to protect his own head.

The sound of the hail on the tarp was deafening, but not loud enough to drown out the sound of the others around them as the hail hit them too. The pellets were slightly smaller than ping pong balls, but were rather soft, if a hailstone could be called such. They began to melt as soon as they hit the ground. Within minutes the hailstones shrunk to the size of peas before the storm waned into a gentle shower.

Rowan stood up, robbing Lauren of his warmth. She rose beside him as they turned to assess the damages. "Is everyone okay?"

Jean-René stood, rubbing his forehead. "I took one to the head," he winced.

"I'm okay," Bahati said. "I think." She glanced over her shoulder, trying to eye a sore spot.

"Let me see," Lauren came over to check, peeling back her rain slicker. A welt had built up on her shoulder blade. "Yeah, that's got to hurt."

"I have something for that," Rowan said. He dug through his pack and found a zip-top bag. He scooped up a couple of handfuls of the ice pellets that had offended them. He made an ice pack. He handed it to Bahati. "Here's a dose of the cat."

"Dose of the cat?" Bahati raised her perfectly arched, and delicately thin eyebrows.

"Hair of the dog that bit you?" Lauren grinned.

"Huh?"

"Never mind," Rowan shook his head. "Put that on your shoulder."

"It's getting late. We need to get a move on it, or we'll be making camp in the dark," Pauline said.

They spent a peaceful evening on the mountain, with no antics from the local fauna. Even the squirrels and rabbits had been quiet. Lauren wasn't sure if that was a good thing or a bad thing. It made stargazing much more peaceful. She and Morrison sat around the fire and drank coffee to prepare for their watch. She had seen a shooting star. She wasn't one to give into whimsy, but she allowed herself a wish — the truth about Sasquatch.

"So how long have you been chasing Bigfoot?" Lauren heard Jean-René ask Pauline as they came to the fire and sat down. She'd founded the local Bigfoot Research Organization, and the fact that she worked for the National Park Service didn't hurt.

"About sixteen years," Pauline said. "I hadn't been working for the NPS very long when I experienced something I'm still trying to explain."

Lauren was immediately interested. She set her journal aside. She rose and refilled her coffee cup, offering up the option to others, filling Morrison's cup before returning to her seat to hear the rest of the story.

"I was nineteen years old. It was my first real summer job. I cleaned bathrooms and took out the trash. Anyway, I was out near Big Pines one night on a trouble call, and something ran in front of my truck. I thought I hit it, but it didn't stop. I thought it was a deer at first, but the next day when I was cleaning up the truck, I found a big swatch of brownish-red hair caught in the grill."

"What did you do with it?" Lauren asked.

"I sent it to a guy at Washington State University who supposedly did Bigfoot research. I never heard anything back. I figured I'd have heard something if he'd found anything."

"That sucks," Derry said. "Would have been nice to know what it was."

"Yeah, right," Pauline said. "Since then, I'm a lot more careful with what I find. I take two molds, if I can. I keep half the sample. I never give up all my cards."

"That's not a bad idea," Rowan nodded, coming to sit by the fire, snagging the pot of hot coffee from the grill where it warmed over coals. "Anyone?"

No one took him up on it.

"Jean-René, how did you get into Bigfoot hunting? Last time I checked, there aren't any Bigfoot in France," Pauline asked.

"Well, I am from Montreal. But it was not *Le Pied Grand* who got me into this work. It was another beast. It was the *Beast of Gévaudan*, to be precise."

"*Je vous dans?*" Rowan arched a confused brow; the translation wasn't making any sense.

"I was working for a small television production company in Loire and was contracted to do the videography for a documentary about the beast. The researchers claimed they could prove it was a hyena, but ... well, I had my doubts. When they weren't around, I talked to the descendants of the villagers who claimed to have killed the beast, but ... they told me a different story. They said that *la bête* told their ancestors to kill a regular wolf and tell the King it was him. The Beast was half man after all. He ordered the people to bring him sacrifice in exchange for his mercy. So long as he was fed and honored, he would not take the life of a single townsfolk. It is a tradition that continues to this day."

"That's a pretty fancy fairy tale." Joshua scoffed. "You don't believe that crap. Do you?"

Jean-René gave him a stern look. "There are stranger things under the heavens, but I have seen these things. I swear it to you all. One night, I went with one of the old farmers to deliver the homage. We waited in the shadows. I was a fool and I took my camera with me. When the *Bestia* came to take his wages, I fired off a few pictures, but the sound of the camera was heard by the monster and he chased us from the forest. I never saw the farmer again. No one has."

"Do you still have the pictures?"

"Unfortunately, I dropped the camera during my escape, and I was too afraid to go back for it, but I swear upon my petrified heart, I have seen this monster." He spoke in a tone Lauren had never heard before, and it sent chills into her soul; she believed him. "Our program on *La bête du Gevaudan* won many accolades. I was hired by the Exploration Channel to work on a new show they were developing called *The Veritas Codex*. Now, here I am, searching for another *bête*."

Rowan looked over and noticed Lauren's face brighten. "What?"

"I know where we can go on our honeymoon."

"Oh no!" Jean-René and Rowan said in unison.

"We're not going to do Gévaudan on our honeymoon," Rowan stated flatly.

A long rant of French profanities poured from Jean-René's lips. Lauren knew she was being scolded, but she smiled to herself, plotting. She usually got her way, and that wasn't about to change any time soon.

"Derry, Lauren, you have first watch," Rowan said. "I'm going to bed. I've had enough of ghost stories by the fire."

CHAPTER 27

THE FOLLOWING DAY, THE SUN SHONE BRIGHT, WITH NO afternoon storms; the breeze provided a break from the heat, and the team made good time getting to Beaver Lake. After dinner, Lauren and Rowan stretched out in their tent to catch a quick catnap before the midnight watch. Lauren was stiff and sore and took advantage of Rowan's offer to give her a proper rubdown. A good massage helped, and by the time Bahati tapped on the tent flap, she wasn't hurting nearly as bad.

"Anything on camera?" Lauren asked, unzipping the flap, pulling on her jacket before stepping out.

"Absolutely nothing," Bahati said, yawning. "I hope you don't get bored and fall asleep. It was everything Joshua and I could do to stay awake."

"Well, go get some sleep," Lauren said. "We've got it from here."

———

Lauren sat in front of the computer screen by the fire, watching the night vision cameras, smiling as something moved into view. She nudged Rowan. He glanced over and grinned. "I don't think that's Bigfoot." He chuckled at the raccoon as it sniffed at the camera before moving on.

"No, I'm pretty sure you're right." she agreed. After a long pause she said, "When I was a little kid, I used to pretend I was a raccoon."

"Hmm?" Rowan had been gazing at the stars above. "A raccoon?"

"I would sneak out of the house at night and run naked through the woods around our house. I would catch crawfish in the river, and climb trees."

"Naked?" She now had his full attention.

"I was just a kid." She slapped his arm.

"How old?"

"I don't know. Five, maybe six?"

He sat chortling. He had learned something new about her. She rarely talked about her childhood, so this was a rare treat.

"There was an old raccoon that lived in a hollow tree. It was the biggest raccoon in the whole county. It had to be. I used to pretend it was a wizard who would tell me stories. I used to hide candies in a hollow log for him."

"A wizard, huh?" Rowan's gaze returned to the sky. He lowered his tone. "Do you suppose we could find us a secluded tropical island where we could lay out under the stars and watch the waves rolling onto the beach? Where I could strip you naked and make love to you in the moonlight?"

Lauren felt her color rise. She smiled at the thought of it. "That would be nice."

"You'd like that?"

She glanced at him sideways. "It would be very romantic."

"That's what I want to do for our honeymoon. Just you and me and no one for days."

She chortled. "Like we don't camp out enough."

He leaned in. "Well, not where we can really enjoy it." He

tried to think of the last time they'd made love in a tent. Now their relationship was no secret and even though they shared a tent, someone was always on watch and there was no way to be discrete. No matter how hard she tried, Lauren was not a quiet lover. He liked that about her ... most of the time.

"So, what do you want to do?" Lauren's eyes remained transfixed on the cameras.

"Fiji. I'm thinking Fiji."

"That's not what I meant," Lauren elbowed him. "I meant about getting married. Do you want a church wedding? Do you just want to go to the courthouse?"

"As long as I've waited for you to say yes, I intend to have a proper wedding." Rowan grinned. "It's up to you if it's in a church or a garden or on a beach."

"How about a meadow like this, with all the Sasquatch invited?"

Rowan laughed heartily. "I was thinking of asking Jean-René to be my best man, but I guess I could get Bigfoot instead."

"Suppose you could get him to wear a tux?" Lauren grinned brightly.

"I'll ask him next time I see him."

"Suppose that will be any time soon?" She asked, shutting the lid of the laptop. She rubbed her eyes. "Two days and we haven't heard so much as a growl from our hairy friend."

"Maybe it's too hot for him." It barely got above 80, but with the humidity and bright sun, it felt much hotter. "They do have a fur coat to contend with."

"It might have been warm this afternoon, but it sure isn't now," Lauren shivered, pulling her jacket around herself.

"I'll put some more wood on the fire." Rowan unfolded his tall frame slowly. The cold left him stiff and he grumbled as he got up and made for the woodpile.

He was just about to sit down when the snap of a limb and a rustling in the trees broke the eerie silence of the night. Rowan paused. An owl hooted. Lauren was at his elbow with the thermal camera fixed on the area where the noise had come from.

"Do you see it?" He whispered. Lauren adjusted the focus and panned the tree line, her shoulders sinking.

"It's a deer." She lowered the camera. "Just a deer."

"Dang it," Rowan grumbled. "What time is it?"

"We have another hour," Lauren said. "I could go for a snack."

Rowan grinned. "Me too."

Half an hour later they both had a cup of hot cocoa and were sticky with chocolate and marshmallows. They enjoyed s'mores by the fire. They kept their playful banter low so as not to wake the sleeping or disturb the fauna.

The time passed quickly. Lauren crawled into their tent while Rowan woke the next watch. He gave them an update on the night's inactivity then bid them all goodnight.

———

Rowan gave the morning briefing. "Today, Lauren and I are going to go scout around the lake and see if we can find any signs of activity in the area. We saw deer and other small creatures last night, but we haven't heard or seen any evidence of Bigfoot activity yet."

Lauren took over. "Team Two I want you to go southeast down to the public area. That's where there were reports of damage to the picnic area you wanted to check out."

"Team Three, there are some caves not too far from here. See if you can find anything over that way, but don't go into the caves. Last thing we want is for anyone to get lost in the lava tubes." Rowan folded up the map. "Everyone should check in with base camp on the half-hour. If you find anything, radio it in. Any questions?"

There were none.

———

Lauren had the forethought to bring a smaller backpack, in which she'd stowed provisions for their mini-expedition. Peanut butter sandwiches were carefully tucked inside plastic containers. With some granola bars and bottles of filtered water and a couple apples they could have lunch whenever they were hungry. Rowan brought his entire pack, with all his emergency supplies. He also had his camera and audio equipment, just in case. The consummate boy-scout, he was always prepared.

The day was clear and cool, and the ground was slick with mud and damp lichens from the rain that moved in after they'd gone to bed. For once, the heat wasn't oppressive. Lauren considered it a pleasant day, despite the damp.

The hike to the lake wasn't especially hard. It didn't take long to get there either. Lauren paused to take pictures as they entered the valley, just to document the sheer beauty of nature. If she had her way, the pictures would appear on their website along with their travel blog.

Deer lifted their heads in the meadow and bolted when they caught scent of the approaching hikers. While Lauren was enraptured by the breathtaking vistas and glens, Rowan was looking down, scanning the damp ground for tracks, traces of anything that might have passed this way.

She paused when they reached the edge of the pond, which was mirror-clear. She could see fish collecting in the still water. "Look, trout." She pointed.

"Guess if we can't find Bigfoot, I can at least catch something to eat," Rowan grinned. He always carried fishing equipment. He could find a good meal almost anywhere there was water.

"Nothing like a broiled rainbow trout over an open camp-fire." Lauren continued her inspection.

Rowan pointed out deer tracks as he worked his way along a small game trail. Lauren lingered behind. She veered out across the field when something caught her eye. A dark form hid in a deep patch of thorny blackberry bushes. She turned, raising her camera, zooming in on the shaded patch. She tried to focus on it. Branches rattled and the smell of crushed berries and stale cat litter assaulted her nose at the same time. She fired off a series of shots with her Nikon. The bleep of her digital camera broke the silence. The form startled and rose, turned and matched her gaze with two dark, cold eyes. Lauren stood transfixed, her finger still on the camera button.

CHAPTER 28

ROWAN KNEW AT ONCE SOMETHING WAS WRONG. HE PUT A HAND on her elbow, but she didn't flinch. He didn't move. His gaze followed hers into the trees. Beyond the clearing, a dark shape disappeared into the cover of the forest. "Lauren? What was it?" He started after it, but she didn't move. He paused, torn between the chase and her thousand-yard stare. "Lauren?" He glanced back at the woods and shook his head as he turned around. Her face was neutral — no fear, no pain, just blank.

Rowan snapped his fingers in front of her face. She blinked slowly then turned. She looked at him, but it seemed to take a split second for her to *see* him. He let out a breath he hadn't realized he was holding. "What?" she asked. She looked down at the camera in her hands and took her finger off the button. She looked back at Rowan. "What?"

"What was it? Did you see it?" He took the Nikon and scrolled through the pictures. Nothing but blurred images.

"See what?" She looked around. He could see her knees suddenly turn to rubber. Rowan forgot about the camera and took her by the arm.

"Come here and sit down." He took her over to a fallen log,

handing her a canteen of water. "Drink this." He brushed her bangs out of her eyes. Her skin was cool, but a mist of sweat collected on her brow and upper lip. Rowan checked her pulse and encouraged her to drink more. "Tell me what you saw?"

"I'm not sure."

————

Lauren was still dazed when they found the others. Rowan did his best to explain what had happened.

"I have heard reports that the Sasquatch have the ability to hypnotize people. To make them forget what they see," Jean-René said, snapping his fingers in front of her face. She blinked a half second slower than someone operating at full capacity might. "Lauren? Are you okay?"

She turned and looked at him. "Hmm?" She answered a beat too late. "Yeah, I'm fine."

"Oh?" Jean-René lifted a brow. "Why don't you come sit down over here?" He took her arm and led her over to a place by the fire.

"Grab her camera," Rowan said to him. Jean-René reached for it, but she drew it back defensively. "Lauren? It's okay. Let him have it," Rowan said kindly. Lauren looked at him with uncertainty. She relented and gave the Nikon to Jean-René. He patted her shoulder and took it over to Rowan.

Jean-René took the memory card and plugged it into the computer. They sat around looking at the pictures on the computer screen. "I suppose that may be why you can't remember anything about what happened to … before."

Lauren wrinkled her nose. "That's nothing more than super-stition and hokum. Don't you think?" she asked. Jean-René tried to improve the resolution on the picture. The bushes obscured the image. She'd done a terrible job getting the subject in focus, much less in the frame. The pictures were useless. She had plenty of shots of the ground and the horizon, even the toe of her boot. But, the one halfway decent shot of a dark form in the bushes was rubbish.

"Score another point for the reigning Hide-And-Seek champion of the world," Jean-René snarked. Bahati chuckled at him, returning to the task of making dinner.

"It's not like you to take bad pictures like this." Rowan came to sit by her. She leaned into him.

"I don't know what happened."

"When I found you, you were just standing there like you were in a trance. Your mouth was hanging open. You had drool running down your chin, for Pete's sake."

Lauren glanced down at the dark spot on her black tank top, and then shook her head dubiously. "Whatever." Bahati brought her a plate, and she wasted no time. Rowan watched her. He noticed Jean-René did too. She shoveled the food into her mouth like she hadn't eaten in a year. While Rowan was happy to see her eat, he was duly concerned. Normally she picked at her food, rarely eating more than a few bites. She was usually more interested in getting back to work.

"Maybe the lab can clean it up," Jean-René suggested, closing the laptop.

———

Lauren gazed into the fire long after the sun had set. She wrapped her arms around her knees, deep in thought. One by one, the team disappeared into their tents. Rowan and Lauren had the first watch. He spent it watching Lauren.

"*Tsi stu wu-li-ga' na-tu-tu'n une'gu-tsa-tu ge-se'i*," she finally said, in a low, soft voice.

"What's that?" Rowan poured himself a cup of coffee and came over and sat across from her. Jean-René and Bahati came over too.

She repeated it. "The Rabbit was the leader of them in all the mischief," she translated. The flames cast a glow on her golden skin. He could almost see her ancestors in her dark glowing eyes. "The Rabbit always got the others in trouble, but never seemed to get caught himself." She continued, resting her chin on her knee. "If the Rabbit was the leader, it was *Tsul'Kalu* who would judge him." Rowan knew that word. He had played the recording from the hospital enough times. "When the ancient Rabbit was caught, the animals demanded justice and brought him before Tsul'Kalu. The Ancient One began to recount the sins of the Rabbit and all his ancestors. Speaking in the ancient language of All Animals, he counted the Rabbit's transgressions. One hundred generations back he went. He told of the time the Rabbit's great-great-great-great-great-grandfather made the buzzard bald. How the Rabbit's great-great-great-great-grand-father stole the bear's tail. How the Rabbit's grandmother spilled the milk and the dog ran through it and escaped into the sky, leaving a trail across the darkness. How the Rabbit himself tried to steal the stars from the sky..." Lauren took a deep breath. "When the Rabbit denied the claims, Tsul'Kalu shook his head, and silenced the mischief-maker with a deep growl. 'It is not a sin to be who you are, Rabbit,' the Ancient One said. The Rabbit smiled to himself, thinking his cleverness was about to acquit him. 'But justice demands repayment for the trouble you and your ilk have caused,' Tsul'Kalu continued. 'Your fate is to dwell among the briars. You will be tormented by thorns for all your days. You will be chased by wolves, snakes, owls and eagles. Never to rest. Never safe in the day. Never safe in the night. Tormented, as you have tormented others. This is the fate for the leader in all the mischief.'"

She was quiet after that. Rowan scratched his chin with his thumbnail. "Who is Tsul'Kalu again?"

"The Ancient One," Lauren's gaze locked on his. "The Tall Man. The one we seek."

"Bigfoot?" Jean-René confirmed.

Lauren took a deep breath and nodded. "The Rabbit will be judged. Tsul'Kalu will ensure it."

"I never heard you tell that story," Bahati said, standing.

"I just learned it today," she said, getting up too.

"From who?" Rowan asked.

"Tsul'Kalu told me," she stopped and turned around. "He will show us. In the north, signs of the Rabbit's mischief are there. We will find it."

Rowan's gaze passed between his team. His brow furrowed and his eyes narrowed. He saw his own concern reflected in the faces of his friends.

"Pauline said there was another camping area to the north," Bahati said. "We didn't have time to check it today. We came back when we got your radio call."

"What did you find at the camping area south of here?" Rowan asked.

"A couple of smashed trash cans. Looks like vandals. Nothing I would chalk up to *Sue Kal* …? How did you say it, Lauren?"

"Tsul'Kalu," she said. "The Ancient One."

"We'll go check it out tomorrow then," Rowan said. He rose, taking Lauren's hand. "Go get some sleep. You've had enough excitement for one day."

Lauren, uncharacteristically, obeyed. Without argument, she went to bed. She didn't fuss or pitch a fit, she just went and crawled into her tent. As Rowan watched from the entrance of the tent, she collapsed into a deep slumber.

CHAPTER 29

Lauren was up before dawn. She had their tent broken down before Rowan could finish breakfast. Her enthusiasm was contagious, and the group made quick work of the morning duties.

"Which way?" Jean-René asked.

"Up through the trees," Lauren pointed.

Rowan stayed close to her. The story she told the night before had him unsettled. He'd been up most of the night, chewing over it. He was trying to figure where it had come from and what she could have meant, if anything at all. Since finding her like a statue in the meadow, she'd seemed — *different*. He didn't like it.

———

Lauren struck off ahead of the group, moving at twice her normal gait. Her pack didn't seem to be weighing her down any. Rowan had to work to keep up. He breathed hard as they broke through the dense underbrush an hour later, into the public camping area.

The campsite stood empty and even the rangers paused in stunned amazement at the devastation they saw. The campsite was in ruins, ransacked. The fire rings were upended. The solid sheets of metal lay crushed like broken wagon wheels. The metal barbecue grills were broken off of their stands and crushed. Even the concrete picnic tables were smashed.

Rowan stood in shock at the devastation. Even the timbers placed as parking barricades at the trail head below lay about as if they'd been tossed aside like cabers at a Highland festival.

From campsite, to campsite the destruction continued. "This was done recently," Katie said. "Look at the trash. Not many animals have gotten at it. This was maybe not in the past day or two, but within the last week."

"I take it this is worse than the reports indicated?" Bahati asked the ranger.

"Much worse," Katie said, as they approached the bank of bathhouses in the middle of the camping area. The frosted glass windows near the rooftops had been busted out, and the doors ripped off their hinges. Inside, the metal partitions between the showers and toilet stalls had been pushed over and crumpled like tinfoil. One of the toilets had been shattered and the floor was flooded. Water gurgled from the broken bowl.

———

Rowan was outside the men's shower, kneeling down by the wall, snapping pictures when Lauren came up behind him. "What'd you find?"

"It looks like blood," he said. "Do we have a DNA sample kit?"

"Of course," she said. She shrugged off her pack.

"Did you know we'd find this?" He asked, looking up at her.

She paused. "Tsul'Kalu did not do this," she stated. "But the Rabbit wants you to think he did."

"Who is the Rabbit, Lauren?"

"*The Leader of Them in All the Mischief,*" she said, handing him the kit.

"You're talking in riddles," Rowan said. "What's gotten into you? Ever since yesterday, you seem to be in a place where I can never go. I feel disconnected from this place in you." He caught her hand. "I can't protect you there." It made him even more determined to protect her here.

Her lips thinned as she hesitated. "Rowan, the People are threatened, and it is the Rabbit who is behind it. We must find the Rabbit and put a stop to his mischief. He must be shown justice … and soon." She took the kit back curtly when he didn't move to collect the evidence fast enough, and bent to take the sample herself. She dabbed at the spatters of blood with the moist cotton swab and then returned it to the vial. She sealed it with the evidence tape, taking a marker from her jacket pocket, initialing it. She placed it in a plastic bag, peeling off the strip that covered the sealing tape. She initialed it as well. She also took out a Chain of Custody form for the lab and filled it out. Whatever had gotten into her, the scientist was still in there too. Despite her agitation, it gave Rowan a sense of comfort, even though he was less-than-happy about this new aspect of his fiancée. She tucked away the sample, looking up when they heard Jean-René's excited shout from a nearby site.

"Wait," Rowan caught her arm, pointing to the print on the metal door that lay crumpled on the ground a few feet away. Lauren's jaw dropped and she rose slowly, taking a tentative step forward. "What the hell is that?" Rowan was on her heels.

"Tsul'Kalu was here," Lauren said. Her voice went shadowy.

A deep rumble echoed through the ground; pine needles showered them from above. The ground lurched beneath their feet. The blood-curdling scream that erupted from Bahati's throat echoed off the trees around them. She threw her arms around Jean-René. In the distance, a mournful bale answered, as the rumbling subsided. Lauren smiled brightly. She patted Bahati's back. "Tsul'Kalu says hello to you, too."

"Was that an earthquake?" Bahati's eyes went wide. "Seriously, you felt that, right?"

"How could we not?" Rowan snapped.

"We are sitting on an active volcano, remember?" Pauline asked.

"It's not going to erupt is it?"

Pauline shrugged. "Eventually."

"Dammit."

CHAPTER 30

"WE'LL MAKE CAMP HERE TONIGHT," ROWAN SAID. THE excitement had worn off. He was tired and hungry. "We'll establish a perimeter, but we need to comb this entire area for additional evidence. We need castings of each of the prints. I want to preserve that handprint somehow. Be sure we photograph everything. Be careful where you sit or step. There are prints literally everywhere. We don't want to disturb any of them before we can get them sampled and make plaster castings."

Morrison stepped up. "We need to be diligent with our watch tonight. Whoever, or whatever did this could come back."

"I agree," Pauline nodded.

"We need to get all this evidence to a lab," Jean-René said. "How are we going to do that?"

"I'll radio the ranger station in the morning and have someone drive up and get them. They can have them delivered via USPS or FedEx," Derry said.

Lauren shook her head. "The chain of custody has to be maintained. No one touches these samples but one of my team."

Bahati stepped up. "I'll take them to the lab. Just get me a ride out of here before this mountain blows up."

Pauline knitted her narrow brows. "You know I was joking, right?"

"I'm not," Bahati said. "Volcanos are nothing to joke about."

"Bahati's right," Rowan said. "She's the best choice for the errand. She knows the procedures. You can take the blood and prints back to the lab and stay there until the results come back in."

"I can't call you back, though," Bahati said. "We haven't had a signal since we got here."

"We should be able to at least get a radio signal to one of the watchtowers. We can have them send a chopper to pick you up and bring you back," Derry suggested. "How long do you think the labs will take?"

"It could take a couple of days once I get them there. It might take me a day just to get to the lab."

"I'll take care of all the travel arrangements," Katie said. "I have some connections," she smiled. "Bahati, we'll hike up to the Bivouac tomorrow. There's a clearing there. I'll stay until the chopper picks you up and I'll meet you back there in a few days."

"I'll go with you," Joshua said.

"The sooner I get out of here the better," Bahati gulped. Rowan could understand why.

———

To keep Bahati busy and keep her mind off the volcano, Lauren had Bahati set up the perimeter cameras and the warning beacon system. They needed to set the trap cams. The evidence around them needed to be processed.

They found large footprints in several locations. It was suspicious to find so many. Lauren insisted they cast them all.

As she was waiting for one of them to dry, she found herself scanning the area looking for anything else out of place. There was a narrow path that beckoned her. It was nothing more than a game trail, but she found herself drawn to it. As she walked, she noticed there were broken branches on the trees. Blades of grass were bent over from something that had passed by less than a few days before.

Then she noticed the beer cans. Crumpled along the trail, they were the cheap kind. The aluminum had been crushed and tossed aside. There were littered in twos or threes here and there. She found more a few hundred yards down the path. In all, she counted almost two dozen. The trail of cans stopped at the edge of a wide, shallow stream. That's where she found the most telling evidence of all, a large footprint set in the mud ... and then she found another. There was a whole series.

She reached for her walkie-talkie. "Lauren to Rowan ..." There was a long pause followed by a wicked squelch and static.

"Where the hell are you? We've been looking for you for the last twenty minutes."

"What? Why didn't you radio?" She glanced at her watch and discovered it was much later than she thought it to be. Sunset would be on them before they could get the evidence collected, if they didn't hurry.

"We have been. Did you have it turned on? Where are you?" She looked up and realized she had no idea. "I followed an animal trail out of the campsite, right by where Bahati and I were casting prints. There are beer cans scattered along the path, there's a small river at the end of the trail. There are prints everywhere."

"Are you ... lost?" Rowan's voice held genuine concern.

"I'm not lost," she snapped. Lauren couldn't get lost. "Are *you* lost?"

The radio squelched again. "Stay where you are, I'll find you."

"Bring more dental stone powder. Have Jean-René bring the cameras. We've got to document this."

———

Rowan's ire faded the moment he saw her. He rushed over and wrapped his arms around her. "You scared the daylights out of me."

"I'm sorry, I don't know what happened. I was following the evidence. Look what I found, Rowan." She pointed to the first print, and then the second.

"Oh my God," he breathed, walking around the tracks. "This is unreal."

"Tsul'Kalu has been here," she said. "He watches over this place. It is sacred."

"Sacred? Why do you say that?"

She turned and raised her hand toward the horizon. The sun over the valley, cast an almost magical glow over the volcano, a plume of steam billowing from its peak. It mixed with the red rays of the setting sun and cast a brilliant pink pallet over the entire valley. Even the trees seemed to glow. The ash beds of pyroclastic flow from the 1980 eruption looked ethereal. Something he could only describe as magic tingled through his nerves. Lauren's face reflected the glow, and her eyes seemed as black as the night sky. She took a deep breath, drinking in the beauty of the scene before them. *"Sacred."*

———

"How many Bigfoots drink beer, seriously?" Rowan picked up one of the cans with a gloved hand, inspecting it. The can was crushed, but not completely flattened. "Let alone skunky beer."

"Now you know why they are called skunk ape." Jean-René chortled.

"Do you think we can get DNA off the cans?" Bahati asked, inspecting one of the cans she had collected.

"If anything, it could be used as evidence if it turns out the same person or persons did all the damage to the campgrounds," Lauren shrugged.

Rowan arched a brow and shook his head. "Alright, let's bag 'em and tag 'em."

Lauren's eye was drawn to something else, and she went to inspect it, leaving Rowan to collect the beer cans. "Jean-René, your camera," she called, gesturing for him to come over.

"What did you find?" He followed, pausing when she stopped and knelt. He raised the camera to his shoulder, clicking it on as he approached and came around behind her. He zoomed in over her shoulder as he neared. He paused. He had to look out over the viewfinder to make sure he was seeing it. "Is that ...?"

"Poop," Lauren said. "It's cold. It's been here a while."

"Human poop or Bigfoot poop?" He took a reflexive step back. Returning his attention to the view finder, panning in as she inspected it.

"Hard to tell," she said. Lauren leaned over it, pulling her long braid back to keep it out of the way. She sniffed and recoiled, turning away. "Smells like poop."

"I thought we'd already established that it was, indeed, poop," Jean-René laughed, and for the first time in a few days, Lauren smiled brightly.

"I stepped in that one. Didn't I?" She chortled, looking up at the camera; pleased at her own joke.

"I sure hope not," Jean-René said. Everyone had a good laugh. Even Lauren relaxed.

"There's not a lot of plant matter in the scat. Our quarry is known to be omnivorous, but I would expect more fibrous matter in the mix," Lauren said. "If the Bigfoot has had good hunting, he could have wiped out a whole elk or deer. That could explain it." Lauren poked the sample with a stick.

Katie came down the trail and came to see what everyone was looking at. "Looks like someone took a dump."

"Someone ... or something," Lauren raised her poo covered stick in emphasis. "I need a sample kit."

"You're bagging poop?" Katie's brow arched.

"We're bagging beer cans too," she stood. "It's all DNA evidence. Maybe it's nothing, but we won't know until we get it to the lab."

"It's probably human poop." Katie said.

"What if it isn't?" Lauren retorted.

"What makes you say that? How can you be so sure?"

"No toilet paper," she pointed around the area. "Not even a hand full of poo-covered leaves."

Rowan gave Jean-René a dirty look and the cameraman grinned from ear to ear. "She has a point," Jean-René snickered.

"Well, then, it's definitely not lady poop," Rowan grinned, his teeth shining in the fading light. "I've been known to do without in worst-case situations."

"That's why I make you do your own laundry," Lauren turned up the edge of her lip and wrinkled her nose.

"Ew. TMI, you two," Jean-René shook his head, recoiling.

"Don't forget to protect the sample in alcohol," Rowan said, before returning to what he was doing.

"I know how to preserve fecal samples." Lauren snapped.

"Silly me. Of course you do."

———

Jean-René stayed with Lauren while she finished her evidence collection. It was dark when she and Jean-René returned to base camp. It was Rowan's night to cook, and the smell of fried eggs, corned beef hash and warm biscuits greeted them. "Breakfast for dinner?" Lauren asked.

Rowan held out a plate. "It sounded good," he smiled.

She held up her hands a moment, still holding the bag containing the poop samples. "Let me wash," she said. He nodded, setting the plate down on the one undamaged picnic table in the whole campground. Lauren disappeared into the bath house, returning a few seconds later. "It sure smells good," she said. She sat down beside him and took a bite from one of the biscuits. Rowan was an excellent cook.

"Coffee?" he asked. He reached for a cup, already knowing the answer.

"Yes." She accepted it gratefully. It'd been a long day, and after all the excitement, she was starving.

Jean-René came over and sat down beside her. "I hope you washed your hands."

"I did," she said between bites. "At least there's running water, despite the damage in there." She reached for her cup and took a sip. "Bahati and I were discussing getting a hot shower after dinner. Pauline said there should be cleaning supplies in the janitor's closet, and it wouldn't take much to get it where we could use it."

"Oh, God," Rowan rolled his eyes. "A shower sounds like heaven."

"The men's shower is wrecked, but you could get into the women's shower after we get done."

"Of course. Ladies first," Rowan said. "Do we have any soap? Shampoo?"

Lauren grinned. "I never leave home without it."

CHAPTER 31

Rowan was waiting outside when Lauren came out of the shower. "Sounded like a regular hen party in there."

"Don't judge." Lauren kissed him quickly. He could smell the perfume of her shampoo. He wished he could strip her naked right there and get her all dirty again, but he resisted the urge to say so. "You're next. You stink." She tilted her head back toward the bath house. "The shower is all yours. You and your roosters can have it."

"Thanks." He grinned. "We drew watch while you were showering. Hope no one cares."

"Not I." Bahati shrugged as she passed.

"Fine by me," Lauren and Pauline said in unison.

"Pauline and Derry have first watch, Morrison and Katie, you've got second watch. Bahati and Jean-René on third, and Lauren and I fourth."

"Sweet," Lauren smiled. "We can watch the sunrise and make breakfast."

"I vote for pancakes," Bahati said.

"In that case, I'm turning in early. I'm exhausted," Lauren said.

"I got our tent set up." Rowan pointed towards it with his chin. "I'll be quiet when I come in, in case you're already asleep."

"Thank you."

CHAPTER 32

"Rowan," the tent shook. He sat up, abruptly. "Rowan!"

"I'm up," he groaned. He threw back the covers and the cold night air hit him. He searched in the darkness for his clothes. "Give me a minute, will ya? I'm up."

"We're getting some activity," Bahati said, urgently. "You're missing all the excitement."

Rowan dressed quickly. He gave Lauren a shake. "Activity! Wake up!" he pulled on his jacket and hurried out with his shoes in his hand.

———

Lauren wasn't a morning person. She certainly wasn't a three-in-the-morning person. The absence of Rowan's body heat urged her to find her clothes. She squirmed in the sleeping bag as she dressed. When she emerged from the tent, her hair was disheveled. Her mood wasn't much better.

"What is it?" Lauren grumbled. She joined the team in front of the computer screen.

"We're hearing tree knocks from two different directions," Jean-René said.

"Tree knocks?" Lauren stood with her hands on her hips. "You woke me up at three o'frick in the morning for lousy tree knocks?"

"Not just tree knocks," Jean-René grinned. "Look at this ..." He pointed to the video he'd just pulled up. "We got something on the FLIR. That's the one we set down by the stream."

Lauren dropped to one knee. The thermal imaging camera assigned a color for the various temperatures with red being body temperature. Hotter temperatures were darker shades of maroon. The cooler tones were yellow, green and blue. Trees showed as almost white, colder than the ground around them which was a much darker blue-black.

The image was hard to make out. It was just a blob. The colors were in the red tones and moved behind the ice-blue trees. The form was large, lumbering. The creature appeared to be interested in something on the ground, hunched like an enormous squirrel foraging for nuts.. When it stood, it was tall. If Lauren had to wager a hypothesis, she might have estimated seven to eight feet. It disappeared behind another tree.

"Is that a bear?" Bahati asked.

Lauren was shaking her head no, but answered, "I suppose it's possible, but ..."

"The arms are much longer than a bear," Rowan finished for her.

"Dang it. The trees are too thick. I can't get a good view of it," Lauren said. She leaned back as the form took several long strides. It turned and worked its way back up the mountain. They lost sight of it all together. "Wait, this is playback? How long ago was this filmed?"

"No more than five minutes ago," Bahati said. "I left to go to the bathroom. Jean-René was making coffee. We didn't think to check the video until we heard the tree knocks."

"We need to get up there." Lauren stood, and turned to look for the equipment. "Wake the rest of the team. We need to get eyes on this thing before we lose it," she said. She brushed her hair back out of her eyes. "Which direction did you hear the knocks?"

"The first one was coming from the left, up the mountain. The other came from the right, towards the river," Bahati handed Lauren the handi-cam from one of the kits. "The second one sounded close, but the video came from trap-cam-six."

"That's the one uphill," Jean-René clarified.

"Put on your shoes, Rowan. We gotta move!"

———

Lauren conducted the hasty pre-hunt briefing. She gave out assignments. "Rowan, Jean-René, Joshua and I will go down the river to check out what we caught on the FLIR. Bahati, take Pauline and the others and go up the mountain with your thermal cam. Keep your voices down. Move as quietly as you can. Use your radios only if you have something. We'll circle around and see if we can find whatever that was on the thermal trap-cam. We'll meet back at base camp before sunrise."

———

Lauren worried about what they'd seen. She had begun to sense the presence of the being she knew as Tsul'Kalu. She didn't trust her senses, though. This feeling was something she couldn't explain using any scientific methods she had been taught. She couldn't sense him at the moment.

The night had gone cold, as it usually did on the mountain. It seemed colder than she would expect. Her breath hung in the air around her as she huffed and puffed her way up the hill.

Rowan led them through the dense trees. He blazed a trail straight to the area where the trap cam had caught their quarry.

"There's the cam," he whispered.

"That's where the creature was," she pointed to the stand of trees ahead of them. "Go stand over there. Let me see if I can determine how tall it was."

Rowan nodded. "Let me know when I get to the right one."

Lauren gave him an owl-hoot to signal the right spot. He stood up right and reached his arm up over his head.

Lauren hooted again and the team met in the middle. "It was every bit as tall as the top of that branch," she said, pointing to one of the high branches on the tree. She pulled up the pictures she'd just taken to give them a better view. "What would that be?'

"That's got to be at least seven feet," Joshua said. "Are you sure it wasn't a bear?"

"No," Lauren said. "Bears don't walk on their back legs. They can stand, but they don't walk."

"Was it your Tsul'Kalu?" Rowan asked her in sidebar.

"I don't think so," Lauren said, trying to find that presence somewhere inside her mind. "But I think there are others of his kind. I do not speak to all of them the way I do Tsul'Kalu." Lauren noticed a look pass between Jean-René and Rowan. They both seemed perplexed and she suspected they didn't believe her. She didn't care.

"Alright, let's keep moving. Watch where you step. Look for prints."

———

They reached the top of the ridge thirty minutes later. Jean-René scanned the distant valley with the thermal imaging cam. The forests were dark. There was no sign of whatever they'd seen earlier. Rowan radioed the other team to check in. Lauren paced, and sat down on a rock, her shoulder aching. She was exhausted and felt defeated. "Son of a ..."

"No one's better at not finding the truth than we are," he shook his head.

"Whatever," she snapped. She turned towards camp, storming away. "We have to get a new fricking catch phrase."

"We're just going to give up?" Jean-René stood fast. It wasn't like Lauren to call it quits so easily.

Rowan started after her, but stopped. "Jean-René, go on. Take the rest of the team and see what you can find."

"But ..."

"She's tired, mentally and physically. I'll talk to her and we'll meet you back at camp later. Go on." He turned and followed her down the hill into the darkness. "Lauren, wait up!"

———

"Let's try some wood knocks," Jean-René said. "We're on the peak, we should be able to be heard across the whole valley."

"I'll radio the other team," Joshua said.

Once the other team had been alerted, Jean-René turned the camera on as Joshua picked up a long thick broken branch and cracked it over the side of a fallen tree trunk. The sound, like an echo of thunder, reverberated over the valley. Three more whacks followed, then ... silence.

Everyone seemed to hold their breath as they listened for a response that never came. "Try it again," Jean-René whispered. Joshua had to find another branch. He'd cracked the first one and it fell apart in his hand. The second gave off a deep, almost musical resonance. Only seconds later, a similar crack echoed from the distant woods. Joshua's eyes lit up and his good-natured smile glowed in the night vision camera.

"It came from that way." Jean-René pointed, and they took off down a narrow trail into the valley on the other side of the mountain. Their enthusiasm increased as a distant howl echoed in the woods. Jean-René didn't hesitate but whooped back in a similar tone.

"Did you hear that?" Bahati's voice squawked over the radio.

"We're on it," Joshua responded.

"We're headed that way too."

CHAPTER 33

I**T WAS A MAD DASH THROUGH THE WOODS, BREAKING BRANCHES** and thundering feet in the underbrush. When Jean-René skidded into the clearing, the teams converged on nothing more than a grassy meadow, heavy with fog as the morning sun cracked over the top of the volcano.

"*Tabernaque!*" Jean-René wanted to pitch his camera into the mist. He resisted the urge. He set it down with more force than he'd intended. "*Merde!*"

"You didn't see it?" Bahati panted, nearly doubled over with the exertion of her own chase.

"Did you?"

"We thought we were right on its tail." She stood with her hands on her hips, catching her breath.

"What was that?" Joshua asked.

"I never got a good look at it," Pauline said. "But it sounded big! Huge!"

"But you didn't see it?" Jean-René asked.

"Just in shadows. It moved so fast." Joshua sat down on a stump, wiping his brow with a bandana. "We're just chasing ghosts out here. Let's go back to camp. I'm hungry."

Jean-René nodded. "I bet Rowan and Lauren will have breakfast ready."

———

When they arrived back at camp, the fire had gone cold, and there was no sign of breakfast, much less Lauren and Rowan. A broad grin spread over Jean-René's face. "That dog!"

"What?" Bahati paused. "Where are they?"

"He said he'd talk to her," Joshua said. "They should have been back by now."

"Oh, I'm sure he's giving her a good *talking* to," Jean-René said. He had a glimmer in his golden eyes and a strongly implied innuendo in his voice.

Bahati shook her head. "Whatever!"

"Come on, I'll cook breakfast," Pauline said. "If they need time to talk, or *whatever*, they can have it. We're not likely to see any more of our fuzzy friend now that the sun is up."

———

"Lauren?" Rowan ran to catch up to her. When he caught her arm, she turned and buried her face into the middle of his chest. He was helpless to do anything more than wrap his arms around her. "Are you okay?"

"You and Jean-René think I'm crazy."

"Nobody said that."

"You don't have to," she sniffed, pulling away. "It's written on both of your faces."

"Lauren," he caught her hand, and pulled her back into him. "Nobody thinks you're crazy."

"But ..." she started to protest.

"Look. We all know something happened to you. I can't explain it, but I will admit that it frightens me. All this talk about the rabbit and Tsul'Kalu ... it's not like you. You and I both know that. We're worried about you. That's all."

Lauren looked down, carefully guarding her feelings. "I have lived my whole life being the odd one. When my brother went into engineering, he was seen as bright and brainy. When I went into biological anthropology I was seen as a nerd. I was told women couldn't do science. They said I should just get my teaching certificate and teach high school biology."

"Look, you're a fantastic scientist. You've never needed to prove that to anyone. Least of all me. I know you think you have to prove something, but you don't."

"I may not have to prove it to you, but I saw the tabloids in the airport in San Diego. I know what they're saying about me ... about our whole team, and I won't have it."

"It's not your job to protect everyone's credibility." Rowan softened his tone, hoping to soothe her. "We didn't need to come back here for you to prove anything. You know that, right?" Rowan knew he'd made a mistake the minute the words came out of his mouth. Fire flashed in her eyes and her jaw clenched.

"You know we had to come back," she snapped. "And you know why."

"But at what risk?" He started, but her eyes flashed in the darkness. "Lauren." He started to rephrase his argument, but she flipped around so fast her braid whipped, smacking him in the face as she stomped off.

Standing in the aftermath of his mistake, Rowan put a hand on his hip and pursed his lips. He took a deep breath, letting it out slowly. He rubbed his face and shook his head. "Lauren," he called after her. She didn't answer. The crunching of the rocks and dirt beneath her boots told him she hadn't even slowed down. He took another moment longer to regain his composure, then set off after her.

———

The terrain grew more uneven as they got closer to base camp. The trail narrowed. He could hear her moving ahead of him, but she still wasn't answering him, and her pace hadn't slowed. "Lauren, please." He heard her come to a skidding stop on the rough terrain, less than a dozen paces behind her. The sliver of sunrise through the trees was just enough to illuminate her features as she froze. She turned towards the clearing. The look on her face told him she'd seen something. He crossed the distance between them before she moved. He came up behind her. A dark shadow melted into the dense vegetation up on the ridge and Rowan was certain he'd seen the flash of eye-shine for a split second. "Did you see that?" Rowan nudged her.

"I did," she said. Her voice was a haunting whisper.

"Was that your Tsul'Kalu?"

"No," she said. "But maybe one of his friends ..."

"Well come on," Rowan pressed past her and started up the hillside. "Let's go find it."

———

They followed the lumbering noises through the woods at a quick pace. Lauren made better progress than Rowan. He was breathless and bathed in sweat. *I'm too old for this*, he thought. There was the sound of a sudden scuffle and Rowan saw a flash off the reflector on Lauren's jacket as she tumbled to the ground. It startled him. He couldn't see her pick herself up.

Frantic, he skidded down the rocky hillside. He wove through the saplings that separated them. When he got to the spot where she'd fallen, or where he'd thought she'd fallen, she wasn't there. "Lauren?" He raised his voice, calling out her name again. *She'd been right there!* He never saw the fist coming at him.

It caught him square in the throat. He stumbled back,

202   BETSEY KULAKOWSKI

turning as he fell to his hands and knees. He gasped. He couldn't breathe. A boot caught him in the ribs. Any air he had left in him, was knocked out. Ribs shattered on impact. Jagged bone grated against his lung. He landed flat on his back, looking up at the face of the man that had kicked him. Beside him appeared the face of none other than Bigfoot himself. "Son of a...!" He heard Lauren swear. The world spun and he lost his grip on consciousness, peering into the eyes of Bigfoot.

CHAPTER 34

"Damn you!" Lauren snarled, falling back against the tree where she was tossed. Her head struck the trunk. The echo of it rang in her ears. "I said leave him alone!"

Bigfoot pulled off his mask. He turned around and roared at her. The man's face had been painted around the eyes to help conceal the fact that it was a mask. It gave him a menacing look. The fact that the guy was as big as a mountain didn't hurt anything either. "You bit me!" The Bigfoot protested, holding his arm. She had, too — as hard as she could. Blood welled up under the marks left behind by her teeth. "You're always mean to me. I don't like you." He moved to strike her, but he didn't.

"You!" Suddenly, everything came flooding back to her. She'd run into these two before. It hadn't been Bigfoot that captured her. It had been this ... this ... *hoax-monger in a monkey suit.* Jess' voice reverberated in her ringing ears.

"Shut up, Billy!" The other man snarled at the fake Bigfoot.

The giant seemed to cower. "Sorry, Mitch. Ain't it bad enough I already got a cut on my hand from that metal at the campsite? I don't need her biting me too."

"You obviously didn't learn your lesson last time. She already kicked you in the gonads," Mitch said.

"I'll teach her another lesson if she bites me again." Billy drew back his fist to strike her again. He didn't. Lauren set her jaw and stared him down defiantly. She realized he was pouting more than anything.

"We'll just have to teach her a better lesson this time, Billy," Mitch said.

"What are we going to do?" Billy's eyes widened. He lowered his hand and stepped away from her.

"We'll take 'em down the lava tube. We'll take em so deep they'll never find their way out. We'll leave 'em there."

Billy shrugged. He put his mask on. He collected the unconscious Rowan and slung him over his shoulder with little effort. Rowan moaned.

"You're hurting him!" Lauren sneered.

"Look at how strong I am." He gloated to Lauren. "I'm stronger when I'm Bigfoot. I'm like Superman or something." He growled. "I can do a lot of things. I can pick up heavy stuff better. I can run faster. I can climb trees better. I can do everything better."

"Zip it already, dork." Mitch snapped angrily. He came over and stood in front of Lauren. She refused to stand. "You gonna walk, or do I have to carry you?" He asked. When she refused to follow his order to stand, he threw his hands down. "Fine." He reached down to pick her up by her shoulders. He hadn't expected her reaction. She came up fighting. He'd left himself exposed. She took advantage of the situation to ram her knee into his groin, then bust him over the head with her bound hands. When he buckled, she kicked him in the face. He fell to his knees.

She ran over and kicked the Bigfoot in the back of the knee. He roared as he fell hard, dropping Rowan, who howled in pain as his ribs shifted. Jagged bone grated against tender flesh. She shoved the giant down and pinned him to the ground, catching him in a sleeper hold. Lauren knew she couldn't defeat a brute his size in a battle of strength. If she could take him out before he could get back on his feet, then she had him.

Lauren never saw it coming. A fist caught her across the side of the face. Her grip loosened as she slumped. Stars danced in her eyes. Mitch stood, still buckled over. His eye was starting to swell shut. He'd sucker punched her just the same. The darkness came for her. The last thing she remembered was seeing him draw back his fist to strike again.

———

When she came to, it was in complete darkness. She could hear a deep voice groaning beside her. "Rowan?" She roused fully. She reached for him. She found him in the dark. He yelped when her hand found him. "Rowan, are you okay?"

"What the hell? I thought I saw Bigfoot." He groaned. "What the hell hit me?"

"That was Bigfoot's buddy, Mitch," she said, pushing herself up to seated, realizing her hands were still bound. "You're wheezing."

"I can't … catch my … breath."

"Think your ribs may be broken?"

"Oh, I'm sure of it," he groaned. "I've got to sit up."

"Let me help you," Lauren said.

"Where … are we?" He asked. She caught his arm, trying to help him sit up. He sucked in his breath as she helped him "Ow...ow..." He wheezed as he leaned back against Lauren's chest.

"I don't know. A cave?" Lauren said, resting her head on his shoulder. "Are your hands tied?"

"Yeah," he said. "My feet too. You?"

"Yes," she said. "But I have an ace in my sleeve."

"You do?"

"A Swiss Army knife in my pocket, actually," she said, getting a hand into the side pocket on her cargo pants. "Idiots made the mistake of binding my hands in front of me, instead of behind my back." A moment later, her hands were free; then her feet. "We have to get you out of here. You need a doctor." She took the knife and carefully cut him loose.

"Where'd the Bigfoot go?" He gasped.

"You mean the *hoax-monger in a monkey suit? Billy* is what the other one called him."

"Oh." He groaned. "Just a couple of guys?"

"Yeah." Lauren said, disappointed by that fact.

"Where'd they go?"

She shrugged. "I don't know. I got sucker-punched too." Her face was throbbing. It was everything she could do to keep it together. Right now, getting Rowan out of here before his condition deteriorated was her only priority. If he did have broken ribs, the wheezing suggested a lung might be punctured. She didn't have to be a trained medic to know wheezing like that wasn't a good sign. She desperately hoped he wouldn't succumb to a tension pneumothorax. She'd taken a human anatomy class in college and had to dissect a human cadaver. Their subject, a vagrant who'd been struck by a car, had died of one. She cringed remembering the look of the dead flesh and the trauma she witnessed.

"Got a flashlight too?" Rowan asked.

"I wish. We've got to get you up. Can you?" She got to her feet. It was an effort to get him to stand. He growled at her, clutching his injured side with the other arm. "Watch your head. There's not a lot of clearance."

Had he been able to stand to his full height, he might have whacked his head on the cave ceiling. Instead, he leaned heavily on her. He doubled over painfully as he shuffled.

Lauren put out a hand to feel the cave wall, so she didn't hit her head or Rowan's. They worked their way along the narrow passageway, but within a few yards, he was gasping for breath.

Lauren paused. "Take a minute."

"Yeah," Rowan panted, but dropped to one knee. "You may have ... to go without me. Get help."

"I am not leaving you, Rowan." Lauren was firm in her resolve on this matter. "If we're down in one of those lava tubes I may never find my way out. Even if I do, I may never find my way back."

He couldn't argue with that logic. "Okay ... okay ..." he said trying to keep his breathing slow and shallow. "Go slow ..." he willed himself back onto his feet.

CHAPTER 35

"We have no choice," Pauline said, "If we're going to rendezvous with the helicopter so Bahati can get the samples to the lab, we have to leave now."

"I'll go with you," Morrison said. "Pauline and I should be back before dark."

Jean-René had been pacing for hours, sitting down occasionally only to pop right back up again. His eyes returned to the mountaintop every time he paused. "Go, then. We'll start the search for Lauren and Rowan. They should have been back by now."

"I agree," Miller said. "I'm assuming they're skilled and trained in wilderness navigation and survival?"

"Lauren lived in Yellowstone studying wolves. Rowan is former military," Jean-René said. "They both know what they're doing. This is why I am worried. They are not lost. If they haven't come back by now, it is because something is wrong."

"We can have the chopper do a fly-over before it leaves," Joshua said.

"Good idea."

"We'll start where we saw them last, and work our way up to

the river," Jean-René said, gathering up everything he might need in his pack.

───────

"Dammit," Lauren swore. She stood for a moment, trying to still her thundering heart. She hated tight spaces, and the darkness made it worse. A rock fall in front of them completely blocked the path. "We have to turn back."

Rowan nodded, but it was everything he could do to focus on his breathing, and she didn't expect an answer anyway.

"Do you remember the pyramid in Egypt?" She talked to calm him as much as to calm herself. "The guide told us the secrets of the maze?"

"Always keep ... your right hand ... on the wall," Rowan gasped softly.

"It doesn't work," she said. "I've been doing that since we started moving."

"Too bad ..." he said. "Worked in Egypt."

"Ow! Dammit!" She gasped when she struck her knee on an outcropping of volcanic rock.

"You have a way of finding the jerks and ticking them off." Rowan chuckled. "I thought ..." he stifled a laugh. "I thought you ... were ... gonna ... punch him. Just like I thought you were going to punch the escort in Peru."

"Don't think I didn't want to," she smiled. "You should have seen what I did to Mitch."

"Who's that?"

Lauren had already told him the names of their attackers. She thought it odd he'd already forgotten. "Here, you need a break," she said, feeling for a spot, helping him sit against the wall of the lava tube. She knew better than to lay him down. She had to get him out of here. It concerned her that she couldn't see him. She suspected his color was poor. He felt clammy when she ran a hand over his brow. "I want you to stay right here," she said. "I'm going to scout ahead just a little and see if I can't find a turn we missed somewhere."

"Just keep ... talking ... to me."

"I will," she said, patting his shoulder, finding his cheek with her hand, noting he'd broken out into a cold sweat. "Just stay with me, promise?"

"Promise."

"So, if we're thinking of a fall wedding ..." she began. Lauren felt her way along the lava tube. "I was thinking maybe an outdoor wedding. I think it would be pretty to be married under the aspen trees. Remember that little place outside of Estes Park?"

"Where you ... fell in the ... river?"

"You're never going to let me live that one down. Are you?"

"No." She could hear his wheezing in the silent darkness.

"I'm lucky I didn't get washed downstream and drowned," she muttered under her breath. "You saved me on that one."

"Saved you ... plenty ..."

She smiled to herself; it was true. He had saved her plenty. From the day they met when he tended her broken leg, to the time her climbing harness failed and she nearly fell 300 feet over a cliff in the Colombian rainforest. He was always there for her. He even nursed her back to health after her recent injuries and illnesses, while she'd been so ungrateful. She owed him her life more times than she could count. She couldn't bear to think about that right now. She was certain she'd start bawling if she kept on this current train of thought.

"Hey, did you ever hear back from the lab on those samples from Peru?" she had to raise her voice a little as she moved farther and farther down the passageway. "Rowan?" he didn't answer. She stopped. Her attention was suddenly drawn to a change in the texture of the cave wall. It was no longer cold hard rock. It was warm ... soft ... fur.

She took a startled step back. A deep growl rumbled beneath her hand. She saw a glimmer of light and realized it was eye shine high above her. "Tsul'Kalu?" she gasped. She took another step back, intent to turn and run, but fell, landing hard, knocking the wind out of her.

The beast grunted. Hands reached down and grasped her. It lifted her effortlessly off her feet. Her heart raced as she recoiled. She could smell the fetid breath of the monster. It blew her bangs away from her face as it growled. It was more than her brain could handle. She felt her blood draining from her head. Her hands turned cold. Dots danced in her eyes *"Ani ... yvn wi ya ... aya tsa-la-gi,"* She gasped before the world around her was lost to oblivion.

CHAPTER 36

"I SEE YOU HAVE MET *TSI-SDU*, THE RABBIT," SHE HEARD THE DEEP voice in her head. She knew it at once. She couldn't move. Her head felt heavy. She tried to force her eyes open, to no avail. She took a deep breath and felt comforted by the aroma of bread and something herbal.

"Rest easy. You are with the People," the voice continued. "You are not badly hurt, but you are weak, *Du-yu-go-dv A-yo-s-di*. I will tend you."

"You call me ... *Truth Seeker*?" She managed, still trying to open her eyes and turn her head.

"You do not remember your time with the People before?" The voice asked. "I am the one who saved you from the Rabbit when first we met."

"*Tsi-sdu* was the leader of them in all the mischief," she remembered the line in the Ancient Language. She could *feel* the words in her head.

"You do remember." A massive hand came to rest on her head, stroking back her hair. "Have no fear, Truth Seeker. Your strength will be restored. *Asi-sde-li-sgi* will be mended as well."

"*Asi* ... *the Protector*? You mean Rowan?"

"He is your *u-ya-hi?*" She felt this word deep in her soul.

Lauren shook her head. "No. He is not my husband yet, but if we survive this ... I will marry him."

"He has given you this promise?"

"Yes." Lauren swallowed hard. "And I have given him mine."

"This is good. Sleep now, *Du-yu-go-dv A-yo-s-di.*" The hand moved down over her eyes, and the herbal smell grew stronger. The voice left her, and she returned to oblivion alone.

———

"Dammit!" Mitch ducked behind a large fallen log. He grabbed Billy by the arm, yanking out a handful of synthetic fur before pulling him down. "There's more of 'em."

"Where?" Billy popped up, reaching for the bottom of his mask. He moved as if to get a better look. Mitch grabbed him by the arm again and yanked him down with all his strength.

"Ouch, that hurt!" He moaned, laying back against the hill to ease the ache in his butt. He found the offending stick underneath the injured muscle.

"Dammit, you dork! Shut up!" Mitch snarked under his breath, punching the ape in his hairy arm.

CHAPTER 37

Lauren lay gazing up at the glistening stars. It took her a moment to realize she was awake. She ran her hand over the soft fur bedding, feeling how comfortable and warm she was.

She yawned and rolled her head to one side. A white-furred creature sat across from the fire, mixing what appeared to be flowers into a cup of steaming liquid. She sat up as everything came flooding back. She found herself in a massive cavern, part of the volcanic underground. She glanced up. Those weren't stars dancing overhead ... but what were they? *Diamonds?*

The beast appeared oblivious to Lauren's eyes on her as she took a long moment to study the softer features of this specimen. It was a female, perhaps older than Tsul'Kalu? The creature looked up suddenly, as if she'd sensed she was being watched and Lauren realized the creature's eyes were blue. She sat looking at her, wondering if she could talk to her like she did Tsul'Kalu. The female returned to her work for a moment then rose, setting what looked like a turtle-shell beside Rowan's sleeping form.

"Truth Seeker, do you remember the story I told you about the Rabbit?" She realized Tsul'Kalu was sitting nearby. He rose and came to sit beside her, crossing his legs. He spoke without speaking, his hands moving in symbolic gesture. She heard his words in her ears. Perhaps it was all in her head?

"Yes." Lauren pulled the fur blanket around her shoulders. "You told me how he was the leader of them in the mischief and that he would be brought to be judged for his misdeeds."

"The time has come for the rabbit to be judged."

"Tell me, what has he done this time to offend The People?"

"He comes to take the stars from the sky." The creature waved his hand above his head. Lauren's eyes went up. "He does not ask or come with respect for the People." Lauren looked at him again. She realized he had white streaks in his beard, heavy wrinkles around his dark, deep-set eyes. He was no monster, but a kind old teacher. A shaman perhaps. "He must be judged. But you must rest." Tsul'Kalu rose and returned to his spot by the fire.

Lauren laid back down and gazed up. Those were raw diamonds; she was sure of it. The female returned to tend to Rowan. She lifted his head and coaxed him to drink from the turtle shell. The she-beast waved a twist of some smoking herbs over him like a fan. In her mind she knew the herbs would ease his breathing. Was she Tsul'Kalu's *wife*?

Rowan's shirt had been removed, and beneath the fur blankets she could see his ribs had been wrapped in some kind of fur cloth. A poultice of some kind was tucked into the wrapping.

"He is doing well," Tsul'Kalu said in her head. He nodded at the female with a gesture. "She will bring you food, if you are hungry."

"Please," Lauren realized her stomach was growling.

The female rose and left Rowan to rest, returning a moment later with a tray of food.

"*Wa-do*," Lauren smiled, thanking her. The female looked at her blankly, but nodded slightly.

"Not all the People speak the ancient All-Language," the shaman said. "She is not of the same clan as you. This is a gift from the gods that we share."

"But how is that possible?"

"I was chosen by the ancient gods who taught me the All-Language. You were similarly blessed," his voice reverberated in her head.

"I was? Wait. What?"

"You were chosen by the ancient gods, Truth Seeker. Chosen to find the resting place of the infant god-child. The infant was given as a gift to the ancient men." Lauren sat up, cross-legged. She watched him as the story filled her head. "He was meant to be a teacher; a leader of men. But the ancient men were afraid of the god-child and what men fear, they must destroy. The child was slain; beheaded to prevent him from being restored by the gods. Fearing their wrath, they buried him in a dark place where the gods would not find him. But the gods exacted their vengeance on those who had betrayed them. The ancient men were slaughtered, wiped from the face of the earth. Only their temples and cities remained, empty and surrendered to the earth. The remains of their cities were devoured by the jungles." Lauren could see a vision of the tale in her mind's eye. She wasn't sure how. She could see the fire raining from the sky. She could smell the acrid smoke and aroma of death. Bodies rotted where they fell, and death came to all the ancient people. She could see the step pyramids entwined in vines and consumed by vegetation. "The ancient gods know you. They have been watching you. You, Truth Seeker, found the god-child; you held his body in your hands. You directed the ancient gods to his resting place. You were repaid with the gift of the All Language."

Lauren was having a hard time processing the whole thing. She had a vision of the headless chicken man from the cavern in Peru ... but the body of an ancient god? An infant? The *god-child*. She gasped as she realized what she had held in her hands.

"Yes, Truth Seeker." The beast had a beatific expression on his face. "The god-child was defiled and abandoned. It was hidden from the ancient gods, who brought down their wrath upon the men who betrayed their trust."

"I still don't understand how you know this. You're a ... a ..."

He nodded. "Our people are an ancient race as well. When the Gods handed down their fury on the ancient men, they came to my father and gave the People warning. We were instructed to flee to the four corners of the world. Our people left the land of destruction and came to settle here, far away from ancient men." He continued, "I was born in the same *b'ak'tun* and recall these events as a child."

"But ..." Lauren hesitated. "That was a long time ago. You were alive then? Centuries ago?"

"For the People, it wasn't so very long ago, Little One." He seemed to smile, but it quickly faded. "Our peace was short-lived, though. Even as our race made its home here, far from the jungles to the south, other men came ... men with yellow hair and eyes like the afternoon sky. They came and made their home in the valleys. For decades, they left us in peace. They came first for the forest, cutting down trees and taking our game. Now, they come for the stars in our sky." He glanced up at the ceiling of the cave and its sparkling gemstones.

Lauren was no geologist, but she knew volcanic processes were responsible for the creation of many kinds of precious gemstones, including emeralds, obsidianite, and even diamonds. Gold and copper were not uncommon either.

"I have so many questions." Lauren was having a hard time taking all of it in. Her head spun and throbbed in her temples. She put a hand to her forehead, turning to examine the cavern, rising unsteadily. There were carvings on the walls that reminded her more of Mayan pictographs than any of the North American glyphs she'd studied. "When the volcano exploded twenty years ago, how did your people survive?"

He understood her curiosity and her confusion as well. "The gods protect us and give us warning. We had time to flee to a safer time place."

She studied his calm expression. "Tell me more..." She sat down across from him, wishing she had her camera. She wished Rowan would wake up. She needed someone else to witness all these wonders — to convince her she wasn't dreaming, or lying comatose in some injured hallucination.

"The Rabbit has been a constant thorn in our toe for the past few years. We could not scare him away as we have the others. Then we found the Rabbit lured others into his deception, using our image to frighten away those who might come in reverence. The People have asked for intercession. I believe this is why the gods brought you to us. I am compelled to bring the Rabbit to judgement. He is of your ilk, but it will be mine who determine his fate; as the ancient gods punished man, so will we."

Lauren took a moment to process the information. Ancient knowledge was hard for her modern brain to take in. She understood that the Sasquatch meant to capture the men who had kidnapped her. Perhaps even kill them.

"So, these men, they have been coming into your home and taking these stones?"

"Yes, Truth Seeker," he said. "They have greed in their hearts. Greed will be their undoing."

"And these are the same men who hurt me several months back."

"I was certain they would kill you. I knew the ancient gods would be furious. I feared their vengeance for all men. I saved you from the Rabbit and would have kept you here to be mended, but there wasn't time. Your own people were putting themselves at great risk, seeking you. I could tell *Asi-sde-li-sgi* was desperate. I could not keep you from him. It pained my heart to feel the hurt in his."

She looked toward Rowan and managed a smile. "We are

grateful for your intervention, Ancient One." She bowed, and he returned the gesture.

"You should rest, Truth Seeker. Your quest is not yet done."

"But I have so many questions, Tsul'Kalu. You are so ancient and wise. I want to know ... know the mysteries of the universe ... the meaning of life."

The beast seemed to smile again. "The meaning of life is a simple one, Truth Seeker. The purpose of life ... is living. Do not wait for life to happen. Live it as it comes." Lauren felt the words sinking in. She realized now how wrong she had been. She thought she had been living, but she'd been putting off life for the sake of her job. She'd put off Rowan. *Oh! How foolish I've been.* She glanced over at him, feeling sorry for every single time she'd told him no. "Eat now," Tsul'Kalu said. "We can talk more later."

"But ..." Lauren seemed desperate. "I still have questions."

"Of course, you do, Truth Seeker. You always will."

CHAPTER 38

Rowan stirred in his sleep. Lauren set her plate aside and rose to check on him. The food was good; simple, but filling. There was meat, and it was well-seasoned. Root vegetables, mostly onions, had been cooked with a glaze of wild berries, sprinkled with coarse salt. It impressed her that Sasquatch had such skills. She hadn't expected any of it. Her favorite was a type of bread, made from what looked to be wild grains. It was hearty and good.

She caught his hand as he rolled his head to the side, wincing. "Rowan, it's okay. We're safe," she said. She pressed her hand to his cheek. A dopy grin spread over his face. "You won't believe where we are."

Rowan's eyes opened. He looked around, but she could tell he wasn't focusing clearly. "Where?" He swallowed hard. She suspected his head hurt as much as hers had.

"Tsul'Kalu brought us to his home. This the most amazing cavern ... it's warm and dry and they have fire. You should taste the food. They cook! And they make blankets from animal skins. Look at the ceiling, Rowan. I think those are diamonds." She could hear the amazement in her own voice. "Tsul'Kalu told me the most unbelievable things. That *thing* we found in Peru? His people know it. It's the child of an ancient god." She spoke quickly, telling him everything. His vision seemed to clear, and he focused on her. "Tsul'Kalu was born in the time of ancient gods. Do you realize what this means?"

Rowan nodded, blinking. "It means that dude with the crazy hair is right? The ancient astronaut theories … are true?"

Lauren's grin spread from ear to ear, as her hands covered her mouth. "I can't believe it either. On top of that, the Bigfoot lived in the time of the Aztec empire."

"Are you sure you didn't get hit in the head, Lauren?" Rowan groaned, trying to sit up.

"No, no. Lie down. You'll hurt yourself even more." She put a gentle hand on his arm.

"Is that water?" he pointed to the turtle-shell cup beside him. Lauren had seen the white she-beast hold it to his lips earlier. "I'm thirsty."

Lauren picked up the cup and sniffed it. It smelled floral and calming. "*De-le-ga-li-s?* Willow bark. I think. It's tea." Willow bark had been known to humans for centuries. It was the basis for modern-day aspirin. The salicylic acid in the bark was a pain killer and fever reducer. She sniffed again, detecting something else she couldn't quite put her finger on … sassafras maybe? Licorice fern, more likely. Sassafras wasn't native in the Pacific Northwest. "Here, let me help you." She lifted Rowan's head holding the cup for him. He drank greedily. He winced as he lay back down, gritting his teeth. "Are you okay?" he asked. He made to reach for her face. He winced as he tried to lift his arm. She leaned in to make it easier. His hand barely grazed her cheek before it fell to the bedding.

"Yes," she said. "Just a few bruises. They'll heal."

He held her eyes for a long moment. She watched as his lids grew heavy again. She wondered if the medicinal tea had anything to do with the stupor that came over him as he drifted back into a healing sleep.

She leaned down and pressed her lips to his, with no response. She sat back on her heels and surrendered. Nothing left to do but watch and wait. Her own body ached, but it wasn't bad. Still, she curled up beside Rowan and pulled the furs up over them and gave in to the need for rest.

CHAPTER 39

"Get that bag, Billy!" Mitch barked orders as they snuck back down to their hideout deep in the cave. "We're gonna have to bug out before it gets too hot to get these rocks out."

"Where are we gonna go, Mitch?"

"My buddy's dad has an old hunting cabin not far from Kelso," Mitch said. "We can stay there until things cool off."

"How are we gonna get there? We ain't got no truck."

"No, we'll have to hike out," Mitch said. It would take them a couple of days to do that. They'd come in from the south last time they'd hiked in, but Mitch decided it'd be better to avoid the roads, and go east, crossing the roads only when they had to, and hopefully late at night.

"Can I wear my Bigfoot shoes? You know I hike better when I have my Bigfoot shoes on."

Mitch rolled his eyes at his cousin. "Sure, Billy. Whatever makes you happy. Wear the whole dang monkey suit if you want. Now, come on. We don't have time to fart around."

"What are we going to do with all these rocks?" Billy hoisted the heavy knapsack over his shoulder. It was full of the uncut stones. The diamonds were worth more money than he'd ever seem. Mitch couldn't wait to cash them in. The last load they'd hauled out had brought in more than ten thousand dollars. He was saving up. He had big plans. Plans that required cash, and lots of it.

"You just let me worry about that, Billy. I think they could be really pretty if we polish them up. We can make Indian Jewelry out of them ... sell them to the tourists," he knew he was lying through his teeth. He didn't care. Billy wasn't all that bright. He had suffered a traumatic brain injury while playing football when they were kids. He had no idea what they'd really been doing for these past few months. He just thought they were digging for rocks. Mitch didn't want him to know what they really were.

"Think we'll make ten dollars?" Billy's eyes lit up in the dim lamp light.

Mitch smiled to himself. "Maybe."

"I could do a lot with ten dollars," Billy said, waiting for Mitch to finish packing his bag.

"Like what?" Mitch sneered.

"Think I could get me a hooker for ten dollars?"

"What would you do with a hooker, Billy?"

"Well I don't know. I never had one." Billy shrugged. "If I found a pretty one, I could take her on a date."

"A date, huh? Come on, let's go."

"What about those people?"

Mitch turned and looked blindly down the dark cavern where they'd left them. There was no way anyone could get out of there in the dark. "We'll come back for them later," Mitch said.

"Promise? I wouldn't like being left down there in the dark."

Mitch wanted to smack Billy, but his hands were too full. "Can we just get out of here already?"

"Promise we'll come back?" Billy stood fast and wasn't about to move.

"I freaking promise, Billy. Now, let's go!"

———

The Ancient One came into the cavern. Lauren was aware of his presence. She could sense he was agitated. His breath rumbled heavily in his chest. She felt her hair prickle on her neck. She lifted her head from Rowan's shoulder, sitting up as he approached. She hadn't realized they were alone in the cavern.

"What's wrong?"

"Danger." His eyes spoke the words in her head even as the cavern began to tremble and debris began to fall. Lauren threw herself instinctively over Rowan's body, supporting her weight on her hands and knees. She shielded his head with her arms, sacrificing her own safety for his.

The Bigfoot did the same for her. She could smell the odor of wood smoke and herbs in his fur, along with an earthy, beastly smell. Had she not been so afraid, she might have gagged at the stink. Instead, she buried her face against Rowan's chest. He didn't smell April-fresh either, but it was somewhat better. It was a more familiar smell.

A piece of debris hit the top of her hand and rolled close enough for her to see. She'd never seen uncut diamonds loose like that before. But she knew that's what it was when she saw it. Being the scientist that she was, she wanted to study it. Without second-guessing herself, she reached out and picked it up. It wasn't until the ground stopped shaking that she had time to question her decision to collect data during an earthquake, but by then it was too late.

"Come." Tsul'Kalu lifted her up effortlessly by the arm. She suddenly recollected him catching her like that once before. He'd caught her to pull her away from the fake Bigfoot who'd kidnapped her. The memory of the pain echoed in her bones, and she flinched. The Ancient One abruptly sat her down. "Forgive me, Truth Seeker. It is easy to forget how fragile you are. I never meant to harm you."

"You saved me," Lauren put a hand on his arm. "I don't blame you."

"We must go. It's not safe here."

"But, Rowan ..."

The beast scooped him up as if he weighed nothing. Lauren shouldn't have been surprised. His arms were like tree trunks. Rowan winced. He looked like a child in the Bigfoot's arms. "Follow me."

More of the creatures fled through the lava tube, and none too soon. The shaking began again as they entered the tunnel that Lauren presumed would lead them out. She fell against the wall, and was shielded again by the Bigfoot. As soon as the quake subsided, they continued.

The passage twisted through the mountainside, weaving left and right, and Lauren was completely turned around. When it got so dark she couldn't see, she clutched a handful of fur on the Bigfoot's arm and let him lead her. It seemed to take forever to get to the surface.

When they broke out of the small entrance of the cave, there were at least a dozen Sasquatch gathered in the dense under-brush. The white Bigfoot tended a wounded Sasquatch's fore-head. She turned to Tsul'Kalu, and Lauren suspected he had communicated with him in a way she couldn't fathom.

In the distance, a fellow tribesman called to the group. One of their band tipped back its head and returned the call. Lauren trembled, stepping closer to Tsul'Kalu out of reflex. She'd heard these calls in the distant, but never had she been so close. It was a bone-chilling cry. She understood now. It was little more than a simple call. "Over here!" or, "We're here!"

The Ancient One grunted something and Lauren sensed, rather than heard, him directing them to scatter into the woods and regroup at another location, the name of which Lauren didn't understand. They did as he ordered; the uninjured aiding the wounded. "We must find your people," Tsul'Kalu said.

Lauren was so turned around, she had no idea which way to go. It was dark, save for moon glow behind thick clouds. *How long had they been underground?*

"Longer than you realize," the beast answered in her head. "Come." They picked their way down the side of the mountain. He could have traveled much faster alone. Carrying a man and leading a frightened woman was slowing him down.

He led her through the dense trees, over outcroppings of rock and then out across a wide plain of volcanic ash. Nothing grew there. The earth was crunchy beneath their feet. Lauren sensed the beast's discomfort at being out in the open. Like a doe with fawns entering a meadow at dawn to feed, he was on edge. He moved quicker. "Keep up, little one," he thought.

"I'm trying," she answered.

They finally cleared the wide expanse of what had been pyroclastic flow from the 1980 eruption of Mount Saint Helen's. Ashen sand made uncomfortable grit in her boots but she had no time to attend to it. At the moment, comfort was less of a priority than safety.

CHAPTER 40

JEAN-RENÉ CAME OUT OF HIS TENT AT THE FIRST TREMBLING OF the ground. The rest of the team gathered around the fire where the morning watch had just put on coffee. He'd just leaned down to pick up the pot when the ground had started shaking again. He landed hard on his butt, startled, but wide awake.

Without warning, a large tree cracked. It snapped at the base and splintered. It twisted and came crashing to the ground. Landing in the middle of the fire at the center of camp, a spray of sparks and flame were jettisoned into the air like firecrackers.

His heart sank in his chest when his eye followed the trunk of the tree to see the remains of his flattened tent beneath the once-tall pine tree. He genuflected blankly, saying a silent prayer under his breath.

Derry picked him up under his arm pits, while Katie stomped out burning flotsam as it came to rest on the ground. "Are you okay?"

"Yeah." Jean-René was alert, though definitely shaken. "Thanks." He wiped the litter from the seat of his pants with trembling hands. He froze when a distant howl broke through the forest. Everyone else froze too. A second call answered a moment later from a different direction.

"Think the quake upset the Bigfoots? Bigfeets?" Katie fumbled for words.

"Oh my God, Lauren is gonna be mad she missed that." Jean-René cussed to himself. As he paced, he debated what to do.

"Your camera wasn't in your tent, was it?" Katie asked, calmly.

"*Tabernaque!*" He nearly doubled over, pounding his fists in his knees. A long string of French expletives rolled out of him like a river. "*Tabernaque!*"

"Surely that's not the only one you brought," Derry said.

Jean-René paused a moment. "Lauren's, maybe."

He climbed over the fallen tree to Lauren and Rowan's tent. He returned with her Nikon. It had night-vision, as well as FLIR. They might need that.

He fumbled with the controls. He was not as familiar with her little gizmo. He raised it to test it just as a giant beast crashed through the trees. It skidded to a stop less than thirty feet away. Jean-René froze, but not before he clicked the camera on.

A second form sauntered out into the clearing behind the beast. The man pulled out a pistol. He leveled it at the group. The rangers already had their weapons drawn, but they were startled by the hairy beast beside him. The creature dropped the heavy bag he was carrying and raised his arms, roaring at them.

"Well look at this, Squatchy." Mitch grinned devilishly, stroking his unshaven chin. "Got us a couple of Rent-A-Cops think they're gonna shoot us."

"Put the gun down," Miller said, pulling his credentials from his shirt pocket, "FBI. You're out numbered."

"Outnumbered?" He scoffed looking smugly at what was clearly a fake-Bigfoot. "I don't feel outnumbered, do you,

Squatchy?" The beast grunted. Katie took a step back, positioning herself beside Jean-René. "The way I see it, Squatchy here is worth two of you. Besides, I know something you don't."

"Oh yeah?" Jean-René felt his blood rise in his face. This guy was ticking him off. *Who did he think he was fooling?* That was no Bigfoot. It was a very large man in a monkey suit. *That was the hoax-monger in a monkey suit! It had to be.*

"Yeah." The man seemed very relaxed. That ticked Jean-René off too. "I know where your people are."

Katie muffled a gasp only Jean-René could hear. Miller spoke calmly. "What?"

"Tall guy and the chick with the long dark hair?" he described Rowan and Lauren. "Oh, she is so sweet." He inhaled, as if breathing in Lauren's perfume, his eyes squinting as a broad, wicked smile spread over his face. "We've met her before," he said. That frightened Jean-René even more. "Hot babe." He made a motion with his hips that made Jean-René nauseated. "I'd tap that any day."

"Where are they?" Jean-René demanded. "What have you done with them?"

The man paused. He stroked the trigger of his gun as he trained it on Jean-René. "I don't think I want to tell you," he smiled, wickedly.

"I will tear your limbs from your body!" Jean-René spat angrily. Katie caught his arm, holding him back. "Where are they?!"

That made Mitch smile even wider. He laughed menacingly, stopping, snapping his aim on Miller. The agent started to move, but froze when the gun turned on him. "They're alive. For now." He pointed with his gun. "Drop your weapons, or I promise you ... they'll never see the light of day."

No one moved.

Mitch pulled back the hammer on the gun and honed his

aim on Katie. He studied her up and down, his menacing gaze softening maliciously. "Oh, you're fine, too."

"Bite me!" She taunted, weapon still drawn.

"Put the gun down!" Mitch started towards her in a near charge, but Miller flipped the safety on his gun back on. He held it up in surrender. He eyed Jean-René with a cautious gaze.

"Fine," Miller said. "Fine." He laid his weapon down and kicked it away from the aggressor.

"Go on, the rest of you. Put your weapons down!" Mitch yelled.

"Do it," Miller instructed. Hesitantly, the rest followed suit.

"We don't have any beef with you. Just tell us where Lauren and Rowan are," Miller said.

"We left 'em down in the caves for the Bigfoots to eat up," the fake Bigfoot chuckled, muffled behind his mask.

"If you hurry, you might be able to find 'em before the squatches do." Mitch turned just as a rock hurled through the trees and pegged Billy in the side of the head. Billy cried out. "That hurt!"

"What the hell?" Mitch caught a flash of movement out of the corner of his eyes. "Don't touch it!" A gunshot echoed. The dirt just inches from Miller's hand exploded. He had almost made it to his gun. He turned with his hands up by his ears. "Another move like that, and I might get lucky. Might accidentally shoot someone," Mitch turned the gun turned towards Katie. Jean-René noticed her stiffen.

"Something bit me, Mitch."

"Shut up!" Mitch snapped. "You think a little bug hurts? Wait until I get a hold of you."

Jean-René had seen the rock flying through the darkness. He strained to see where it had come from. He was debating making a dash for it. But he had no idea what these two were up too. He didn't care. He just wanted to find Rowan and Lauren. He moved behind the others, lifting the camera. He scanned the trees. There was something there. He flipped over to thermal imaging. There was a form behind a nearby tree, and he tried to discretely pan in on it. He waited until he was sure no one was paying him any mind. He zoomed the lens in.

"Pick up the bag, dumb ass," Mitch rebuked his partner.

His large companion, still holding his wounded head, bent down to collect his bag. He fumbled with it. Its contents spilled out amidst the pine needles. The remaining fire light made the stones sparkle. "Are those diamonds?" Katie asked.

"So it would seem," Mitch chortled.

"We're gonna make ten dollars!" the Bigfoot said. He scrambled to get the stones back in the bag. Most of the stones were no more than pebbles, a couple might have been the size of acorns.

"Ten dollars? That's got to be a half-a-million dollars' worth of uncut stones!" Katie gasped, her voice rising. "You can't take those. It's against the law. This is a National Park."

Mitch just laughed. "I figure in the right market, I've got more than a million," he said. "And I can take them. You can't stop me."

"What are you going to do? Shoot us? You can't take out all of us," Miller said. "You pull the trigger and you might get one of us, but the rest of us will take you down before you get off a second shot."

Mitch laughed even harder. "In that case, I think I'll start with you," he raised the gun, and cocked back the hammer. Suddenly, a large stone flew through the trees and struck Mitch in the side of the head. He was sent tumbling. The gun fell from his hand. It landed at Katie's feet. Everyone scrambled but she managed to grab the weapon and trained the gun, first on the fake Bigfoot, then on Mitch. He rolled over and moaned. "Son of a …"

"Don't move," Miller and Derry had their guns again too.

"What the hell was that?" Jean-René swore. He turned the

camera in the direction the rock had come from. A smaller form appeared from behind a tree. A hand raised then flipped him off. He sucked in a breath, forcing himself to maintain his composure and stifle a smile. That could only be one person. A wide grin spread across his face.

CHAPTER 41

MILLER HELD THE GUN ON THE FAKE BIGFOOT. "TAKE OFF THE mask."

"But it's my lucky Bigfoot mask ..."

"Leave him alone," Mitch snapped.

"Shut up," Katie snarled. She glanced up at Jean-René, catching the end of his smile. His attention returned to the scene in front of him. She shrugged. "What?"

"The Federal Agent told you to take off the mask. I suggest you do it," Jean-René said. His thick accent added to the command.

"Aw, man." Billy reached up and pulled it off.

"What is your name?"

"Don't tell him!" Mitch snapped.

"Billy." He swallowed hard, wringing the mask between his hands, looking down at his toes.

"Billy what?"

"Billy Birdsong," he whined. "Billy Alex Birdsong, I live at 19 Mountain View Road, Seattle, Washington. My phone number is ..."

"That's enough." Jean-René glanced back at the rest of his

party. All weapons were trained on Mitch. "How do you know this piece of garbage?" He looked at Mitch.

"He's my cousin, Mitch."

"Mitch what?"

"Sheesh, Billy!"

"*Mitch-ell*." Billy was sobbing as he shuffled his feet. He twisted the mask between his hands.

"Keep going," Jean-René encouraged him

"Mitchell Wayne Anderson. Please don't shoot him. He's my best friend," Billy cried.

"Anyone got any handcuffs?" Pauline asked.

"I've got some zip ties," Katie said, holstering her weapon. She went to find her knapsack.

Jean-René turned his attention back to Billy. "I won't let them shoot him, Billy, as long as you both do what you're told. Can you do that?"

"Yes, sir." Jean-René realized he was the sort to be respectful of orders and probably did whatever he was told. Mitch probably told him what to do often. He probably wouldn't even be here if Mitch hadn't brought him.

"Okay," Jean-René said. "Stick out your hands and let the agents do their job."

"You're not gonna take me to jail, are you?" He cried. "My momma will whoop me with her belt if I go to jail."

"We just have to ask you some questions." Katie came over and took the mask, watching him as he held out his hands and let her bind them. He cried pitifully.

"You didn't tell me we were going to get in trouble, Mitch. I'm gonna tell your Daddy on you!"

Miller didn't get the same docile response from Mitch. As the agent bent down to secure him, Mitch kicked him in the knee. He punched him in the stomach. It was pandemonium. Mitch bolted, tackling Derry. He knocked the gun out of his hand. Someone shouted, "Get him!" Mitch scrambled to his feet intent on escaping into the darkness. Jean-René ducked, feeling the wind rush past him as a much larger rock came from over his shoulder and clobbered Mitch in the back of the head. The man's momentum carried him a few feet. He fell flat on his face.

"Jean-René, did you throw that?" Katie asked.

"I felt it come over my shoulder," he raised his camera and saw the thermal figure of Lauren still standing in front of him. He turned the camera the direction the rock had come from. There was nothing there. It must have been Rowan, but why was he hiding? Only the thermal would have been able to see him in the dark.

Miller, angry and hurt, pounced on the unconscious Mitch. He got ahold of his hands. He had them zip-tied behind his back. "You got him this time?" Jean-René demanded to know.

"That jerk isn't going anywhere!"

"You killed him." Billy came over and dropped to his knees, sobbing over the unmoving form on the ground. "Mitch?"

"He's not dead yet," Miller said. "He'll stay that way as long as he stays on the ground. Same goes for you. Don't move. Don't try anything."

Convinced the situation was under control, Jean-René started towards Lauren. She stepped out from the shadows. Even in the dim light, he could see her face was black and blue. Her hair was a wreck. "Are you okay? Where have you been? Where's Rowan? What happened to you?" He hugged her.

"I'm okay," she said, catching her breath. "Those two numb-skulls left us in a dark cavern. Rowan's hurt."

"You're hurt."

"It's nothing," she said. "Rowan needs a doctor."

"Where is he?" Jean-René looked around. The first rays of sun broke over Mt. St. Helens.

"He's ..." she scanned the trees. Rowan staggered out of the tree line holding his injured side. "Rowan!" Lauren dashed toward him. She caught him, as he lurched forward. Jean-René caught his other arm, taking some of his weight from Lauren. A cry escaped the back of his throat all the same.

"Nice shot, man!"

"Shot of what?" Rowan's eyes weren't quite focused.

"You threw that rock, right?"

"What rock?"

"Never mind," Jean-René said. "Come sit down before you fall down."

"What happened to your tent?" Rowan paused at the sight of the fallen tree.

"I'm just glad I wasn't in it." They got Rowan settled. He groaned as he was lowered to sitting. Jean-René steadied him.

"Who's that?" Rowan asked. He pointed at the guy in the Bigfoot costume.

"That's who kidnapped us," Lauren sneered. "That goon in the monkey suit is the one that broke my arm."

"I'm sorry," Billy sniffed, sitting down next to Mitch, still teary eyed. "It was a ... a ... a ... accident. I didn't mean to."

Jean-René looked up the hill as something caught his eye. He thought he saw something move, but after a moment, he decided it was nothing.

"Who triaged your injuries?" Katie asked, kneeling at Rowan's knee.

"I did," Lauren lied. "I think Rowan has some broken ribs. But I can't tell if his lung is punctured. He's breathing better than he was when we were in the cavern."

"Your head is bleeding, Lauren!" Katie got up to grab the first aid kit.

"A rock must have hit me during the earthquake," she said. She put her hand to her forehead. The knot on her head sure did hurt.

"What are these? Rabbit skins?" Derry examined the wrappings around Rowan's chest as Katie returned with the first aid kit.

"I found them in the cave." Lauren came up with a quick lie. "It was so dark, I couldn't tell what they were. They seemed clean enough. I didn't have anything else."

"Where's my shirt?" Rowan asked.

"Lost it in the dark," Lauren lied. Katie knelt in front of her to tend to her injuries. "We need to get Rowan to a hospital."

"When's Bahati coming back with that damned helicopter?" Katie swore under her breath, but loud enough everyone heard it.

"I'm better," Rowan grunted. "I just wanna lay down. I'm so sleepy."

"Don't do that," Lauren said. "You need to stay awake."

"I'll see if I can radio out for help," Derry said, glaring at the rousing Mitch. The injured man moaned on the ground. Suddenly, the ground shook again. Rowan yelped as he nearly fell off the tree trunk. Leaves and pine needles rained down around them.

"Look at the mountain," Lauren tried to steady Rowan as she nodded over Jean-René's shoulder.

Everyone turned. A plume of ash boiled from the top of the barren volcano. It billowed up into the atmosphere.

"What the ..." Lauren turned at a startled grunt from Miller, who'd been pushed to the ground by the fake Bigfoot. Billy scooped up his cousin and threw him over his shoulder. He made a dash for freedom in the middle of the chaos.

"Stop!" Derry yelled. He fired a shot over their heads, but the frightened man didn't stop. He disappeared into a dense bank of trees. Miller took off after him.

"We have to get out of here," Lauren said. The team hesitated, debating what to do. "Rowan can't wait for him to come back."

"Miller!"

"Let's get to the clearing where the chopper can land. They

know we're here. They'll come to evacuate us," Katie said. "Miller will find us, if he can. If not, we'll come back for him."

Lauren took Rowan's arm. "Lean on me, we have to move."

"What about our stuff?"

"Emergency supplies. Only what you can carry," Lauren ordered. The continued trembling waned and peaked intermittently. "If nothing happens, we'll come back for it. If something does happen, well, it didn't matter."

Jean-René hesitated. When no one was looking, he picked up the backpack full of diamonds. He tucked it into his camera bag. "Hurry!" He rushed to catch up with Lauren, and gingerly took Rowan's other arm.

CHAPTER 42

KEEPING ROWAN ON HIS FEET WAS A CHALLENGE. INTERMITTENT quakes were enough to keep everyone moving. The mighty pine trees cracked and toppled around them. They dodged falling timbers more than once.

Prevailing winds carried the ash cloud to the south, away from them. The sky darkened. Lauren realized the rumbling of the earth had grown to a deafening cacophony of shaking ground and tumbling rocks, cracking tree trunks and skittering stones. She felt her lungs burning, and her muscles screaming.

Even when it grew quiet, her heart was still hammering. "Come on! Come on! Come on!" She urged Rowan on.

"Lauren!" Derry yelled "Lauren! It stopped!"

"Lauren! Stop!" Jean-René's voice snapped her out of her panic. Rowan dropped to one knee, taking her down with him. Lauren fell back on the ground, her head throbbing. Her lungs burned. She struggled to catch her breath.

"Rowan needs a break. Are you okay?" Katie asked. Rowan looked pale, but her face had gone bright red.

"Yeah," she panted. "I just need a minute. We need to keep moving. There could be more aftershocks."

Derry shook his head. "Take a minute, though."

"Can you radio out?" Jean-René came over and dropped to one knee in front of Katie.

"I'll try again, but I probably won't get a response. Once we get to the meadow, we should be closer to the radio relay tower. I'll try there."

"We have to keep trying," Lauren said, catching her breath. She accepted a canteen of water. She held it to Rowan's lips, letting him take a sip first.

"We'll be okay," Derry said.

Lauren nodded. Tears welled up in her eyes, but she blinked them away. She didn't want the others to see her moment of weakness. She was near her breaking point. She wanted nothing more than to see that helicopter come over the rise.

"Lauren," Rowan lifted her chin. He inspected her black eye and bruised cheek. "It's … okay. We're going …to be okay."

She sniffed and nodded. "I know," she said, stoically. Rowan held onto her and pulled her into him, leaning on her heavily. She reached up under his shoulders and clung to him. It was all her fault Rowan was hurt. She knew he wasn't the kind who liked to admit to being vulnerable, but he was just as mortal as the next guy. She couldn't bear thinking how badly hurt he was, even though he seemed improved under the care of the Bigfoot healer.

"What is it?" Rowan asked.

"Can we please just keep moving?" She sat back on her heels.

"Okay. Just not … such …a break-neck … speed, okay?"

Lauren nodded. She got to her feet and helped Rowan up. He grimaced as she steadied him. She kept her back to the others as she turned and headed up the mountain toward the meadow.

CHAPTER 43

BILLY STOPPED RUNNING WHEN THE SHAKING QUIT. HE SAT HIS cousin down against a tree. "Mitch? Wake up, will ya?" He shook him. He sat back on his heels when Mitch groaned and opened his eyes tentatively. "I thought you were dead."

"Not yet," Mitch grumbled. "Get these things off me."

"I got my hunting knife on under my Bigfoot costume," Billy said. "But I can't reach it." He held up his own bound hands.

"You're telling me you can't break those off?" Mitch patronized him. He scooted himself up off his hands. While Billy's hands had been bound in front of him, Mitch's were bound behind him.

Billy strained against the plastic zip tie until his face turned red and a bead of sweat ran down his forehead. They wouldn't budge. "I can't do it, Mitch." He panted.

"Come on, buddy." Mitch's voice softened. "You're a big bad Bigfoot. You can do anything. Remember? You're stronger. You can run faster and do all kinds of smart stuff when you have your Bigfoot costume on."

Billy smiled, blushing. "I am stronger."

"Prove it, man."

Billy gritted his teeth and set his jaw. He pressed his arms apart until the plastic stretched and finally snapped. He nearly punched Mitch in the face before he caught himself. He looked surprised but quite pleased. "I did it! Mitch! Did you see me? I did it!"

"Good job, Billy. Now get the knife and cut me loose."

Billy struggled with the zipper in the back, dancing around trying to reach it. Once he got a hold of it, he was able to work it down. He only had to shrug his massive shoulders to get the zipper to slide the rest of the way down. From there, he was able to peel out of the fake fur suit. He left it hanging at his waist as he found the Buck knife on his belt.

"Don't cut me. Okay?"

"I'll be real careful, Mitch," Billy promised. With a careful hand, he cut the zip-ties and Mitch was free.

Mitch smacked him affectionately on the head. "Good job, dork," Billy smiled. "Now give me the knife. We're gonna go get our loot."

"But the policemen took it."

"They weren't real police." Mitch took the Buck knife and waited for Billy to hand over the sheath so he could put the knife on his own belt.

"But ... we can come back and get some more rocks," Billy said. "I don't wanna be in any more trouble."

"Don't be such a baby, Billy. We're not gonna get in any trouble in the first place. Let's get our rocks. Then, we'll get the hell out of here. No one's gonna tattle on us. We'll be long gone before anyone finds out."

"Where we gonna go?"

"Wherever you want to go, I guess," Mitch said.

"Can we go to Portland?"

"What's in Portland?"

Billy shrugged. "I don't know. I've never been there."

Mitch smiled. "Okay," he said. "We'll go to Portland. Just as soon as we get our rocks back."

The sound of a broken branch cracked behind them. Mitch ducked, pulling Billy behind a tree. Someone was following them. Mitch had only seconds to get his bearings and figure out where they were, and where to find the idiots who stole his diamonds. He wasn't about to let them get away with his loot. He'd worked too hard to get the whole ruse set up. They'd scared away hikers and tourists, and even other jokers like Billy in fake Bigfoot suits. This was his payload. He had plans to go to Mexico. He would find a beach and get drunk every day. He might find him some sweet little señorita with big boobs and let her screw him to death. That was how he wanted to go out. Hopefully that would take a long time.

———

An hour later, Mitch was sure they were lost, but he was certain they'd lost whoever was tailing them. He didn't blame Billy for getting them lost. He'd done a good job getting them out of that camp, but he must have run willy-nilly through the forest. It didn't help that the ground kept shaking or that the volcano acted like it might blow its top any minute. He didn't care about that. He just wanted his rocks.

"Do you think they're alright?" Mitch heard the voice before he saw anyone. He managed to grab Billy and pull him back down behind a large boulder.

"I hope so," Pauline said. "We should have found them by now."

"Could you tell whose tent was flattened?" The people didn't see them as they passed. Mitch knew they had the drop on them.

"I think it was Jean-René's," Pauline said. "Why would they go off and leave all their supplies?"

"If the ground was shaking as hard here ..."

Mitch jumped out from behind the boulder and clobbered the man over the head with a rock. The woman jumped and yelped, backing into Billy, who wrapped his arms around her and held his hand over her mouth, growling at her.

"Hello, Doll-face," Mitch smiled.

"What the ..." The curse was muffled as Pauline struggled. The hand wrapped around her arm was humongous and unyielding, not to mention hairy.

"Shut up," Mitch ordered. He pulled the knife out of its sheath. He held it up as he walked over to her and pressed the blade against her face. "If you scream or make a peep, I will cut you. Understand?"

She nodded, wide-eyed. Billy took his hand away from her mouth. She kept her lips pinched tightly shut for a moment before demanding "Who are you? What do you want?"

"You know the people that were there at the camp site?" Mitch asked. She nodded. "They took something from me, and I want it back. You're going to help me get it."

"Okay," she said, not fully understanding the predicament. "I'll get it for you as soon as we find them."

Mitch smiled. "Good. Then I don't need him." He reached down and caught the unconscious FBI agent by the hair and tipped his head back. He drew the blade across his throat in one swift motion. Blood gushed and Pauline gasped, covering her face with her hands. Mitch tossed the dying agent to the ground. He drew back his fist and struck her in the stomach. She dropped to her knees but moved to roll the agent over. She felt his life ebbing from his veins as she clamped her hand over the wound, trying to save him.

"Get up!" Mitch pulled her up by her ponytail, putting the bloody knife to her throat. She could smell the blood and almost taste iron on her lips. She struggled in vain to free her hair from Mitch's grasp. "On your feet, and not another peep!"

CHAPTER 44

MITCH WAS EMBOLDENED BY HIS HOSTAGE. DESPITE BILLY'S protests about killing the FBI man, he pressed on. They caught up with the other group just shy of the meadow. He marched right up to them, with Pauline in front of him. He held the knife pressed firmly to her throat.

"Give me my backpack!" he demanded. "No discussion. No arguments. Just give me what's mine and I'll let her go."

"He killed Joshua," Pauline sobbed.

Rowan and Lauren stopped. Rowan struggled to catch his breath. Miller and Katie took a more offensive stance, while Jean-René turned so the guys couldn't see he had their pack in his camera bag. Lauren put up a cautious hand. "Just let her go."

"Not without what's mine," Mitch dug the blade into her skin. She yelped. Fresh blood ran down the front of her fern-green uniform shirt.

It appeared to be superficial, but it was frightening none the less. Lauren backed up. "Okay. Okay!" She glanced at Jean-René. "Give it to him." He pursed his lips and hesitated a moment. He didn't think she'd seen him pick it up. Begrudgingly, he unshouldered his bag. He took out Mitch's bag of stones. He held it out, taking a tentative step towards him. A deep rumble reverberated all around them. The ground heaved, nearly upending them all. Mitch didn't even flinch. He narrowed his eyes coldly at Jean-René. The camera man looked towards the volcano. His jaw dropped.

Mitch's gaze followed Jean-René's gaze. Above the barren dome, a silver object appeared from behind the plume of ash. Then there was another ... and another.

Three objects arranged into a V formation circled the volcano. They maneuvered like a flock of geese. Below, everyone on the ground were momentarily blinded by a glowing blue light as the three objects came together into a unified disc. It hovered above, seeming to lower. It kicked up dirt and rock, sandblasting them with grit.

Mitch took the momentary distraction to make his move. He dropped Pauline and snatched the pack from Jean-René's outstretched hand. He grabbed Billy's sleeve. They turned and bolted from the edge of the clearing. They disappeared into the woods.

Lauren rushed to Pauline's side, shielding her from the dust storm around them. Her gaze returned to the disc. It hovered a moment longer before lifting higher. It shot off and was gone.

"Are you okay?" Lauren asked Pauline once the dust began to settle.

"What the hell was that?" Pauline gasped.

"God only knows," Lauren said, under her breath. She moved Pauline's hand to inspect the wound on her neck.

"How bad is it?"

"It's not as bad as you'd think," Lauren said. "Nothing more than a flesh wound." Lauren found a tear in Pauline's untucked shirttail and ripped a section of it off. It was clean enough for her purposes. She tied it gingerly around her neck, creating a temporary bandage. "You're okay. Keep pressure on it until the bleeding stops."

The team froze as Miller dashed out from the tree line, breathless. "Where'd they go? Everyone okay?"

Pauline nodded and pressed her hand over the wound. "He killed your partner," she gulped, her lip trembling.

"Who?"

"The mean one," she sneered. She let Lauren help her to her feet. She was understandably shaky.

"We need to get back to the rendezvous," Lauren started, but a deep mournful howl echoed through the trees and it sounded close.

Lauren peered up from beneath her lashes at Rowan. "Tsul'Kalu?" he asked.

She nodded. "And he's close," she said. Chills ran down her arms and made the hair on the back of her neck rise. "The judgement is at hand."

She turned and ran toward the sound. Jean-René caught Rowan, steadying him. "Lauren?"

———

Lauren dashed through the trees. She climbed over rocks and up the hill. She skidded to a stop at the sound of the Ancient One's bone-chilling roar. It reverberated in her chest and snatched her breath away. She hurried towards the sound.

She hesitated as she found Tsul'Kalu in a battle to the death with the angry man. Mitch slashed at him with the knife. Despite the Bigfoot suit, Billy cowered on the ground next to a tree. Mitch was holding his own. The blood dripping down Tsul'Kalu's face was a testament to that. A wicked cut bisected his face.

The great beast had brute strength on his side. One well-placed blow with the back of his mighty forearm sent the man flying. The bag of diamonds landed at Lauren's feet. The beast leapt and landed on top of the flailing man. There was a bone-jarring crunch. The man's form went limp beneath the beast.

Lauren gasped as Tsul'Kalu rose. He turned and roared at her, still in a blood-rage Lauren gasped, stumbling backwards, landing on her butt with a thud. His expression softened to the wise old Shaman she knew him to be.

"Truth Seeker," she heard his voice in her head. "The Rabbit has been judged."

"You're hurt." She got to her feet. She took a step towards him. He shied away.

"You and your people should be leaving. The mountain has awakened. It is not safe to remain."

"But ..." Lauren moved closer. "What about you?"

"The People are taking shelter. We will go to a safe place."

He allowed her to reach for his face. She ran her hand along the side of his large cheek bone. He leaned his face in her palm, cupping her tiny hand in his. "But ... I still have so many questions, Tsul'Kalu."

The beast managed a faint smile. "Truth Seekers always do."

CHAPTER 45

THE GROUP STOPPED IN THEIR TRACKS. ROWAN AND JEAN-RENÉ followed a moment later. Rowan was wheezing as he sunk to one knee, gasping for breath, wincing in agony.

Before them, one body lay broken and bleeding on the ground. Another cowered in abject horror beneath the cover of branches. Then there was Lauren. The researcher stood encircled in the embrace of the mythical monster. The creature looked up and gazed at them softly. Lauren turned too.

Rowan was unable to move. He folded and melted to the ground, panting in quick, shallow gasps

———

"Tsul'Kalu," Lauren withdrew. She turned and stared at her friends, who all had the same blank expression on their faces. Rowan was the exception. He was too involved with trying to breathe. She was torn between wanting to tend to Tsul'Kalu or rush to his aid. "What did you do to them?" She took a few steps toward Rowan. Tsul'Kalu moved with her. As she knelt down to inspect him, Tsul'Kalu's voice filled her head.

"There will be time for answers another day. The gods have come to warn us to flee from this place. You must do the same, little one. You must go, now. When the time is right, you will find me again. This is my promise to you."

Lauren realized she had found the truth, but it was a truth she could never tell. She couldn't risk it. The protection of the species was too important. Lauren leaned into the Sasquatch, He embraced her again. "This is my promise to you, Tsul'Kalu. Your secret is safe with me."

His hand rested on the top of her head, his palm completely covering it, his long fingers cupping her head affectionately. "Be well."

"Go, Tsul'Kalu, find somewhere safe."

He nodded. "And you, Truth Seeker," he patted her head. "Stay curious, always."

The beast fled from the scene and Lauren bent over Rowan. It wasn't until she started snapping her fingers that he seemed to focus on her. "What?"

"What the hell just happened?" Jean-René snapped out of his euphoria too.

"I don't know," Lauren said. She ran her hand down her frazzled braid. "Help me get him up. We have to get Rowan out of here."

"My God. What could do something like this?" Miller asked. He walked over the broken body. "His neck is snapped." He looked at the man in the Bigfoot suit, who was obviously in shock.

"He was like that when I found him," Lauren said. No one gave any sign that they remembered seeing Tsul'Kalu.

The ground rumbled once again. Lauren looked up as the sound wave passed. A distant whir followed. She realized it was helicopter blades cutting through the air.

"We've got to go! The chopper's back!" Katie shouted. "Come on! We have to go!"

The ash cloud that broke from the mountain's peak was now black and ominous. The roar of it became deafening, as the eruption intensified. "Come on!" Lauren shouted, grabbing Rowan's arm. She shoved him towards the rendezvous point. No one argued and everyone raced to meet their escape-craft.

"What about the dude in the Bigfoot costume?" Jean-René pointed at Billy.

"Bring him with us," Lauren said as the helicopter door opened.

Lauren could see Bahati's frightened eyes in the cockpit as they approached. She knew they couldn't afford to wait any longer to get the hell out of here.

Lauren got Rowan on board carefully, then made sure everyone else was coming before she took the seat behind the co-pilot.

Bahati handed her a pair of headphones. "Where's Joshua?" She asked, as soon as Lauren had them on.

"He didn't make it," Lauren responded. She hadn't let herself think about it. She'd liked the fair-haired FBI agent. She wasn't prepared to deal with the repercussions of his loss, or the details behind his death.

"Is everyone else okay?" Bahati asked.

Lauren glanced back, inspecting the team. "Minor injuries. Rowan has some broken ribs, but nothing life-threatening." She took his hand

"We'll get him to the base hospital," Bahati said.

———

Jean-René had gotten Billy into the very back seat of the helicopter. He was grateful to have the back seat. The backpack full of diamonds had been dropped in the confusion. This time, no one saw him duck back for it. He was sure of it. He sat now, with it hidden in his camera bag.

Billy was still in a stupor. He wasn't paying any attention to anything. Jean-René watched him for a moment, just to make sure. He opened the bag and stuck his hand into the midst. He relished the rugged feel of the stones against his skin. He knew they'd never be allowed to keep all of them. He pocketed a handful. He wasn't sure what he'd do with them, but that wasn't the point. *Why shouldn't he have a couple?* No one would ever know.

———

Ben was on duty in the ER when the chopper arrived. This time, it was Rowan on the stretcher. "Lauren?" He looked puzzled. "What are you two doing back?"

"Rowan's hurt," she said.

"Let me guess, he got mugged by a Bigfoot too?"

"No," Rowan grimaced as the gurney clipped the door jamb as they wheeled him into the exam room. The gurney came to an abrupt halt. "Just a hoax-monger in a monkey suit."

EPILOGUE

LAUREN CROSSED THE BRIDGE OVER THE BIG THOMPSON RIVER IN a shower of leaves. Golden swirling ribbons of aspen caught in her hair. The tiny heart-shaped foliage crowned her with their beauty. Rowan and Jean-René waited for her in a clearing. A minister stood behind them. Their friends and families gathered around, smiling. Some eyes were red with happy tears.

Bahati helped her with her skirts as she walked across the meadow. She carried a bouquet of wild pasque flowers and daisies. It had been dressed with blue ribbons tied in eternal knots.

Rowan took Lauren's hand when she reached him. His eyes were glistening. "You look beautiful," he said. A tear tumbled down his cheek.

She smiled. "You clean up pretty good yourself."

"Wanna get married?"

She smiled. "I'd love to."

"Dearly beloved, we are gathered here in the sight of God." The minister began, but Rowan's gaze held her in a trance stronger than any magic Tsul'Kalu could do. She didn't hear a word of it. She was lost in Rowan's eyes, and he in hers. She'd never seen him in a tuxedo before, but then, he'd never seen her in a white dress.

Her hair had been curled and piled up on her head, a circlet of Swarovski crystals kept most of the tresses from spilling down her back, though a few had escaped, framing her strong face. The same knotted ribbons in her bouquet had been tied into her hair. He reached up and freed a leaf from a curl.

"We come today to witness the union of Rowan Charlemagne Pierce and Lauren Diane Grayson." She gazed into her groom's eyes. He couldn't seem to stop smiling any more than she could. His dimples dug craters into the corners of his cheeks.

Yes, this was the right choice. Her heart was his no matter how long nor how hard she'd fought against giving it away. No one else deserved it. She knew it now. Her heart had *always* been his. She would spend the rest of her life proving her commitment to him, not that she needed to. She was happy to do it.

"With this ring, I thee wed ..." she came back to herself, realizing Rowan was slipping the ring on her finger. She glanced down. Her brow furrowed and she looked up at him. This wasn't the same ring he'd given her a year ago. This one was a much larger emerald cut diamond with a smaller diamond on each side of it.

Rowan exchanged glances with Jean-René, then winked at Lauren. Lauren turned to Bahati, who handed Lauren the ring for Rowan. His was a thick white-gold band inlayed with smaller chips taken from the same diamond in Lauren's stone. She inspected it and puzzled a moment, looking at the ring on her finger. Finally, she reached for his hand. "With this ring ... I thee wed ..." her voice trembled, not in fear, but in disbelief that this day had finally arrived.

"Lauren," Rowan squeezed her hands.

She came to herself realizing she'd drifted away again. "You may now kiss your bride," the minister repeated. Rowan made sure he had her attention. She leaned in to him. Rowan took her in his arms and pressed his lips to hers, lingering a lot longer than anyone expected.

Cheers rose from their families and the whole *Veritas Codex* production team who'd come to witness the nuptials. Lauren came up for air, feeling light-headed; practically giddy. She leaned on Rowan and smiled at everyone who'd assembled. Her mother stood at the edge of the gathering, smiling at her. Her brow furrowed. But her gaze moved past her to the mountain. Dark eyes peered out from the trees and as the cheers raised across the valley, they were answered with one somber yowl after another from all around the mountains. Lauren glanced at Rowan. She sensed the presence of the unseen figures in the trees. Rowan leaned in and whispered, "We have a flight to catch."

"Didn't you hear that?" Jean-René furrowed his brow. It wasn't like Lauren or Rowan to ignore something like that.

"I didn't hear anything," Rowan held her and kissed her again. "Let's go, or we won't make it to Denver in time." She took Rowan's arm. She turned one last time looking past her mother into the darkened forest. Tsul'Kalu stepped out a moment, then faded back into the shadows.

"Where are you heading on your honeymoon?" Bahati asked Rowan, trying to keep up with them.

"It's a secret," Rowan smiled.

"But..."

"He won't tell me either," Lauren said. "See you in three weeks."

"Three weeks?"

———

"I need another piña colada," Lauren lifted her empty pineapple cup without looking to see where he was.

Rowan had pulled every string he could tug to make their dream honeymoon happen. Now, they lay on the beach of an isolated island in the middle of the South Pacific. There wasn't another soul for a hundred miles — living or dead.

Lauren had made a cabana from branches and coconut leaves and was lying with her face in the shade and her naked body in the sun. It felt warm and safe, and she was at peace.

Rowan arrived, dripping water on her leg as he returned holding up two large fish by the tails. "Room service," he grinned. Lauren sat up on her elbows, shading her eyes with her hands.

"Yummy," she said, sitting up. "I'm going to need a fresh cocktail before dinner."

Rowan bowed. "Yes ma'am." He grinned. "One more piña colada coming right up."

Despite the remote location, Rowan had thought of everything. They had plenty of alcohol and mixers, even ice. He'd had a screened-in bungalow erected with a hanging bed. A portable generator provided power for the few appliances needed to keep them relatively comfortable. There were fairy lights strung around the cabana and torches all up and down the beach. Lauren got up and followed him to the beach front table, tying a sarong around her body as he took the fish over to the prep table by the gas barbecue grill. He had everything he needed to prepare a gourmet meal. A golden statuette stood at the corner of the table.

"Why did you bring this?" She picked up the Emmy, inspecting it.

"I intend to take it everywhere." He grinned. He ran the blender and poured the thick concoction into her cup. "Your drink, Mrs. Pierce."

She raised her cup to him before putting it to her lips. "*Doctor* Pierce."

"Of course." He shook his head. "Silly me."

"What day is it? How much longer do we get to stay?"

"How much longer do you want to stay?"

"I guess forever is probably too much to ask," Lauren shrugged.

"We have enough booze for about three more days, the way you're going at it," Rowan said, chopping the head off first one fish, then the other. "The boat will come back in a few days. We can decide if we want them to get us more supplies or if we want to head to Hawaii."

"Hawaii?" Lauren arched a brow. "What's in Hawaii?"

"Our next assignment," he grinned.

"Oh really?" she leaned her chin on her fist. "What's that?"

"We've been asked to investigate some paranormal activity around the Kilauea volcano," he grinned. "Interested?"

"Another volcano?" She seemed to hesitate for a moment as she leaned back. "Why not? But what will Bahati have to say about it?"

"Is she an Executive Producer of the show?"

A curl formed in the corner of Lauren's cheek. "Nope, that would be me. She's just the Lead Researcher." Bahati had earned a promotion too.

"Did I mention we got renewed for another twelve episodes?"

Lauren's head snapped around. "You did not."

"Maybe we got nominated for the People's Choice Awards too." He spitted the fish and put them on the grill.

"Oh yeah? What else don't I know about?"

Rowan rinsed his hands off in the bucket of water he'd brought up from the beach. "I heard some scuttlebutt about a live show in Scotland at some old castle next Samhain."

"I liked Scotland," Lauren came around and put her arms around his neck.

"You just like men in kilts," Rowan grinned, leaning into her. Her lips hovered just inches from his.

"You look very braw in a kilt," Lauren smiled, playfully. "Not sure how I feel about the ghosts, though. Even in kilts."

"Don't worry," Rowan kissed her. "I'll protect you."

"I'm counting on it."

"Ye'r verra bonnie. Ah'll no' let harm befall ye." He did a fantastic Scottish brogue.

"Save it for the cameras, silly."

He reached down and peeled off his shirt, reaching for the button on his shorts. "There's no cameras here."

Lauren laughed and bolted, but he caught the hem of her sarong. It fell to the sand as she leapt for the waves. The sun set across the clear blue lagoon as he caught her and pulled her down into the water, careful not to hurt her. She rolled him over and pinned him in the sand, kissing him.

He lay beside her in the warm shallow waters with the sunlight golden on her skin. "So, tell me the truth," he said between kisses. "Did we really see a Bigfoot in Washington State?" He'd been trying to get the truth out of her for months. All the evidence suggested they'd encountered something, but no one could really remember what it was. Fans swore they could see a big hairy shadow in one of the video clips and their social media posts had trended for weeks. They got millions of hits. News reporters had been clamoring for interviews and they'd appeared on every major network. But Lauren had been less than forthcoming with information, though he knew, eventually, he'd get the truth out of her.

"We saw something," Lauren said. That had been her standard response the whole time.

"Come on, Lauren." He insisted.

"You want the truth?"

"Isn't that what we're all about? *Veritas?*"

She sat up. "Okay. The truth is, Bigfoot is friends with the little green men from Mars. He's been around since the age of the Aztecs and Mayans. Oh, and our radioactive headless chicken corpse was the infant child of the ancient gods."

Rowan had a stern expression, studying her dark eyes that glowed in the setting sun. Then he broke out laughing. "That's the biggest load of BS I have ever heard."

"You wanted the truth!"

"I don't believe it," Rowan said, flatly. "Tell me the real truth."

Once, Lauren might have been wounded by his lack of trust. But now, she didn't need him to believe her. She knew the truth, and that was all that mattered. It was enough. "The real truth?" Lauren softened, reaching for his cheek "The real truth is, I have loved you from the moment you first smiled at me."

That same smile broke like the dawn across his face. "Now that, I believe."

ABOUT THE AUTHOR

Betsey Kulakowski has thirty years of experience as an occupational safety professional and recently completed her degree in Emergency Management. She lives with her husband and two teenage children in Oklahoma. Betsey has been writing since she could, and created her first book at the age of six—cardboard cover, string binding and all. This is her first published novel.

Babylon Books is an imprint of Bernhardt Books, Inc.

Editor-in-Chief: Alice Bernhardt

Chief Financial Officer: Harrison Bernhardt

Marketing Director: Ralph Bernhardt

Made in the USA
Middletown, DE
16 September 2020

18939684R00161